MOUNTAIN DREAMS

CHERYL HOLT

ZEBRA BOOKS
Kensington Publishing Corp.
www.kensingtonbooks.com

ZEBRA BOOKS are published by

Kensington Publishing Corp.
850 Third Avenue
New York, NY 10022

All Kensington titles, imprints, and distributed lines are available at special quantity discounts for bulk purchases for sales
promotion, premiums, fund-raising, educational, or institu-
tional use.

Special book excerpts or customized printings can also be created to fit specific needs. For details, write or phone the office
of the Kensington Special Sales Manager: Attn. Special Sales
Department. Kensington Publishing Corp., 850 Third Avenue,
New York, NY 10022. Phone: 1-800-221-2647.

Zebra and the Z logo Reg. U.S. Pat. & TM Off.

ISBN-13: 978-1-4201-0128-7
ISBN-10: 1-4201-0128-5

First Printing: November 2000
10 9 8 7 6 5 4 3 2

Printed in the United States of America

Chapter 1

Allison Masters climbed the stairs to the second floor, looking for the door with the doctor's name on it. She didn't see it. Just her luck—it would be clear at the end of the walkway, where God and everybody else could see her enter. What was this idiotic physician thinking, renting space in a building where her door faced an outdoor balcony instead of an indoor hallway? Anyone strolling by could look up and see who was stopping by for an appointment.

A car door banged, and she jumped. "I'm just nervous," she muttered, although there wasn't any reason to be. Most people went to the doctor all the time. She just didn't happen to be one of them.

In the Masters family, members were expected to charge full steam ahead every moment of the day, and illness was considered the ultimate sign of weakness. *Weakness* was a commodity her father had certainly seen her exhibit lately. If he heard she had now sunk so low as to be seeking treatment from a doctor for a *rash*, he'd do much more than just

banish her to the end of the earth in Jackson Hole,
Wyoming. He'd disown her, rewrite his will, change
the locks, revoke her last name, cut her face out of
all the family photos hanging around corporate
headquarters . . .

And that would be just for starters.

He wouldn't think something as simple as hives
was a real ailment, and heaven forbid his ever
learning that the horrid itching could be brought
on by stress. She'd never live it down. If he suspected that it was all in her head, she'd seem even
more crazy in his eyes. But she was past the point of
caring. If she didn't get the itching stopped, and
soon, she was very likely to start screaming, which
would definitely be a mistake, considering how
many people would be witnesses.

Down below, the busy thoroughfare bustled with
the July throng of tourists who had stopped in the
small mountain resort community on their way to
exotic destinations like Yellowstone and Grand
Teton National Parks, which were both just up the
road.

Not that Allison had ever been to either of those
places, or would ever go to see them. She had no
desire to. Sightseeing on all those wide-open country highways held no appeal whatsoever. It was bad
enough to have been forced to move to Jackson,
and she refused to spend any of her free time visiting the local points of interest. She had settled in at
the family summerhouse, and later today she would
begin the duties her father had assigned her. When
her exile ended, she'd be gone in a heartbeat. She
had no intention of staying one instant longer than
he'd mandated.

On the corner across the street, she heard the clopping of horse hooves and the jingle of bells, and a stagecoach pulled to a stop. Several tourists jumped down onto the sidewalk, laughing and talking about the ride around the famous town square, while others hurried to take their places for rides of their own.

Their fascination with the town was a mystery to her. Sure, the scenery was pretty in a rural isolated sort of way. The streets were charming to those who liked that log cabin, folksy type of scene. Supposedly, this was where the Old West met the New West, a fact about which she could not have cared less. All those horses and boots and hats didn't do a thing for her.

It was a warm beautiful day, and she'd have given anything to be sitting on the veranda of her father's beach house out on Long Island, sipping ice tea and watching people strolling along the sand. Now, that was the way to pass a summer day. Not here, fighting elbow to elbow with all these tourists searching for the cheapest place to buy a hamburger.

She walked along the balcony railing, itching terribly but trying not to scratch, past the row of office doors, vaguely noticing an accountant's name, an insurance agent's. Below, a couple of tourists exited an ice cream shop with dripping cones in hand and looked straight up at her. Quickly, she turned her face toward the wall. They walked on without giving her a second glance, and she breathed a sigh of relief.

Ahead, several feet away, she could see gold lettering on the door of the doctor's office: Dr. Pat Beaudine—Family Medicine.

A few more steps and she'd be safely inside!

The glass on Beaudine's door caught her reflection, causing her to stop and stare, thinking she certainly looked every one of her thirty-two years. Luckily, her nasty red rash was mostly hidden by her clothing so that it wasn't visible, but her blond hair, pulled back in its usual workday chignon, had lost its sheen. Behind her glasses—the ones she didn't need, but wore to give herself a more professional air—her blue eyes were magnified, looking dull and lifeless, and there were dark smudges underneath them, clearly indicating fatigue. The navy suitcoat hanging on her shoulders barely hid her recent loss of weight.

When had she gotten so thin?

At five-feet, six-inches, with an adequate rounded figure, she'd always been the picture of health. Now, she looked the way she felt: haggard, tired, worn down and out by the events of the past weeks.

But who wouldn't be? she asked herself, giving in to a moment of self-pity before straightening her backbone and getting a grip.

Her hand reached for the knob, but she hesitated, realizing that during the exam the doctor would ask questions about how she'd gotten hives. Since Allison was a poor liar, she'd have to tell the woman the truth—that she'd broken out before, on occasion, but only during times of intense personal stress. If Dr. Beaudine was like any of the other doctors Allison had seen, she'd ask one question after another, expecting Allison to simply spill the contents of her sorry situation all over the room.

Was this what she really wanted? To bare her soul to a stranger? To talk about personal and family business as though she were just an ordinary person? To reveal private yearnings and hurts as though she were simply another member of the masses who couldn't control the petty day-to-day foibles of existence?

She wasn't just *anybody*, for heaven's sake. She was Allison Margaret Emerson Masters. Her family had been a leader in American commerce for over a century. They controlled fortunes, destinies, lives. They built empires, started dynasties, created kingdoms. Great-great-grandfather Herbert, who'd opened his first rooming house next to the Union Pacific line in the 1880's, had seen to that.

Over the decades, that humble beginning had blossomed until the family owned exclusive hotels in every major US city and in many spots around the globe. The company's advertising slogan—Stay With The Masters—said it all. Theirs was the top name in upscale overnight accommodation.

Generations of Masters blood flowed through her veins. She was strong, tough, determined. Raised by the most sought after nannies. Educated at the finest schools. Imbued with the strictest standards of excellence, and a taste for only the best. Wealthy, admired, and perpetually ready to take on the world with every expectation that whatever she wished could be accomplished simply because she willed it.

That woman, the woman she was supposed to be, would never break out in a rash simply because she was experiencing a run of bad luck.

"God, I can't do this," she murmured to her silent reflection, but a door down the walkway opened just then, and a person exited. Mortified at the thought that someone might see her, she stepped into the office before she could change her mind.

It was dreadfully quiet inside, and she was alone. She'd planned it that way, scheduling her visit after hours so she wouldn't have to meet the receptionist or any other patients. Her ploy had worked. The place was deserted.

For a few minutes, she paced back and forth, expecting the doctor to welcome her, but no one appeared. Never one to be kept waiting, she walked down the hall. There were several doors, all closed but the one at the end. It was open, and sporting a sign that read The Doctor Is In. She stepped to it and paused.

Behind the desk sat a man who could only be Dr. Beaudine. Besides the facts that he had a stethoscope around his neck and a medical journal open and resting on his chest, the way he comfortably filled the space kept him from being anybody else. He was leaning back in the chair, his feet propped on the desk and crossed at the ankle. At first glance, she thought he was young, but the smile lines around his mouth made her realize that he was probably closer to forty. His eyes were closed, and he was apparently enraptured by whatever music he was listening to through a pair of CD earphones.

To her absolute dismay, he was dressed in typical Jackson Hole western garb, complete with cowboy hat, boots, and denims. He wore all black, giving him the air of an Old West outlaw. The hat, made of felt or some such fabric, looked soft, brushed, and expensive. The shirt had fancy pearl snaps, the boots were polished to a high sheen, and the jeans looked freshly pressed. The severe dark color of the ensemble was broken by a splash of red flowers embroidered across the shoulders and collar of the shirt and a red bandanna tied jauntily around his neck.

He's too handsome for his own good, she thought with no small amount of disgust, instantly reminded of her fiancé, Richard.

Ex-fiancé, she scolded herself. He'd taught her well how deadly a handsome man could be.

With her trust in men completely shattered, she had no doubt that this cowboy doctor was the same, a scoundrel who commanded his surroundings through the sheer force of his good looks. Women probably swooned over that hair, all thick and wavy, the color of golden wheat, worn long to where it curled casually and just brushed his shoulders. A bushy mustache, a shade darker than the hair on his head, framed his full sensuous mouth, which probably curled deliciously when he lied like a dog and broke hearts left and right. And his eyes . . . well, she couldn't see them, but she just knew they'd be blue, blue as a summer sky, piercing and shrewd, the kind that could look right into a woman's soul and crush every secret desire hidden there.

His broad shoulders filled up every inch of the distinctive shirt. That flat stomach, the bulging sex, those long long legs and thick powerful thighs . . .

For some reason, the room suddenly felt too hot, and she took a deep breath, needing a bit more oxygen in her lungs.

He didn't look like any doctor she'd ever seen. Of course, she was forced to admit, this was Jackson Hole. Things were different. People were different.

Still, she'd been sure that Dr. Beaudine was a

female, so she'd been expecting . . . well . . . a
woman. If she had been expecting a man, she'd
have pictured someone in a tweed jacket and khaki
pants, with loafers and soft eyes, and maybe some
serious-looking eyewear. That was the kind of man
she could tell her troubles to.

This is a mistake. The message rang inside her
head. She must have been crazy, thinking some
stranger could help her. Thinking that she could
talk about what had happened. Thinking she could
ask the question that had plagued her for weeks
now, the question to which she didn't really want an
answer because she feared the answer might be *yes.*

The only thing to do now was to get out of there
and pretend she had never made the appointment
in the first place. So what if she'd broken out all
over? So what if she felt as if fire ants were biting
her a million times a second? So what if she was sad,
heartbroken, feeling lost and betrayed by those
who were supposed to love her? So what?

Bad things happened to others all the time. They
had happened to her, and she would just deal with
all of it logically and stoically, as she always had in
the past. Through the sheer force of her will, plus
some over-the-counter extra strength cortisone,
she'd have herself back on track in no time.

Her mind made up, she was poised to flee. Just
then the doctor opened his eyes and saw her. Like
a deer trapped in the headlights, she couldn't
move, and she stood paralyzed by his assessing gaze.

Sapphire blue, she thought petulantly as she stared
into those magnificent eyes. *Bluer than the summer
sky, like the deep dark waters of the Mediterranean.*

"Hello, darlin'," he welcomed her in a deep rich

baritone that sounded like honey poured over velvet. "I didn't see you standin' there. You're Allison, right?"

She'd never heard her name pronounced in quite that way, all slow, long, and drawn out with a western drawl. It sounded as if it should belong to a different woman than the one she was, maybe one who wore dangling earrings and hand-painted clothing and let her hair blow free in the wind.

"Hello, Dr. Beaudine," she offered in return, giving him her frostiest, most professional Masters smile. "I just stopped by to tell you that I have to cancel. I know you'll understand how these things happen. I realize it's terribly rude of me to wait until the last minute, and I'll certainly be happy to pay you for your time. It's just that . . . well, something's come up, and, ah . . ."

Suddenly, she was overcome with the urge to explain herself. "I have to be at my office, and I just can't meet with you right now. I'm very very busy, what with starting a new job here in town and all that entails, and taking a few minutes for myself is clearly impossible. I wanted to tell you personally, so you wouldn't think I skipped our appointment."

She was babbling like a fool, but she couldn't seem to stop. "I mean, I wouldn't want you to think I was *afraid* of coming here, or anything like that, because I'm not. Afraid, that is. There's nothing frightening about visiting the doctor, now is there? It's just that this has turned out to be a horrendously inconvenient time. So, if you'll excuse me, I'll just show myself out."

She dipped her head in a gesture of good-bye, hoping to make a graceful exit. Before she could escape he unfolded himself from the chair and rose to his feet. She remained rooted in her spot, watching all six-feet, two-inches of him stretch and rise like a lazy cat. There was something strangely beautiful about the way he did it, almost as if his normal speed were slow motion, as if time itself waited for him to take his next step.

"Beau," he said in his honeyed drawl, tipping a finger to the brim of his hat like an old-fashioned cowboy.

"Pardon?"

"Not Dr. Beaudine. Just *Beau*. That's what everyone calls me."

"Oh . . . well . . ." This was really too much. An oversexed, overdressed, overbuilt professional who didn't even use his title. All the more reason to get the hell out of there. Fast. "Doctor . . . I mean Mr. . . . ah, Mr. Beau—"

"Beau, darlin'. Nothin' else."

"Well, *Beau*," she managed, forcing the familiar means of address past her lips, "thank you for agreeing to see me, but I really must be going."

"Are you sure you want to go and do that?" he asked, rounding the desk which placed him directly in front of her. He leaned his hips against the edge, crossed his booted feet at the ankle, and evaluated her carefully.

"Quite sure."

"But you just arrived, and I can't imagine you'd want to leave so quickly."

"I do. I really do," she murmured, wondering why she felt the need to convince him of anything.

"Honey, you look so worn out. And you've definitely lost a few pounds. If I'm any judge of women—which I am, by the way—you're having a real hard time right about now. It sure might help to have somebody to talk with for a spell."

Did she look so terrible, so rundown, that a virtual stranger could see her distress? How utterly embarrassing! All the more reason to pull herself together and go. "Be that as it may," she said, trying to sound firm, "I don't think you're quite what I'm looking for."

"That's not the first time I've heard that comment from a woman." His chuckle was low and soft, and the sound drifted across her senses and tingled through her nerve endings. He spread his palms out, welcoming assessment. "What's not to like?"

"It's not that I don't *like* you, Dr. . . . ah, Beau. It's just that I was expecting someone a bit more . . ." What? What adjective could she select that wouldn't sound completely rude?

He put her on the spot, asking, "A bit more what?"

"Well, typical, I guess."

"You don't think I'm *typical*?" he asked with a mischievous gleam in his eye, and Allison couldn't help feeling that he was teasing her.

"Well, you have to admit you look different. I mean . . . take your mode of dress." She ran a hand up and down, indicating his western attire. "It's a tad unusual."

"This is Jackson Hole, honey. You're in the heart of what's left of the Wild West. What should I be wearing?"

There was that twinkle in his eye again. Why was she even having this conversation? "Your costume just seems a bit odd, considering your chosen profession."

"I always wear something like this to work."

"See? That's what I'm getting at. I was expecting someone a little more . . . sedate."

He looked down at the shiny black fabric of his shirt, the stitched red roses, and laughed. "Well, this shirt is certainly not *sedate*."

"I'm sure many people would consider it a perfectly fine shirt," she added hastily. "It just makes me uncomfortable."

"For heaven's sake, darlin', you make it sound like we're courtin'."

"And another thing. You keep using such familiar terms of address."

"Like what?"

"*Darlin'* this, and *honey* that. I don't care for it. I really don't." That was a lie. No one had ever called her *darlin'* before, and the word poured out of his mouth like a sweet ambrosia. She wouldn't mind hearing it over and over again. "That method of address may be acceptable out here in the *Wild West*, as you call it, but it doesn't work for me."

"You know, darlin'," he said, completely ignoring her last statement, "the longer I listen to you talkin', the more I'm sure that I'm exactly what you're lookin' for."

"I don't think so."

"I could probably do something about those smudges under your eyes. Put a little sparkle back in those baby blues. You're way too pretty to look so sad."

How does he see all that? she wondered. He reached out and ran his thumb across her cheek, just brushing the fleshy part, and she had the oddest desire to turn her face toward his hand and kiss the center of his palm. Since such an overt physical act was completely foreign to her character, she couldn't help wondering if she'd lost her mind entirely.

They stood so close to each other that she had only to lean forward and she'd be in his arms. In some secret cavern of her heart, she wished she could let him enwrap her, shelter and protect her from the current storms in her life. The hurt little girl buried deep inside her would love nothing more than to curl up on his lap, where she felt she could burden him with all her troubles.

The idea shocked her to her core. She wasn't a child anymore. She was an adult, with grown-up problems. Seeking solace and comfort from this sexy forward stranger would be the worst kind of mistake. Hadn't she learned anything in the past months?

Nevertheless, he was a man. If she couldn't allow him to provide succor or medical attention, perhaps he could be useful in another way. She recognized his type. Oh, he might dress differently from the "blue suits" with whom she generally consorted, and he might talk and act differently than them, but at heart he was exactly the same: a virile male whose every other word was a come-on line to any woman he desired.

If his behavior was any indication, he went through life expecting women to fall at his feet. Men like Dr. Beaudine were all alike, and, with any luck he might actually turn out to have some insight into her situation.

While she'd wanted to speak with a woman doctor, it was entirely possible that a man would suit better. Wouldn't a man be more likely to understand another man's thinking? Wouldn't a man be better able to provide an explanation for what another man had done?

She was already there. If she left, she'd never find the courage to return. This might be her only chance to ask the questions she wanted answered.

"I suppose I could stay for a few minutes."

"Good girl." He crossed his arms over his chest. "Now, why don't you tell Beau your troubles? Let me see if I can help."

How does one begin this sort of thing? she wondered. And where? At the beginning? Where was that?

She opened her mouth to start, then hesitated. "You won't tell anybody what I say, will you?"

"Wild horses couldn't drag it out of me." With a laugh, he added, "Although I do see that you look mad enough to kill somebody."

"And you'll never tell anyone that I've been here, or what's wrong with me, will you?"

"Never."

"Good. I expect this to be private. Very private."

"I'll always keep your secrets, darlin'."

With that small reassurance, she faced the opposite wall, unable to look him in the eye, and admitted, "I have a rash."

Remarkably, the itching eased just from mentioning it to him.

"I don't see anything."

"Well, it's . . . it's . . ." She blushed, unable to mention the private spots where it was located. He might be a doctor, but, first and foremost he was a handsome man, and she absolutely was not going to discuss her body parts! "It's kind of under my clothing." The tight spots were the worst, like where the elastic from her bra and panties rubbed on her skin.

"Were you hiking?" he asked.

"No," she answered, confused.

"Did you fall into a patch of poison ivy?"

"No," she said again, now understanding his thinking. "I've had it before, usually when . . . well . . ." *Buck up!* she ordered herself. *Quit being such a coward! Tell him what's happening!* He was a medical professional, and could certainly help. She declared steadily, "I've been under a lot of stress lately."

"I thought so," he responded kindly. "What from?"

"I'm engaged. Well, I was, until last month."

"But you're not anymore?" At the shake of her head, he asked, "How come?"

"I'd taken a trip to check on one of our hotels in San Francisco." She sighed, surprised at how the words were poised on the tip of her tongue, begging to be released. "And the trip went quicker than I'd planned, so I came home two days early. To New York. I live in New York. Well, I *did* live in New York. There was Richard. In my bed, in my apartment, with another woman!"

"Richard is—was—your fiancé."

"Yes!" The words began to tumble out, and she couldn't remain still. She started pacing back and forth across the small office, hardly noticing Beau resting patiently against the desk. "And not just any woman, mind you. My secretary! He was in my bed! With my secretary! They were . . ." Blushing furiously, she thought of where Cindy's mouth had been when she'd walked into the room.

It had been a horrible scene, and she simply couldn't share it with Beau, not even when he was listening so intently. There were some things that were too humiliating to say aloud.

"He wasn't even sorry! He said it was my fault! That he was unfaithful because I wasn't woman enough to satisfy him! That I didn't give him what he needed as a man! That pig. Ooh!" She paced faster.

All these weeks, she'd not been able to say anything to anyone. As the reigning princess of the Masters family, she was supposed to be tough as nails, able to take a hit as hard as she could throw one, never showing weakness to others. So, she'd hurt and fumed silently, and now it felt so good to let it out.

What a catharsis! Perhaps this was why Catholics were so devoted to the confessional. What a feeling of release!

"I went to my father and told him what happened, and he wasn't even surprised. He said I was being a baby to fuss about such a thing, and that Richard was a handsome powerful man who would always have a few flings on the side. My future marriage would never succeed if I couldn't learn to live with a little infidelity." Her cheeks burned with the admission, and she was too ashamed to mention the rest—how her father had said she should work a little harder to keep Richard's interest, perhaps get a makeover, try softer colors, wear sexier clothes, try to be more feminine.

"Can you believe it?" she continued, not waiting for Beau's answer. "He talked about infidelity as if it were a bad rash that needed to be scratched every so often." Scratching her own as she said it, she wondered why, if someone had to break out, it couldn't have been her wayward ex-betrothed. If anyone deserved such misery, he did.

"A lot of men feel that way, honey."

"A lot of men don't."

"That's true." He nodded in agreement. "So, what did you do?"

"Nothing."

"I thought you said Richard was your ex."

"He is now, but it took another three weeks before I broke it off. My father said I should calm down before making any hasty decisions."

"Is that what you wanted to do?"

"No. I wanted to fire Richard and Cindy." Actually, she'd wanted to do much more than that. Castration, poisoning, and a wooden stake through the heart were a few of her leading choices. "Or at least move them to other sections, so I wouldn't have to face them every day."

"Richard works with you, too?"

"For the family," she said distractedly, thinking instead of how awful it had all been. Richard had refused to move out of their apartment, saying he didn't consider the engagement broken and that everything would get back to normal once her "hissy fit" had ended. Her father wouldn't let her transfer Cindy, insisting that Allison was making too much of an incident that meant nothing.

Not knowing what to do or where to go, she'd hidden away in a hotel for a week, ordering room service, huddling under the covers, thinking her life was over. Then her father had discovered her location and smothered her with his intimidating presence, which she'd never been able to resist. She'd forced herself back to work. For the next two weeks, she'd appeared at her desk every morning, her head held high, ignoring the whispers, snide remarks, sympathetic looks, Cindy's smirking, and Richard's fawning.

Blindly, she'd moved through her days, pretending nothing had changed and that she was coping just fine, that she could care less that her fiancé was a philandering slug or that her secretary was a woman of low moral character. Eventually, she'd become so numb that she thought she might be able to pull it off. Either that, or she'd shatter into a million pieces and vaporize into the cosmos.

"What happened?" Beau prompted, bringing her out of her reverie.

"We had a board meeting. Everyone was there. All my cousins. My uncles." She had no siblings, or they'd have been there to witness her humiliation, as well. "The handful of others, like Richard, who my father brought in from outside. Cindy was handing out a report I'd completed, and I handled that just fine."

"Handled what?"

"The little whispering with Richard. The wink he gave her when she moved on. It was the other that really set me off."

"What other?"

"My father promoted him! To senior vice president!" No one outside the family had ever risen so high. It was an unspoken, but confirmed, rule. Only family could work in the inner circle. Allison had hoped to become the first female to earn such a spot, only to see it given to Richard. Her father had gone on about how it was unprecedented, but, since Richard was about to become one of the family, he'd decided to promote him.

Allison could still feel the flash of rage the announcement had ignited. At that moment, she'd hated as she'd never thought it possible, hated her father and Richard, and the family, and the company. The surge of emotion had been frightening in its intensity, but it had felt good. It felt even better now to be able to talk about it.

Beau raised a single eyebrow. "How did you take the news?"

"Not well. I grabbed the stack of papers in front of me and tossed them around the room. I grabbed all the papers around me and tossed them, too. I grabbed the water pitcher and doused Richard thoroughly." Beau laughed long and hard at that, and she couldn't believe how wonderful it felt to hear such simple acceptance. "I was going for my father next, but three of my cousins grabbed me and wrestled me down on the table before I could reach him."

"I wish I'd been there to see it."

She saw approval in his eyes, and liked the way it made her feel—confident, and in the right. "I was pretty mad."

"What would you have done if you could have reached your daddy?"

"I'm not sure," she answered honestly. "Scratched his eyes out, probably. As it was, I had to settle for throwing my engagement ring in Richard's face while I was dragged from the room kicking and screaming."

"Whooee." He blew out a long breath. "That must have been quite a scene."

"It was. It was," she answered, running a hand anxiously across her hair and realizing that somewhere in all the pacing and haranguing a few strands had come loose from her chignon. She tried to tuck them away, missing a few. "I've never been so embarrassed in all my life."

"You shouldn't have been," he offered kindly. "Everybody needs to blow off a little steam now and then. Especially when they've been treated as badly as you were. You had every right."

"Do you really think so?" she asked. No one in her own world had ever thought she had the right to do anything—certainly not the right to disrupt a board meeting or to throw emotional family secrets out into the open where everyone would be forced to look at them.

Her antics had upset everyone, and she'd heard several of her uncles whispering that her behavior was the reason female cousins were never allowed into the upper echelon; women were simply too hysterical, and couldn't control themselves.

"Yes, I do. You did all right for yourself."

"Thank you," she said with quiet pride.

"What happened after the meeting ended?"

"I was banished here. To Wyoming."

"To do what?"

"To run our hotel."

"Which one is that?"

"The Masters Inn."

"Interesting," he said, giving her a look she didn't understand. "You're going to be the new manager?"

"Yes. The last one quit on the spur of the moment, and my father is looking for someone to replace him. He said I had to come here in the meantime, stay for six months, and then he'd *reevaluate* my position." She was still wondering if that meant in the company or the family. Could he, would he, fire her as his daughter?

"Then what?" Beau asked. "Would you go back to New York?"

"Supposedly."

"What if he says you can't?"

He'd just asked the very question she'd avoided asking herself ever since the moment her father had first mentioned Wyoming. When he'd put his position on the table, insisting she take it and go, she'd agreed with hardly any argument. That was the way it had always been between them, the way it was between her father and everyone else. Randolph Masters said *jump,* and people asked *how high.*

From the moment it became clear he was serious, she'd never dared to ask herself what would come later. What if he never let her come back? Her job at the company was her entire life. If she wasn't a vice president at MasterCorp, who was she?

"I haven't thought that far ahead," she lied, unable to discuss this formidable dilemma. "I'm just taking things one day at a time for now."

"That's a good idea. You've had the rug pulled out from under you these past few weeks. I'd say you need time to settle. Put things in perspective."

"My feelings exactly," she agreed, giving him a hesitant smile.

"You've moved to a new town. You're starting a new job. That's enough of a burden right there. You don't need to be obsessing about all the other stuff."

"Yes," she agreed again, liking him more now. He had an amazing ability to see to the heart of a situation.

"Besides, I'm a great believer that time heals a lot of deep wounds. Things will look better in a week. Even more so in a month. Why, in six months, you might like it here so much that you'd never consider going back to New York."

"Well, I wouldn't go that far."

"No, I suppose you wouldn't." The force of his smile lit up the room. "You do have the air of a city girl about you," he said, taking in her blue suit, white silk blouse, heels, and stockings. In small town Jackson, the outfit was definitely out of place.

His gaze had taken on a new look, one she recognized well. Even with the weight she'd lost, it was hard to hide her figure. Her breasts had always been a little too full, her hips a little too curvaceous, her legs a little too shapely. Male admiration was something she'd begun to notice at an early age.

As her desire to succeed at her father's side had blossomed, she'd done everything she could to play her appearance down, wanting the men in her professional circle to appreciate her for her hard work, not her physical attributes. The boxy clothing in which she usually attired herself did a fair job of hiding her figure, but men still noticed, just as Beau was now. Self-conscious under his assessment, she glanced at her watch.

"My . . . look how late it's getting," she said, wanting to distract his attention, which seemed to have focused on her bosom. "I haven't even mentioned what I came to talk about."

"I'd say you've talked about plenty." He chuckled

in that pleasing way he had, his eyes no longer on her breasts, but his scrutiny continuing to unnerve her. "What could possibly be left?"

"Well, it's a problem I've been wondering about for a long time. And . . . do you know very much about women, Beau?"

"A little," he said, one corner of his mouth curving.

"I'd say more than a little. You seem to be a man who is thoroughly familiar with women."

"I'd say you're probably right," he said, crossing his arms over his chest again, apparently amused by her ideas about his character.

"So, you might be able to give me your opinion about something."

"What is it, darlin'?" he asked gently.

There was no easy way to lead into it, she decided, so she took a deep breath and just blurted it out. "Do you think a woman can really be frigid?"

Chapter 2

"Oh, honey, who told you that?" Beau asked, staring at the distressed woman standing before him. He had not seen a prettier one in a long time, and he'd seen plenty. Rarely had there been one who was more beaten down, although her pride prevented her from showing it. With her shoulders squared, her fists clenched, and her jaw firmed, she looked ready to take on the world. Only the sheen of tears in her eyes gave away the tender heart she struggled so valiantly to hide.

There were the circles under her eyes, too, the haggard look to her hair and skin. The girl wasn't taking care of herself. That was fairly clear. Those who were supposed to love her didn't. Despite how hard she tried to act unconcerned and unaffected by the story she'd shared, her pain and sense of betrayal were obvious. Beau knew of her family—who didn't?—and she seemed too gentle a soul to come from such aggressive ruthless stock. How had this precious morsel survived for so long among the sharks in the ocean where she swam?

"Did Richard say such a terrible thing to you?" he prodded tentatively.

"Yes," she said, swallowing hard and taking another deep breath to keep from suddenly bursting into a flood of tears. As it was, a few were stinging behind her lids, begging to erupt. They'd been conversing so easily that she'd thought the important part of her visit would be just as easy to talk about as the rash and its causes, but she'd been wrong. It was bad enough to discuss how she'd failed as a professional. It was worse to discuss how she'd failed as a woman—so much worse.

"When I caught him with Cindy . . ."—she swallowed again, needing to go on, but hating to— "there was a dreadful scene. He said that it was impossible for me to show physical affection, that he'd always had other women because I just didn't know how to satisfy a man, and never would." She looked down at the floor as a torrent of shame washed over her. Of all the things Richard had said, this was the worst—because she was so afraid he was right.

She'd never liked being touched; it just wasn't in her nature. As a young girl, growing up with governesses instead of a mother, she'd had no hugs or embraces. There were no pats on the head or rubs on the back. Touching was an odd chance encounter. As she grew older, she'd come to expect her personal space to be respected, and had never enjoyed physical intimacy because of that.

All through college, she'd remained a virgin, surrendering only at the ripe old age of twenty-three. The experience had been so unfulfilling that she'd waited another five years before trying it again.

That one had been just as bad. So she'd waited some more, wondering what was wrong, why she didn't enjoy what others obviously did.

Then came Richard, the wonder boy from an old Massachusetts family with a Harvard degree and all the spit and polish that went along with it. From the first moment they met, she'd been attracted to him. Six months later, by the time they were dating and ready to take the first steps toward a sexual relationship, she'd been sure Richard would ignite the spark that had been missing.

She'd been wrong.

Sex with him was just as boring and lackluster as it had been with her first two partners. Try as she might, she was hard-pressed to discover just what women saw in the act. All that thrusting, moaning, and sweating, just so the man could enjoy a few minutes of pleasure. When it ended, all she wanted to do was take a shower and creep into her own bed, where she could spend some time alone. She never did, though.

Knowing how important sex was to Richard, she'd never denied him, never feigned a headache, never pleaded fatigue. Within reason, she'd done everything he'd asked, worn whatever lingerie he requested, watched whatever kinky videos he brought home.

Then, to find out that he'd detested every moment of their intimacy! To learn that he found her lacking as a woman in every way! That he'd never been faithful, and never intended to be! Tears overflowed and ran down her cheeks. God, she was so embarrassed to have someone see her like this. She never cried! Never!

"Come here, honey," Beau purred, opening his

arms wide, and she stepped into them, resting her forehead against his chest. He'd never been able to stand watching a woman cry—not his mother, not his sister, not any of the women who flowed through his life. He enveloped her with his body, shifting her between his thighs and holding her there with his hands balanced lightly on her waist.

She smelled good, sweet and tangy at the same time, like a mixture of flowers and lemons. Up close, she was even prettier than she'd been from across the room. Her skin was smooth and baby soft, a lovely touch of temper still blushing her cheeks. That glorious blond hair was falling out of her bun. It matched her condition, he thought— tightly controlled, but gradually falling apart. How he'd like to pull the pins and let the whole mass swing down around her shoulders so he could run his fingers through it.

"Do you think it could be true?" she asked, finally raising her gaze to meet his. "That I could be . . . you know . . ."

Those eyes! Shielded behind her glasses, they were magnified by the lenses shimmering with tears. "No, I don't think it's true," he responded without hesitation.

"But what if Richard is right, and there's really something wrong with me?"

He might have laughed if she hadn't been so serious. Any man could see the passion bubbling beneath the surface of this woman. She exuded sexuality, with all those curves and valleys in just the right places and just the right amounts. And that was on the outside. Inside, she was a veritable inferno of sensuality, the fire shoved so deep down that she wasn't even aware it existed.

Richard must be a total ass.

If Beau knew anything, he knew that this woman was vulnerable and hurting, and needed a good shot of self-esteem. "You know, honey, I was thinkin' we ought to do a little test."

"What kind?" she asked warily.

"A passion test," he answered, snuggling her a little closer, liking the way she fit so well between his legs. She was so near that her breasts nearly brushed his chest every time she took a breath. She was so distressed that she hardly noticed.

"I've never heard of such a thing."

"Let me show you."

"What are you going to do?"

"I'm gonna prove to you that Richard doesn't know what he's talkin' about."

"How?"

He raised his hands from her waist to her face, his fingertips barely resting against her cheeks. His eyes widened in surprise when he realized that he was getting a serious jolt of sexual energy just from the light contact. "You trust me, don't you, honey?"

She was caught in the power of those mesmerizing blue eyes. Like a beacon, they held her, and she couldn't look away. All she could do was nod. "I do."

"Good. Just hold steady now," he said quietly, as though gentling a skittish mare.

"For what?" she managed to ask.

"I'm gonna give you a little kiss."

"I don't think that would be appropriate." With every breath in her body, she knew she should move away, but she felt permanently attached to him, as though some invisible thread bound them, the touch of his fingers on her face and his thighs against her legs acting as magnets.

"Why wouldn't it be?"

"I hardly know you."

"That's true," he was forced to admit, "but you did ask for my professional opinion, and I think kissin' you would be a great idea."

"It would?"

"Of course it would," he said, running a thumb across her bottom lip. "I happen to know a thing or two about women, honey, and I can tell you that Richard doesn't have a clue. Let me give you one little kiss, and I'll prove it."

Wasn't this what she had wanted all along? Some proof that Richard was wrong? That she wasn't cold and unfeeling? Beau was ready to supply confirmation, so why not let him? It wasn't as if kissing him would repulse her in some way. Far from it.

Her brow wrinkled enticingly. "Well, if you're sure."

"I am." He removed his hat and laid it on the desk. "I like to take off my hat when I kiss a pretty girl."

The way he said *pretty* made her heart do a little flip-flop. When he looked at her, she felt exactly that way—pretty, and desirable, and sexy. She blushed at the thought. Had she become so pathetic that flattering words from a stranger could make her feel better?

Apparently, the answer was yes.

Sounding serious and stern, like a soldier ready for battle, she insisted, "I'm ready."

"So am I." He chuckled. "Close your eyes."

She did, expecting to be instantly grabbed, pressed tight, crushed in a thoroughly male, overwhelming embrace.

Nothing happened, though, not right away at least, and the waiting only heightened her tension and sense of awareness. Every sound was magnified. The tick of a clock, a car horn, a bird chirping, the frantic beating of her heart. His touch, when it finally came, was soft as a butterfly. Not the groping hug for which she'd braced, but a light cradling of her face, as if she was something delicate and fine.

Her first thought was that she'd never been kissed by a man with a mustache. In her world, the men were all clean-shaven, and it had never occurred to her that a bit of facial hair could feel so erotic. The bristly ends tickled her just a brief moment before his lips met hers. After that, she was lost.

He made no move to deepen the kiss. There was no melding of torsos or stroking of his hips against hers. Their bodies touched in only two places: where his palms cradled her face, and where their mouths were joined. But, oh, how those two spots sizzled! She could feel the gentle press of those lips from the roots of her hair to the tips of her toenails.

She'd never felt anything like it before. Her head was pounding, her ears were ringing, and the room felt so hot she thought she might ignite, and she had a brief vision of the two of them standing there until they burst into flames.

Time seemed to have stopped, and she couldn't have said how long they stood there. A minute? Ten? Thirty? She didn't know, and didn't care, as long as this glorious sensation never ended. It did, though, eventually. As his lips parted from hers, she

sighed in resignation, strangely bereft at the loss
of something so sweet and wonderful.

"Oh my . . ." she whispered. Her eyes fluttered
open, and she blinked, then blinked again. She
couldn't see anything! For one panicky moment,
she thought she'd been struck blind. Then Beau
brought her back to her senses by gently removing
her glasses, which had completely steamed over. He
set them on the desk next to his hat.

"Oh my, indeed," he said, giving her a strange
look which was impossible to read.

She opened her mouth to speak, but no sound
emerged. She closed it, swallowed, tried again.
"Could we . . ." Her voice was a high squeak. She
cleared her throat. "Could we try that again?"

"With pleasure, ma'am." Beau was in a state of
shock, never having imagined that kissing her
would be anything unusual. He'd kissed thousands
of women in his life, always liked it, never tired of
it, and had figured she'd be an innocent flirtation
and a bit of fun on a boring afternoon.

Everyone who knew him realized he never took
anything seriously except his work, but something
about the woman's story had rung a bell with him,
and he couldn't bear to see her so sad. For some
unfathomable reason, he had desperately needed
to make her feel better about her day, about herself. A jolt of confidence was just what the doctor
ordered.

But Beau had been the one to receive the jolt.
Their innocent kiss had affected him right down to
his toes, which were even now curled in his boots.
When was the last time a simple kiss had curled his
toes? The tips of his fingers tingled, his skin was

on fire, his heart was pounding, and God, he was aching and hard as a rock.

He flicked his thumb under her chin and raised her face to his. This time, when their lips met, there was no holding back. His mouth claimed hers with fiery possession, taking her, branding her. Teasing her lips, he bit at them, played with them, giving them all the fierce attention they deserved. His hand found the back of her neck, and he tilted her head back and deepened the kiss. His tongue flicked in and out, asking, asking again, and she opened wide and welcomed him inside with a hearty groan of surprised pleasure.

Allison was in heaven. She had never imagined that something physical could feel so wonderful. Reeling, she threw her arms around his shoulders and gave her entire self into the force of the kiss. As deeply as he kissed her, she kissed him in return, running her fingers through those delicious blond curls, tracing his broad shoulders and chest, his flat stomach. For a moment, she even considered moving lower and touching him where she could feel his arousal straining against his jeans.

Excited as she felt, though, she couldn't take that extra step. Instead, she circled her hands around his waist and hugged him as tightly as she could, the move bringing her breasts into contact with his chest. They swelled and ached, her nipples turning into hard buds, and each slight move he made shot her full of a flood of wanting.

Finally, she understood why a woman would need a man to caress her breasts, to suckle there. Instinctively, she knew that Beau would be able to ease the ache that often came to her but was never assuaged.

She could imagine lying in a deep bed covered with red satin sheets, looking down to see his beautiful head hovering over her bosom, his mustache tickling her, his lips wet and hot, his tongue rough and playful.

The very idea made her knees weak, and if he hadn't been holding her so tightly she might have fallen.

"More," she thought she heard herself begging. Perhaps she said it, or perhaps it was simply the rhythm of her heart pounding in her ears. "More, more, more . . ."

Beau wasn't sure what was happening. He was always the one in control, taking the woman in whatever direction intrigued him. This time, his body refused to follow the path he'd set, instead forging a new and exciting course, as though knowing there was something precious to be explored, something he'd never encountered that needed to be cherished and savored.

While his mouth learned everything about hers, his hands were busy, moving across her shoulders, her arms, up and down her back, to her small waist, her rounded hips, urging her closer, and, finally, finally, easing some of the building pressure by moving her against him. He felt like an adolescent with his first girl, ready to explode without notice. Her mound pressed against him, and he could imagine how tight she'd be, how wet, how soft. His ability to fantasize had always been vivid, but he'd never known it to be quite this stirring. He knew exactly how she'd look, how she'd taste, how she'd feel, how she'd sound when he entered her, when she came.

He wanted her—without thinking, without planning, without regard to the consequences. If he'd had more than a few minutes of time on his hands, he'd probably have forged ahead and taken her right there against the desk. And again on the couch. Somehow, common sense prevailed. He removed his lips from hers, taking small love bites as he whispered words and kisses along her cheek, chin, and forehead.

Leaning back against the desk, he pulled her closer, the shift in their weight stretching her body out the entire length of his. She fit perfectly, as if she belonged right there and nowhere else. If it was this good standing up in an office, just imagine how it would be in his big bed at his house, when they had all the time in the world to get to know each other.

With a growl of pleasure, he smiled down at her. Never a man at a loss for words, he surprisingly could only offer, "Whooee."

"Did I pass?" she asked breathlessly.

"Pass what?"

"The passion test."

"With flying colors." He chuckled. "You are mighty fine, honey. Mighty fine."

"Do you really think so?" she asked with undisguised pleasure.

"No doubt about it. You are one hot sexy woman." He kissed her on the mouth, then pulled away. "The next time you see your buddy, Richard, you tell him I said so."

She smiled, started to chuckle, too, then laughed. Her voice was full and husky, and he couldn't help laughing, himself, just because he liked the sound of it so much. "I like seeing you smile," he said. "You should always be happy enough to laugh like this."

"I can't believe how that felt. Like . . ." She gave up searching for words to describe what had just occurred. There weren't any. "I've never had anything like that happen to me before."

Me, either, Beau thought, but didn't say. He was too experienced with this type of situation to admit that it had been something out of the ordinary. Well, he had been feeling a bit blue himself, lately. That's probably all it was; he refused to credit it with being anything more.

Instead, he simply said, "Good."

"It's amazing, but my itching has stopped." She looked down at her torso as though it belonged to someone else. "I haven't felt better in a long long time."

"I'm glad I could help." He flicked a finger against the tip of her nose. It was so cute, tiny and turned up at the end. Just looking at her made him want to start kissing her all over again, but the sound of a throat being cleared, coming from the direction of the doorway, rescued him from himself. Glancing over, he smiled in recognition.

Allison heard the sound at the same time and turned slightly in Beau's arms, looking over her shoulder toward the door. A cute blond woman stood there—mid-thirties, about Allison's size, with a short pert haircut. She looked interesting and friendly in a casual sort of way, dressed in khaki slacks, plaid shirt, and corduroy blazer. Her hands were slipped into the pockets of her pants, and she rocked back and forth on loafer-clad feet.

"Hi, I'm sorry I'm late," she said. "I'm Dr. Pat Beaudine. Are you Allison? I'm glad you waited for me."

Allison jumped away from Beau as if she'd just touched something red-hot. Sometime during their encounter, he'd pulled the pins from her hair without her realizing it. It was hanging curled around her shoulders, and she ran a nervous hand through it. "*You're* Dr. Beaudine?"

"Yes," the woman answered, puzzled.

"Then who the hell is this?" Allison asked, nearly shouting, pointing at the man who had just completed his seduction.

"My brother, Harley," the doctor responded slowly, looking back and forth at the two of them and obviously not liking what she saw. "Do you two know each other?"

"We do now," Beau offered with a smile.

"You bastard!" Allison spat out as she wheeled around, pulled back a hand, and slapped him across the face with all the force she could muster. She seriously considered continuing the attack, wrapping her fingers around his worthless neck and squeezing until there wasn't a breath left in his body.

"Harley, what did you do?" Patty Beaudine groaned just as his head snapped to the side with a resounding smack.

"Ah, honey," he griped to Allison, rubbing his stinging cheek, "what'd you go and do that for?"

"You told me you were Dr. Beaudine!"

"I never said any such a thing!"

"You did!"

"You were the one who asked if I was Patty. I told

you my name was Beau. Can I help it if you came to the wrong conclusion?"

"I asked about your clothes," she said, looking scathingly at his overdone western attire, the kind she'd always detested and detested even more now. "And you said that's what you always wear to work."

"It is, and I'm heading there in just a few minutes."

"He plays music," Patty offered softly, "and sings."

"He does *what?*" Aghast, Allison whirled to face her.

"He's a musician."

"What kind of musician?" she asked, ready to kill.

"He has a country band."

"Ooh . . . a lounge act!"

"I'm not a lounge act," Beau provided, terribly offended at not being recognized. "I'm Harley Beaudine."

"I've been standing here pouring my heart out to a lounge act!" Allison roared to the ceiling, his flip attitude causing her fury to grow by leaps and bounds. "Of all the dirty, lowdown, disgusting, filthy tricks. You're a pig, a pervert, a slug. You're slime. No, you're lower than slime." She frantically looked around the room for something she could brandish as a weapon, but nothing looked useful. "I'll murder you with my bare hands."

"I don't know what you're so all-fired upset about," Beau said. "Just a few minutes ago, you were telling me that your itching was gone, and that you hadn't felt better in ages."

Allison's jaw fell open in shock. A loud humming started deep in her ears and moved to her eyes until she saw red. She charged him, fists swinging out to pummel his chest, but before she could land

any blows Patty jumped forward, wrapping her in a
bear hug and holding tight.

"Let me go," Allison begged. "Let me kill him."

"Much as it would make you feel better, your
pleasure would only be temporary."

"No, I'd be happy for a long long time."

Patty held on until Allison quit struggling, then
dropped her arms and rested a comforting hand
on Allison's wrist. "Allison, please. I don't know
what happened here, but I can tell how upset you
are. Let's all just calm down for a minute while we
sort this out."

"Calm down! Are you crazy?" Allison hissed.
"You'll be lucky if I don't sue you for this." Even as
she threatened it, she knew she never would. How
could she ever relate this humiliation to another
soul? Pointing a condemning finger at Patty's
brother, she insisted, "That man is a menace."

"I know," Patty agreed.

"You know?" Allison shrieked. "Then what is he
doing here in your office where he can prey on unsuspecting women?"

"It's my fault," Patty admitted readily. "I had an
emergency, and I knew I couldn't get here on time,
so I asked him to come by to tell you I'd be late, and
to ask you to wait." She looked over at her brother,
flashing him a look that could have melted lead.
"I'm sorry." She shrugged. "Whatever he did, I'm
sorry. I thought he could behave himself for two seconds. Obviously," she said caustically, "I was wrong."

In his own defense, Beau offered, "I didn't do
anything she didn't want me to do."

"You're not helping, Harley," Patty said in a tone
that brooked no argument, though it had never

worked on him before and she didn't expect that it would now.

Allison was shaking all over. The force of her rage was matched only by the size of her mortification. "You're blaming this on me?" she asked Beau. "I innocently came in here needing some help and advice, and you took advantage of my distress. I told you everything! Everything! Oh, God . . ." she trailed off, holding her fingers tightly against her lips, thinking she might be sick right there in the middle of Dr. Beaudine's carpet.

"It's a good thing I convinced you to stay, too," he continued. "After hearing your story, I've got to admit that I've never met anybody who needed Patty's help as much as you do."

"Shut up!" both women shouted at him at the same time.

"Oh, God, oh, God . . ." Allison cried as the tears that had threatened to overflow finally did. "I've got to get out of here." She looked around as though lost, saw the hallway, and started to run.

"Allison, wait!" Patty begged, taking a few steps after her, but the woman was already out the door, and Patty wasn't about to further her humiliation by chasing her down the walkway for all of Jackson to see. She stood there silently, leaning against the doorjamb, watching her go until she disappeared around the corner.

First, she counted to ten, then twenty, before turning back to face her brother. While she would have loved to scream and shout at him, long experience had taught her that it wouldn't do any good. He was the incomparable, immovable, unchangeable Harley Beaudine.

Taking a deep breath, she closed the front door and returned to her office. Beau was already relaxed in the chair behind her desk, still wearing her stethoscope, his feet propped up, leafing through a magazine as though nothing untoward had just happened.

She walked over to him, yanked her stethoscope off his neck, and shoved his legs hard, snarling, "Move!"

"Ouch," he winced, the western drawl in his speech suspiciously absent now that Allison had departed. Getting up in slow motion, he walked over to the opposite couch, where he flopped down, looking terribly put out.

"What the hell did you do?" she asked.

"Nothing—" he began, but she cut off whatever else he might have added by raising her hand.

"Save it," she said, rolling her eyes. "I saw you kissing her."

"Then why'd you ask?"

"It's just a funny quirk I have. I like to see how many different ways you can come up with to justify the way you act."

"Hey, that woman needed a kiss like nobody I've ever met. I gave her one. What's wrong with that?"

"What's wrong with that?" she asked, rubbing her eyes in frustration. Why did she even try to have a serious discussion with him? "She came to see me because of a physical condition that's very likely being aggravated by personal problems."

"Don't I know it!"

"Most likely, they're very distressing."

"Extremely distressing."

"Since you realize that, couldn't you have kept your hands off her?"

"Why would I want to?"

"Maybe because you're a grown man, and it's way past time you started acting like one?"

"What fun would that be?"

Patty rolled her eyes again. Most days, she could tolerate his ability to skirt along the edges of adolescence, even though he was quickly pushing forty. Today was not most days—not when his juvenile behavior had jeopardized a client's health. "Just tell me what you did, so that when I call her to apologize, I'll know exactly what happened."

"She came in here all panicked and tense, saying she couldn't stay and she was sorry she'd made the appointment. I could tell what a bad time she was having just from looking at her, and I knew you should see her. So I got her talking to pass the time."

"That was all?"

"Yeah. Pretty much."

"Didn't you leave something out?"

"What?"

"You were kissing her when I walked in!"

"Oh, that," he said, waving a hand as though their embraces had been the least important part.

"Yes, that." Patty waited, then waited some more, knowing he'd break down and spill the truth. She was probably the only person in the world who could make him feel guilty about anything, even though her success at it was limited. He seldom thought he did anything wrong.

"She was having some troubles with her fiancé."

"What kind of troubles?"

"The guy keeps telling her she's not sexy. He's been doing such a number on her that she's started to believe it."

"Oh, no," Patty groaned.

"So I just took a few minutes to show her the guy was wrong."

"What? You couldn't just say I was late, and leave it at that? You had to start in on your version of bedroom therapy?"

"Don't knock it. She was pretty happy till you showed up."

Patty shook her head in disbelief, rubbing at her temples to ease the throbbing headache that had started when she first entered the room. "Allison is right. You're a menace." She reached into a drawer, searching for aspirin but not finding any. Tired of dealing with him, she asked, "Don't you have to be somewhere?"

"I was just leaving." He stood, stretching, giving no outward sign that what had happened had any affect on him at all. Casually, he glanced at his watch, noticing that he needed to be at the hotel in about ten minutes. Jackson was a tiny community, but in the middle of July, trying to drive across town was like trying to maneuver Manhattan at rush hour. He scooped up his hat, moved to the mirror behind her desk, and fussed with it until he had it adjusted just right. "Are you going to stop by to listen?"

"I ought to say no. It would serve you right if I didn't."

"Now, Patty," he said, turning around and rubbing the back of her neck where he could see her muscles tight with tension, "don't be like that. You know if you don't come, you'll fuss for days over the fact that you missed it."

"Would not."

"Would too," he responded in the way they'd often spewed at each other as children.

Patty ground her teeth, irritated by the fact that he was right. He hadn't performed publicly in almost ten years, and the chance to hear him again was too enticing. Despite all the ways he constantly played on her emotions, yanked her chain, and messed up her life, she was and always would be his most devoted fan. Seeing Harley Beaudine perform in person was like no other experience on earth. Grudgingly, she said, "All right. I'll be there."

"I'll play 'Willow Blossoms' for you," he promised. She was a sucker for hearing her favorite songs, and any snit that might still be festering would quickly vanish.

"You don't play fair," she said, hating that he could read her so well.

"Besides," he added, "if you come, you'll have a chance to talk to Allison again."

"Why would she be there? It sounded as if she hates country music."

"She just said that because she's never heard *me*," he said without any trace of humility. "Once she does, she'll change her mind pretty quick."

"It must be nice to be so sure of yourself," Patty said. Just to needle him a bit, she added, "I say she won't show."

"Well, you'll be wrong. She has to be at the hotel. She's my new boss."

"What?"

"She's Allison Masters. You know, *the* Masters

family? This wingding tonight is a welcome reception for her, and the office manager asked me to
stop by and play a few songs—sort of a coming attraction for my new show. They haven't had such a
bigwig from the company show up in a long time,
so they want to make a good first impression."

This was sounding worse by the second. "Tell me
you're kidding."

"Nope. Seems like Daddy Masters sent her out here
to run the hotel for a while." He smiled the Beaudine
smile that had made female hearts pound all over the
west for nearly two decades. "I suspect she and I are
going to be spending a lot of time together."

"If she doesn't kill you first."

"She won't kill me. She loves me." He winked, totally serious. "She just doesn't know it yet." He
snatched Allison's glasses off the desk, stuffed them
in his front pocket, then walked to the door and
opened it. "Let's go. I need to get there early to get
my fiddle tuned."

Chapter 3

Allison stood in front of the hotel and looked up at the discreet sign over the door. The Masters Inn at Jackson Hole was all it said. It was simple, wooden, hand-carved, and stained. Those who came to stay at the small mountain inn—whether for winter skiing or summer touring—didn't need a loud announcement at their arrival. They knew what they were looking for.

The clientele was wealthy, dramatically so, usually famous if not infamous. On any given night, their guest book might include an Arab sheik, a world famous model, an author or two, and several movie stars. The Masters standard of excellence drew them, but the quiet service and small town ease, where they could just be themselves for a while, always brought them back. As more and more of the world's elite fell in love with Wyoming, it had became one of their most popular properties, and reservations had to be made months in advance.

Sitting in her New York office, Allison had been aware of all these facts, but she had never actually entered the inn until this very moment. Before being exiled to the town, she'd never had the desire to set foot in the cowboy community, which was world famous for its nightly rodeos and main street outlaw "shoot-outs."

As she faced the door, trying to find the courage to enter, she scanned the grounds. She was forced to admit that the place held a certain crude charm. The building looked like an old log cabin, complete with rounded logs and pegged corners. There were dramatic rock chimneys visible in several spots, white windowsills set against the dark logs, and window boxes filled with bright red geraniums. Wild yellow rosebushes in full bloom added color across the front and sides.

The architecture had been so skillfully executed that it was hard to tell it was a fifty-room hotel. It blended perfectly with the neighborhood where it was tucked away, a serene blissful haven for those who had too much noise and excitement in their lives.

She looked at her watch and realized she could no longer avoid the inevitable. The staff was expecting her, and they'd be waiting.

Taking a deep breath, she walked up the three steps and opened the screened door. A screened porch, complete with rocking chairs, served as the entryway. The lobby was cozy, with a fireplace in the center and plush armchairs grouped around it. It being a warm July evening, there was no fire, but she could just imagine it in the winter with tired skiers lounging around in bulky sweaters and heavy slippers. Surprisingly, it was an inviting image.

At the front desk, she introduced herself, and the

clerk immediately summoned the office manager, a thin blond man in his mid-twenties.

"Miss Masters?" he asked, extending his hand in a friendly greeting.

"Yes. Chad Hastings?" She'd talked with him on the phone, but they had never met.

"Welcome. We're so glad you're here," he said, and Allison watched him carefully, trying to measure the enthusiasm behind the comment. He appeared to mean it, but then she'd never been good at reading people. "I take it your flight was uneventful."

"Everything was fine."

"And things at the summerhouse were satisfactory?"

"Yes, perfect." The summerhouse was one of several owned by Allison's father, and staying in the huge monstrosity was going to be difficult. Built at a cost of three million dollars, it was twelve thousand square feet of opulent luxury, with a full-time staff and such amenities as an indoor pool, a movie theater, and bedrooms with Jacuzzis.

As far as she knew, her father had stayed there exactly one time. In his circle, it was chic to be able to say he owned a house in the exclusive mountain community. Whether he actually used it or not was beside the point.

"I know you'd like a tour," Chad was saying, "but I thought we could save that for tomorrow."

"That would be fine," Allison agreed, wanting to appear interested. In all actuality, she wished she could just turn around and go back to her life in New York.

"Guests are already arriving for the reception.

Everyone's thrilled about this chance to finally meet you."

She could barely contain a groan. She'd never been good at working crowds. Somewhere along the line, she'd lost out on the natural charisma that seemed to come so automatically to the men of her family. Seldom knowing the right thing to say or do, she often felt tongue-tied in social situations. "Where is it being held?"

"In the bar," Chad said, pointing over her shoulder across the lobby. "And we have a special treat for you, too."

"What is it?" she asked, imagining the worst. What kind of surprise would these small town people think appropriate?

"You'll see," he said, trying to sound mysterious.

"Can I freshen up somewhere?"

He was flustered by his failure to foresee her request, and brought her behind the desk to the administrative offices. Real estate in the valley was at a premium, so no space had been wasted on them. Her office was tiny but functional, and, luckily, had a small bathroom she could call her own. She closed the door after promising to meet Chad in a few minutes so they could head into the reception together.

A quick assessment in the mirror told her that the effects of her encounter with the Beaudines had been minimal. Her hair was down, the wayward pins left scattered on the doctor's floor. The mascara around her eyes was a little smudged. Her feet were sore from walking in her high heels. Her toes were pinched and blistered, and one heel had a raw spot where the strap had rubbed the skin.

After running away from the doctor's office, she'd spent nearly an hour on the bustling streets of downtown Jackson Hole. She'd needed the opportunity to get her careening emotions under control, and the warm pleasant evening had proved to be a soothing balm to her aching soul.

There were thousands of people out, eating, sightseeing, and enjoying the summer weather. For a time, she'd sat on a bench in the town square. A peacefulness had crept over her as she watched tourists go in and out of the designer shops, children lick their ice cream cones, the stagecoach stop to drop off passengers.

Silly, but she'd envied those who were taking the short ride in the old-fashioned, horse-drawn carriage. Not that she'd ever do such a thing, but sitting there, all alone in the midst of so many, she'd been reminded once again of how desperately alone she was.

Her little episode with Beau had only underscored her isolation. She was so starved for a bit of attention, a shred of kindness, a crumb of understanding, that she had poured her heart out to the first stranger who acted as if he'd listen. Just thinking about what a fool she'd made of herself brought a new flood of tears to her eyes, a flood she thought she'd taken plenty of time to suppress. She refused to start crying again.

She repaired her eye makeup, fixed her hair and lipstick. Anger was what she needed. Pure, bright, red-hot fury was a better solution than tears. When she thought of the lowdown, disgusting way Harley Beaudine had used and abused her, she saw red all over again.

Chances were rare that she'd cross paths with him again, but if she did—ooh, if she did! The bastard had better be ready. She was through playing doormat for every womanizing scoundrel who thought he could walk all over her.

Before she could go too far down that road, she forced herself back to the present. Chad was waiting just outside, ready to introduce her to the senior staff and whoever else he felt she should meet on her first day. Much as she wished she could simply go back to the summerhouse, take a long soak in the Jacuzzi, then bury herself under her covers, she had obligations.

"Chin up, girl," she murmured to her reflection. "You can do this."

She opened the door and stepped into the hall. On seeing her, Chad snapped to attention.

"All set?" he asked.

"Yes. I'm ready." She pulled on the bottom of her suitcoat, straightening the hem. "Is there anything I should know before we go in?"

"No. It's very casual tonight. Along with the staff, I've invited some civic leaders, a few of the more important business people. The bar is open, too, so there may be a few guests present. We'll have some live music a bit later."

"How nice." She smiled, not meaning it at all. The event sounded dreadful. Chad seemed unaware of her sarcasm, though, as he moved her through the lobby and into the bar. To her surprise, it was full of people. They were a pumped up crowd, the members obviously in a festive mood. Since she knew they couldn't possibly all be there to meet her, she wondered what the attraction was.

It was a glorious, long July evening. Why would anyone want to be inside if they didn't have to be?

The bar was small, matching the hotel in ambiance and style, with only twenty tables or so, six stools at the bar itself, but people were packed in from end to end. Fireplaces were strategically located on either side and, despite the current crowd, she could picture how cozy it would be in the winter with skiers huddled around, sipping their hot drinks.

At the far end there was a stage, where a guitarist and bass player were fiddling with their equipment, readying themselves for the concert Chad had promised. She could just imagine how a performer would sound in the tiny space with a limited audience. It was an entertainer's dream, and she closed her eyes for a moment, hearing the music in her head—a solo guitar or piano, something bluesy, moody, and quiet, to help the crowd unwind after a hard day on the slopes.

Chad worked her through the crowd, introducing her to everyone he felt she should meet, but there were simply too many people.

Glancing discreetly but impatiently at her watch, she saw it was nearing eight. Thinking she had spent enough time saying hello, she hoped to plead fatigue and slip away. To her dismay, Chad chose that instant to steer her to a table in the very front, next to the stage. She was completely boxed in, and wouldn't be able to escape.

As though the rest of the crowd sensed what was coming, there was a definite increase in its animation. Through the loud drone of bar noise, she managed to ask, "What's happening?"

"It's time for your surprise." Chad pulled out a chair, then sat himself next to her.

"What is it?" she asked, simply wanting the horrid day to end. Before he could answer, a third chair was pulled back, and Allison looked up to see that Patty Beaudine had joined them.

"Oh, hi, Patty," Chad exclaimed. "Dr. Patty Beaudine, this is Allison Masters, our new manager. She just arrived from New York."

"Hi," Patty said casually, as though they'd never met before.

"Hello," Allison answered automatically.

"Patty's the town's favorite doctor," Chad felt compelled to add, laughing, "so she knows everybody's secrets."

Patty groaned, and Allison turned pale as a ghost. If only the floor would open and swallow her. A wave of nausea coursed through her, and she truly thought she might be ill, which worked to her advantage. It gave her the excuse she needed to leave.

Just as she was about to turn to Chad and tell him so, Patty said gently, "You don't know what's happening, do you?"

"I've kept it a surprise!" Chad crowed, all enthusiasm. Allison shot them both a deadly look as he continued. "It's such a coup for the hotel. We can use it in our national advertising. Tickets are already sold out for the first three months."

"Tickets for what?" Allison asked.

"For Harley Beaudine! He's come out of retirement just to play here in the lounge. Exclusively! Isn't that great?" he asked, failing to notice that neither woman agreed with him.

I never should have gotten out of bed this morning, Allison thought. *This nightmare just keeps getting worse.*

Behind her, she could hear the crowd chanting. Different groups had been doing that the past few minutes, and, in her naiveté she'd thought they were drunkenly saying, "Oh, Oh, Oh." Now, she realized they were saying, "Beau, Beau, Beau."

As if summoned by their siren call, in a bright spotlight illuminating the stage, he burst through a curtain, looking more handsome and dazzling than he'd been in his sister's office. His blond hair was silver against the shiny black of his cowboy shirt, and much of the red stitching across his shoulders and chest was embedded with sequins, making him sparkle every time he moved.

He didn't just step onto the stage. He seized it, captured it, appearing larger than life, a man obviously and completely in his element. There was an aura around him of energy and tension that defied onlookers from turning their attention elsewhere. When he stood in front of a crowd, nothing else mattered. Everyone felt it immediately—even Allison, much as she didn't want to.

"Hello, Jackson," he said into the mike, his voice once again oozing that slow western drawl, "it's good to be back."

The local crowd hooted and hollered as though they were in the middle of a stadium rock concert, and Allison winced at the volume of his welcome. Patty, seeing her reaction, leaned over and placed a comforting hand on her forearm, leaning close and whispering, "It will be all right."

Allison shot her a look that had slain lesser mortals,

and Patty dropped her hand. In a deadly tone, Allison said, "Leave me alone."

"Sorry." Patty shrugged in defeat, knowing the situation could only go from bad to worse.

The guitarist and bassist began playing a typical western beat, the kind that made people want to get up and dance. Allison hated the way her body responded to it. She curled her toes into her shoes and forced her feet against the floor, refusing to tap her foot in time with the music, succeeding well until Beau stepped to the microphone and began to sing.

She'd intended to hate it. She'd intended to ignore him. But, once he started, it was simply impossible not to listen, and not be moved. His distinctive baritone filled the small bar, coursing off the ceiling, walls, and floors, making her skin tingle, her blood throb in her veins, her eyes moisten.

Good as it was, it got even better after he raised his violin to his chin and began to play. The smooth resonant vibration of the instrument soothed her raw nerves like warm molasses, giving off a rich timbre she had never heard matched, not even by the finest concert violinist.

Grudgingly, she was forced to admit that she'd never heard anything like it. Why did he have to be so good? And so obviously adored because of it?

The song ended, and the crowd came to its feet, stamping and cheering. Being terribly conspicuous, she felt forced to join them, a brittle smile on her lips, daggers in her eyes. She clapped politely, refusing to show any hint of enjoyment.

Before the applause could begin to fade, the ensemble began another song, this one slow and poignant. Because Beau seemed to be looking right at her, Allison glanced away, only to notice Patty Beaudine smiling so hard she was crying and wiping tears away with the back of her hand.

"I'm just so glad he agreed to do this," Patty murmured, and Allison was shocked by the lump that formed in her throat. The love Patty felt for her brother was so apparent that it hurt to watch, and she tried to find somewhere safe to rest her gaze. She made the mistake of looking back at the stage. Beau smiled and winked at her, quickly bringing her back to her senses.

"Bastard!" she said aloud, the noise of the crowd too loud for anyone standing nearby to hear. He read her lips, though, raising her ire when he merely laughed, winked again, then continued hamming it up.

For the next half hour, she suffered silently, listening to a dozen more songs, the crowd growing louder and more boisterous with each one. The tunes were varied, some raucous and rowdy, some melancholy and sad with beautiful melodies and lyrics. Many times, those in the assembly of listeners sang along. Apparently everyone but Allison was familiar with Beau's repertoire.

Who was this man? How famous was he? Chad had mentioned that his presence could bring national recognition for the small hotel. Could Beau really be that illustrious?

She couldn't be the only one who realized he was a disgusting pervert. Knowing how fickle the public was, most in the room probably overlooked his flaws because of his good looks and talent. Having grown up in a family known for its rich, alluring men, she knew the phenomenon well.

So, Beau thought he was going to perform at her hotel, did he? Well, she'd see about that!

When the song came to an end Beau's two backup musicians continued to play while he addressed the crowd.

"Man, do I feel good!" he said over the sound of the closing music. He smiled, just the curve of his lips sending the room into a clapping frenzy. "I start my show right here on Saturday night. I hope y'all will make it a point to come back reg'lar." Dozens of fans shouted that they would, and he said, "Thank you, and good night."

With a few draws of his bow across the violin strings, it was over. Amid thunderous applause and excessive whooping, Patty and numerous others rushed to the stage.

Chad, a truly enraptured fan, obviously wanted to run to Beau's side, too, but Allison stopped him. They exited the bar together, and, despite herself, she couldn't help peeking back toward the stage, where Beau was surrounded by adoring women, one of whom had him in a tight lip-lock. She was young and blond, with a body to die for, and it was pressed against his from mouths to breasts to knees.

Allison was shocked by the flash of pure unadulterated jealousy that shot through her at the sight, her best intentions notwithstanding. Two hours earlier, he'd been holding *her* like that, kissing *her* like that, and, much as her mind wanted to forget the entire humiliating episode, her body remembered in full force.

She shook herself back to reality. The man was a

pig! He'd kiss anything or anyone! God, he'd probably kiss Chad if he had the chance. Yet she stood there mooning over him like a sick dog.

Forcing her gaze out into the lobby, she walked determinedly to the executive offices, with Chad following along behind. He was still excited from the short concert.

"Wasn't that great?" he asked once they were behind a closed door.

"Yes, great," she answered with none of his enthusiasm.

"It's such a boon for the hotel. I can't believe we were able to get him signed!"

Chad went off on a detailed explanation of the events leading up to Beau's contract, relieving Allison of the embarrassing trouble of pumping him for information that she should have already known, since she was supposedly a bigwig at corporate, and the new inn manager.

Beau's fame had evidently come from being part of a band when he was in his twenties. For some reason, a decade earlier, he'd quit performing and touring. Instead, he'd tucked himself away in Jackson, a local enigma, doing nothing more than living in his house and sticking pretty much to himself.

The previous inn manager had gotten the idea of having him perform in the intimate setting of the hotel bar and had approached Patty with the idea. Patty, in turn, had spent nearly a year convincing her brother to come out of retirement. Apparently, Beau was such a renowned personage that Allison's father had involved himself in the negotiations.

"How long is the contract for?" she asked, interrupting Chad's monologue.

"Only six months!" he said in dismay. "That's all we could get him to agree to!"

Allison hid her consternation. Six months! That was the length of time for which she'd been banished to Jackson Hole. The thought of him working in the hotel the entire time she was in Wyoming was too dreadful to contemplate. Something had to be done.

Trying hard not to rain on Chad's parade of devotion, she said, "Six months seems like a long time to book the same act."

"Not Harley Beaudine. He *is* Jackson Hole. He's a veritable living symbol of the New West."

She could hardly keep from rolling her eyes. He sounded as if he were quoting from a magazine one might find tucked behind an airline seat. "Really, Chad, you make him sound like a legend or something."

"He is!" Chad insisted.

"He's just a singer," she shot back more nastily than she meant to. "I want to see the contract. Could you have it on my desk in the morning?"

"Sure."

There had to be something the lawyers could do to terminate it. "Are we on for tomorrow with the department heads?"

"Yes, ma'am. Everyone will be here at seven o'clock."

"I'll want individual meetings with them during the day after that. Tell them to be prepared to make themselves available."

"I'll make sure everyone knows."

"Thanks, Chad. I know this will be a difficult transition. I want to make it as easy as possible on everyone." *Especially myself,* she thought. The first day had been a catastrophe, and she couldn't take many more like it. "Now, I'm exhausted. Could you call me a cab to take me out to the summerhouse?" The house was several miles out of town, on a gravel road lined with mind-boggling, overdone country mansions that all looked more or less like her father's.

"I could drive you."

"That's all right. It's too far out of your way."

She'd only been in Jackson a day, but it was already clear that transportation was going to be a problem. Making a mental note to deal with it in the morning, she turned to go. "I'll wait for the cab out in front."

"Good night, Miss Masters."

"Good night, Chad." A white lie slipped out as she added, "Thank the staff for the reception. It was very nice."

Outside, it was quiet. She stood listening to sounds she'd never heard before. Some kind of insects were humming. Crickets? They were soothing in an odd sort of way. The air was filled with the green odors of summer. Roses wafted their light scent from the bushes along the front of the hotel, and there were other smells, all strange and unknown, and she felt as though she'd stepped into some foreign exotic land where everything was new and different.

"It's beautiful tonight, isn't it?"

The male voice coming from right next to her could only belong to one man. She whirled around to see Beau materialize out of the shadows. He was so close that she could have reached out and touched him. Wasn't she safe from running into him, no matter where she went?

Through gritted teeth she asked, "What are you doing here?"

"Looking for you."

His answer stopped her. But only for a second. "Well, you found me. What do you want?"

"You were upset when you left Patty's office. I just wanted to make sure you're all right. I brought you your glasses. You left them in Pat's office."

Renewed embarrassment and anger tinged her cheeks pink, and she grabbed the glasses. "Mr. Beaudine—"

He cut her off. "Just call me Beau."

"Mr. Beaudine," she began again, "I'm going to buy a knife. A great big one. And if you ever mention that incident again, I'm going to gut you with it and scatter your innards on the ground so some of the wild animals for which Jackson is so famous can pick away at them at their leisure. Do I make myself clear?"

He took a step closer, and she stood her ground. There were only inches separating them, and electricity seemed to spark from him to her.

"I like your hair down," he said. "You should wear it this way all the time."

He exuded a sexual energy to which her body instinctively responded, and she couldn't prevent her senses from kicking into overdrive. She was instantly aware of everything about him. The sparkle in his eye. The width of his shoulders. The tang of tobacco and whiskey he carried with him from the bar. Underneath it all, she could detect a musk that was all his own, one so distinctive that she could be standing blindfolded in a crowd of a thousand and be able to pick him out.

Nothing like this had ever happened to her before, and she didn't know why it was happening now.

"You're so pretty," he said softly, reaching out with his fingers and running them through her hair.

Like a thunderstruck virgin, she let him do it, relishing the feel of his heat, the touch of his hand, the tender words that made her feel as attractive as he said she was. But only for a moment. Reason quickly prevailed, and she slapped his hand away and took a step back to put more space between them. "Don't touch me again, either. I don't like it."

"Liar." He laughed.

"Tell me why you were looking for me, Mr. Beaudine, then beat it. It's been a long day, and I don't have any energy left to put up with more of your nonsense."

"How'd you like my singin'?"

She paused, searching for a word she knew would deflate some of his enlarged ego. "It was very . . . very *adequate*."

"Adequate!" he began, offended, then stopped himself. "Honey, you're lyin' again. I watched you through the whole thing. You loved me."

He'd watched her through the whole thing!? Little warm butterflies swarmed in her stomach, then she quashed them. "I know my predecessor was completely enamored of you and was dying to have you perform here, but I'm not sure your kind of music is appropriate for the image we're trying to project for the hotel."

"Are you still mad about our little misunderstandin'?"

"Little misunderstanding?" she hissed, quickly

reining herself in when the front door of the hotel opened and a group of people exited. Several of the women called their good nights to Beau, and he smiled and waved. After they'd passed out of earshot, she said quietly but fiercely, "A little misunderstanding? Is that what you'd call it?"

"We could call it something else, if you want."

Intrigued by the huskiness that had come into his voice, she turned, ready to give him what-for, but stopped when she saw how near he'd moved. He hovered like a big, silent, predatory cat, ready to pounce, ready to devour.

"I'm free for the rest of the night," he said. "How about if I give you a lift home? It's on my way."

She snorted. "I wouldn't get into a car with you if you were the last man on earth."

Beau ignored the insult, choosing instead to raise a hand and rest it against her cheek. His thumb played over her bottom lip. "I'd like to finish what we started."

Allison was caught. She couldn't move away or push him back. All sensation was centered on the touch of his thumb against her mouth, and it shot a charge of desire through her breasts and down between her thighs. The temporary paralysis gave her plenty of time to think.

What caused this completely unreasonable desire to fall into his arms? What was it about him? The elevation in Jackson was around six thousand feet. Perhaps the thin oxygen at the high altitude had affected her brain.

In a voice that sounded nothing like her own, she insisted, "We didn't start anything."

"Didn't we?"

The front door of the hotel opened and closed again, and Chad hustled out, chatty and oblivious, breaking the cord of control Beau seemed to exercise over her.

"I thought I'd better check to see if you were still standing here. The cabs aren't always so reliable. Oh, here it is."

Just as he said that, a battered beige station wagon with a dent in one of the fenders and no sign on top pulled up to the curb. Allison stepped away from Beau, welcoming the commotion that set her free of his spell, but eyeing the car with some distaste. Beau reached around her and opened the passenger door.

"My offer still holds," he said, seeing how dubiously she regarded the backseat.

"No, thank you," she said, firmly refusing both the ride home and the myriad of other activities a ride might entail.

"Are you sure?" he asked, his tone oozing sexual promise. "Lonely nights in Jackson Hole can get pretty long."

Allison was furious at the come-on, made right in front of her assistant. Just what she needed was for word to get out that she was the kind of loose woman who would fall under the spell of Harley Beaudine on her first day in town. That was *exactly* what she'd done, she was forced to admit, but she'd slit her wrists before she'd let anybody know about it.

If Chad thought they were involved, she'd never earn any respect from him or her new staff. Time to put Beau in his place. Time to let Chad know that Beau was just an employee, nothing more. She glared at Chad. "Has Mr. Beaudine been advised of the meeting in the morning?"

"Ah . . . no," Chad hesitated. "I didn't think he'd be one of the people you'd expect to attend."

"Why not?"

Chad fumbled around, his hero-worship obvious. "Well, he's . . . he's Harley Beaudine. We can't ask him to get out of bed at the crack of dawn like a regular . . . regular person."

"Isn't he the new *lounge* act?" She stressed the word, making it sound like an epithet. "Won't that place him in a position to have a maximum effect on guests' enjoyment of their stay?"

"Well, I guess," he hedged. "But everyone knows Beau never gets up before noon."

"Why?"

"He works at night," he explained, stating it as though it was one of the Ten Commandments.

"I hardly consider that my problem." She was being a bitch, but she couldn't seem to help it. "He'll be there, or I'll know why."

Chad looked as if he was, once again, going to jump to Beau's defense no matter the personal cost, but Beau stopped him with a look, one that made it seem as though the two of them were sharing a little man-to-man joke at her expense.

"That's all right, Chad," he said, adding slowly and with special emphasis, "whatever Miz Masters wants, I'll be more than happy to provide."

"Seven A.M. Sharp!" she said to Beau, ignoring the blatant sexual offer.

"See you then," he said with that irritating smile.

Without saying anything further to either one of them, she got into the cab and left.

Chapter 4

Beau walked into the dark and quiet of his empty house. The place had been his home for years now, long before it had become popular for wealthy men to build dream getaways in Jackson. He stood in the center of the living room, wondering what to do. Even though it was mid-July, there was a chill in the air. For a moment, he thought about lighting a fire to chase it away, but couldn't seem to find the energy to do it. The clock on the wall chimed softly, telling him it was already one o'clock.

After his performance, he'd been too jazzed to come home right away. It was always that way after he'd been on stage. The adrenaline provided by the crowd's energy, the synergy with the band, the unequaled joy of playing well and sounding good, was the ultimate. He'd never been able to sit still after he finished.

A decade earlier, he'd have partied till closing time, picked up one or two women, gone to a motel room with a box of condoms, a bottle of Jack and a case of Bud, and made a night of it. Not anymore, though.

Somewhere along the way, he'd lost the desire. Once, he'd thought of his life as a continuous party, but now he felt too old to suffer through the hangovers, too tired to get by on no sleep, too set in his ways to wake up in a strange bed.

There'd been so many women over the years, and he had no regrets about any of them. Being in a band, a famous one at that, was as great as it could get for a man in his twenties. Women threw themselves at his feet, whispered their room numbers in his ear, slipped their phone numbers in his pocket, fondled him in the backseat while their husbands sat in the front.

That kind of stuff had been fun when he was twenty, but now, looking at it through thirty-nine-year-old eyes, it seemed kind of pathetic. Maybe he should get a life—a topic which weighed heavily on his mind these days. He couldn't remember the last time a woman had truly turned his head. Oh, he still looked a lot and played occasionally—he was human, after all—but there was a sameness about them all, and had been for a long time. Turn the lights off, and he couldn't tell one from another. Turn them on again, and they all looked so damn young!

For several years now, he'd tried to ignore the fact that he was old enough to be a father to many of them. Some of the young ones had screwed his socks off, but, much as he liked that when it was happening, he had come to want something more—like conversation when it was over.

Who would have ever thought? Harley Beaudine,

the great lover and user of women, wanted to find one who could carry on a conversation when it was over.

There was one small consolation in this change. At least he wasn't going to turn out like his father. God forbid that he'd walk into his bedroom when he was pushing seventy only to see some twenty-year-old stretched out on his bed. He absolutely refused to become a lecherous old man like his daddy.

He went to the kitchen, popped a beer, and stood for a long time feeling lonely and out of sorts, which he hated. Lately, he detested being alone, and he couldn't find enough ways to pass the time. Contentment was elusive, and he couldn't seem to figure out what pieces were missing so he could get it back.

Outside, the clear summer night beckoned, and he thought about taking his fiddle into the backyard and playing to the moon. It would be full in a few days, right during the tenth anniversary of the plane crash. He was entitled to howl a little, wasn't he?

He couldn't work up the energy he needed, though. It was this way more and more. The old pleasures simply didn't hold the thrill they once had.

Beer in hand, he trudged up the stairs to his room and walked out on the balcony. His property bordered Grand Teton National Park, and he looked out across his yard to the forests on the edge of the park. Far off in the distance, the upper peak of the Grand Teton itself was visible in the bright moonlight. The magnificent piece of rock and snow called to him like nothing else, almost as if it had cast some sort of magical spell.

After the plane crash, when he'd finally been discharged from the hospital, his world shattered, his friends and fellow band members dead, he hadn't belonged anywhere. The world seemed empty, moving too fast, so it wasn't surprising that he'd been drawn back to the mystery the mountain offered. His house and the small town peace and quiet of Jackson had been the balm he'd needed, and he'd stayed—the weeks gradually turning into months, and then to years.

On the railing, his telescope perched, waiting for him to peer far off into the distance. He used it to watch climbers nearing the peak of the Grand, to observe them moving in silent slow motion as they pounded their pegs and rappelled on their ropes. They were up there now, sleeping in their little bivouac tents, waiting for the morning and their final assaults on the summit.

He adjusted the viewfinder, but even with the radiant moon he couldn't see any of them, so he lowered the lens, looking out across the woods for animals that might be on the prowl. Near the edge of the trees he hesitated for a long time, thinking he saw a moose, waited, then decided it was just the shadows. He turned it the other way.

Across the valley he could see the mansions set along both sides of the road. The Masters family's summer home was one of them, and he brought the house into sharper focus. Except for the yard and landscape lights, the place was dark. He scanned the windows on the upper floors, wondering which one belonged to Allison.

No doubt about it, having sex with her would be a far cry from doing it with the twenty-year-olds he kept running into. With all that temper and sass, she'd actually have something to say when it was over.

Casually searching the windows, he let his imagination run free, trying to picture the room she'd select for herself, what she'd wear to bed.

Red, he decided.

Hell, it was his dream. He could dress her or undress her anyway he wanted. So, red it was. Something thin and sheer that would hug every inch of those great tits and that lush ass. It would have a long slit up the side, so some of that creamy white skin would show whenever she moved her leg. She'd have on some red earrings and a gold necklace, so that when he took off the slinky negligee, that's all she'd be wearing. The necklace would have a blood-red, heart-shaped pendant, and he'd use the tip of it to tease her nipple until . . .

"Well, hell," he murmured, looking down at the sudden bulge in his pants. Damn if he hadn't started to get hard just from thinking about her. Maybe he should have accepted one of the offers he'd received while he was in town. He patted his front pocket, knowing he carried a few phone numbers, knowing he could call and find some comfort.

He hesitated for the longest time, standing in the moonlight, staring into his bedroom at the phone on the nightstand. Finally, he flopped back down in a chair and sipped on his beer. Whatever those ladies offered would be fine while it lasted, but he'd still be antsy in the morning. He wanted . . . what?

A slow smile curved his lips as comprehension gradually dawned. He wanted that sizzle again. The one he used to feel when he was twenty, when a hot babe caught his attention, when a new song came together with the band, when he played a lick so sweetly that it brought tears to his eyes.

He wanted that sizzle, the same one he'd felt when he was kissing Allison Masters in Patty's office. He couldn't remember the last time anything—a woman, music, life—had made him feel that way. So alive. So vital. He wanted to feel it again.

He didn't know what it was about Allison that yanked his chain, but it was something special. Something about the way she looked, maybe, or the way she smelled. Whatever it was, she set his senses on full alert. When he got close to her, he felt like a bull elk sniffing out the prime female in his herd. It was primal. Ancient. Uncontrollable. Therefore, impossible to fight. So, why even try?

Hadn't she said she'd been sent to Jackson for six months? Perfect. He'd work on her, spend some time wearing her down. And he had no illusions about that. He *would* wear her down. They all said yes sooner or later.

Eventually, she'd welcome him into her bed over in that fancy house of theirs. He'd take advantage of what she offered for the few months she was in the valley, let their connection set him on fire. Get her back on track as a woman, so she could forget all about what her idiotic fiancé had done. Then, about the time the excitement started to fade and he began to get bored, she'd be scheduled to leave. No strings. No hassles. Just a pleasurable good-bye.

Just the way he liked things.

Relieved to have a plan, he sat back in his chair, letting a rustle of wind chill his skin. A small herd of deer came across the yard, worked the salt lick, then disappeared as quietly as they'd come. He smiled at the sight. Then he went down, snagged another beer, and brought it back outside. When he'd finished that one, too, he grabbed his fiddle and played a few tunes for the night animals, who liked to listen.

He was a sight, he supposed. An almost forty-year-old man who had no real friends and only a sister he'd claim as family, sitting by himself in his big empty house, with only wild animals to keep him company. But his life was just how he wanted it. It wasn't that he was lonely, or feeling sorry for himself, or anything like that. No, he was fine. He just needed a little diversion from his routine, and Allison Masters was going to provide it. Then, he'd feel better—happier again, less alone.

It was coming up on four o'clock when he remembered the promise he'd made to show up at the hotel at seven. Now, why had he gone and done that? He hadn't been up at seven since . . . well, he couldn't remember when. It was an ungodly hour. When he was younger, he usually stayed *up* till seven. One of the privileges of the life he'd built was that he could get up any damn time he pleased, and that sure as hell wasn't at seven in the morning.

He fell asleep grumpy, tossed and turned for a few hours, and woke up even grumpier. He had to scramble to shower and dress, and barely made it to the hotel on time. In the lobby, the desk clerk motioned him behind the counter and toward a conference room at the end of the hall. As he entered, he glanced at his watch and saw that it was fifteen minutes after the hour.

Allison was standing at the far end, a small lectern in front of her, an overhead projector lighting up the wall behind her. A dozen people were packed around the table. Heads turned and the various hotel employees murmured welcomes and voiced surprise at seeing him up so early, interrupting the flow of Allison's speech and obviously causing her a great deal of irritation.

"Mr. Beaudine," she said caustically as he found a chair in the corner and slouched down, "how nice of you to join us."

"Mornin', ma'am."

"You're late," she said. "Don't let it happen again. I don't tolerate tardiness in employees. This is the only warning you'll get about it." Hardly taking a breath, she returned to her notes, ignoring him completely.

Well, wasn't she a bitch and a half first thing in the morning?

She sure was cute, though, dressed in red as he'd imagined her in his fantasies, although in a power suit with a long jacket and short skirt. Whenever she shifted sideways, he got a great shot of thigh. She seemed to like high heels, and wore a pair of red ones that set off the length of those glorious legs. Her hair was up again, pulled back in that bun.

She was talking about corporate image or some such nonsense, and he leaned back in his chair, resting his head against the wall. Her voice was low and husky, and he thought with a smile about how great she'd sound as one of those late-night deejays on a big city radio station. The rhythm and cadence of her speech was like the gentle rocking of a boat.

Before he knew it his eyes closed, and he fell into a deep sleep, the first he'd enjoyed in a long time.

Allison hadn't intended to talk as long as she did. It was her first speech, after all, and she didn't want her new employees to think she was boring or dull. Plus, they all had places to be and things to do. But, ever since her meltdown at the board meeting in New York, she'd felt unsure of herself, as though she needed to prove at every turn that she really did know what she was doing.

She couldn't help glancing over at Beau. What had she been thinking, insisting that he come to her inaugural staff meeting? Wasn't she nervous enough lately about what other people thought of her?

Her temper was the culprit. Everything set it off these days, and she allowed it to rule, instead of her better judgment. So, he'd hit on her in front of Chad. So? He was a consummate womanizer, and his attempt to solicit an evening of pleasure shouldn't have shocked her, nor should she have allowed him to goad her into demanding his presence.

The last thing she needed was to see him so early in her day, looking scrubbed, tired, rumpled, and adorable. It was a sin the way he filled out that western shirt and those tight Levi's, the way they hugged him in all the right spots. Worse yet was how he smelled like fresh mountain air, so clean and crisp that his scent beckoned to her from clear across the room.

She'd spent the night tossing and turning, trying to focus on her new job, her new home, her new town, but all she'd really done was flick back to

wondering about Beau and whether he'd gone
home with the young gorgeous blond she'd seen
him kissing when she left the bar.

From the moment he'd entered the meeting—
late, but what had she expected?—she'd had to
find someplace else to rest her gaze. Just looking in
his direction caused too many confusing thoughts
and images, and made it hard to concentrate.

She'd just begun to wind down her comments
about guest enjoyment and its connection to prof-
itability when a noise coming from the back caught
her off guard. It was followed by a snicker, which
she ignored. The small commotion caused her to
lose her place, and she shuffled through her notes,
trying to get back on track to work toward the end.
The noise came again, followed by more snickers,
and she looked up. The handful of people surrounding Beau were whispering and shaking with
soft laughter. Forcing herself to brave it out, she
looked directly at him, ready to hear some smart
remark from that delicious mouth of his.

He let out a soft snore.

Asleep! The creep was sound asleep!

The first emotion she felt was hurt, hurt that he'd
embarrass her like that, that he'd show her such
disrespect at such an important moment in her
new life. Quickly, she buried the emotion, and replaced it with red-hot anger. Fury worked best in
her relationship with him.

How dare he treat her like that? In front of her
staff! In her own hotel! She was Allison Masters,
and, by God, she wasn't going to stand for that kind
of treatment anymore. Not by him. Not by anyone.

She cleared her throat, held up a hand, silencing

the employees as she said, "We're through here. Thank you all for your attention this morning. Now, let's leave quietly, shall we? So we don't wake him." There were smiles as everyone silently gathered up their belongings, then tiptoed out.

Allison and Chad were the last. Chad, looking horribly worried, asked, "Shall I wake him?"

"No, he'll be all right, just where he is."

"I'm sorry, Miss Masters. I know he didn't mean . . ."

Whatever apologies he might have made on Beau's behalf she cut off, giving him a smile that was pure innocence. She whispered, "Could you please have housekeeping send up a blanket? And bring me our copy of his contract."

He hesitated. "If you're sure—"

"I am." She waited in the doorway until he returned with both. "Go on to my office. I'll join you there in a few minutes."

"What about Beau?"

"Don't worry. I'll take good care of Mr. Beaudine."

Chad looked back and forth several times as though he didn't believe her, but she was the boss, and a Masters to boot. He shrugged in resignation, and left. She closed the door behind him, turned the lock, and shut off the lights. The room was illuminated only by the glow of the overhead projector, which was still on at the front of the room. She walked to it and raised the black pen, ready to write.

Absurdly, she paused, for some reason remembering the look on Patty Beaudine's face when she'd stood in the bar listening to Beau play. It had been filled with so much love and affection. What

Allison was contemplating would hurt Patty very much, and Allison had never been a cruel person.

She scoffed at her equivocation. She didn't owe the woman anything. She didn't owe Beau anything.

Returning her gaze back to the overhead projector, she wrote her message in big letters: YOUR'RE FIRED!!

After adjusting the focus until it was easily readable, she tore his contract into several pieces and placed it on the table directly in front of him. Then, she unfolded the blanket and tucked it around his legs and chest so that he was nice and comfortable. She hoped he'd sleep for a long time, so he would be extremely lucid when he woke and received her message. Let there be no misunderstanding of her intent.

As she left the room, she was surprised that she didn't feel any of the elation she thought she would. She should have been rejoicing. Instead, she was itching at her rash, and felt irritated and out of sorts.

With a word to the desk clerk not to let anyone disturb Beau, she walked on to her office, finding Chad waiting patiently, the files she'd asked for neatly placed in the center of her desk.

"Is Beau all right?" he asked.

"Perfectly." She smiled. "He's still sleeping."

"Oh, I thought you might have—"

"What?"

"Woke him up."

"I didn't need to wake him for him to get my message."

"What message?" Chad asked, cautious.

"He's fired."

"Fired?" Chad choked, his voice coming out an octave higher. "But he's Harley Beaudine. You can't just fire him."

"Can't I?" she asked, and began counting off his transgressions on her fingers. "He's rude, unmanageable, and offensive. He's a born womanizer who's bound to upset many of our female guests. His type of music is too loud and raucous for the image we wish to present, and will draw the wrong type of crowd into the bar. Why anyone thought he would be an appropriate addition to the hotel is completely beyond me. I've chosen to rectify a situation which never should have occurred in the first place."

"You fired him?" Chad asked, apparently not hearing a word of what she just said.

"Do you have a problem with that, Mr. Hastings?" Her tone made it clear that he could also hit the road if he didn't like her decision.

"No . . . no, ma'am," he answered slowly. "I have no problem with that."

"Good. Let's get to work then, shall we?"

She had no idea what time Beau woke up, or what he said and did when he realized what had happened. Because of her position, she couldn't ask anyone. He left the hotel at some point, and, thank goodness, she'd not seen him again. No one mentioned his name or asked about him, but he hovered over everything like the memory of a beloved family member who had just passed away.

Try as she might, she couldn't concentrate all day. She had never fired anyone before, and, doing it for the first time at thirty-two made her feel depressed.

It didn't help that she could feel the employees watching her. When they thought she wasn't paying attention, they stared at her with varying looks of dismay, shock, or disapproval. They all valued their jobs too much to say anything to her face, but she felt their anger all the same.

At last, the horrid day ended, her second in Jackson. All in all, it had been just as terrible as the first, if not worse. With one swift decisive move, she'd managed to alienate her entire staff—even Chad spoke to her only in monosyllables. In a matter of hours, she'd become a walking pariah.

With the greatest relief, she escaped the hotel at dusk, once again taking the nasty taxi out to the summerhouse. She tossed and turned all night, so that when she arrived for work on her third day she was grouchy, stressed-out, and tired.

It was midafternoon before she remembered that she needed to eat lunch. The shortcut to the dining room took her through the bar, and the sight she witnessed there was so shocking that she thought she must be dreaming.

Speechless, she stood in the shadows and watched Beau on the stage, looking as though he didn't have a care in the world and talking with two men who were centering a neon sign which would hang behind him when he was performing. It spelled his name, B-E-A-U, in muted greens and blues.

For a long time, she listened to them chatter. Finally, no longer able to remain silent, she stepped into the circle of light surrounding the stage. "Hello, Mr. Beaudine."

"Hello, honey." He smiled at her. "How do you like my new sign? These boys designed it special."

"Did you understand my message yesterday?"

"I surely did, and I'm sorry you were so upset."

Allison took a deep breath, biting the inside of her lip, refusing to lose her temper, but it was so difficult to remain calm when he was staring at her like an innocent choir boy. "In my office, Mr. Beaudine. Now!" She spun around and stomped out of the bar.

Behind her, she heard Beau remark, "She sure is pretty when she's mad, isn't she, boys?" He murmured something else she couldn't distinguish, and the two men laughed. She absorbed the sound, letting it sink in and fuel her fire.

She passed the front desk, not pausing as she said to the clerk, "Find Chad, and tell him I want to see him immediately." Then she continued on to her office, where she stood behind the desk, impatiently tapping her foot. Waiting. Then, waiting some more.

From a long distance away, she could hear Beau coming. Apparently, he had all the time in the world, stopping to chat with a few people in the lobby, talking to one of the maids, asking the desk clerk about her boyfriend's new motorcycle. Finally, he sauntered in. At the same moment, Chad entered behind him, looking sheepish and worried.

"Shut the door," she said to Chad, which he did.

"You look a trifle upset, darlin'," Beau said. "Why don't you calm down?"

"Let's start with me saying this—I am not your *honey* or your *darlin'* or whatever good ole boy word you feel like using. Do I make myself clear?"

"Yes, Allie," he said, shortening her name to the nickname she had always hated. The way it rolled off his tongue stopped her short for a moment. How did he do that? How did he manage to distract her just by talking, just by walking, just by being?

"It's *Miss Masters* to you."

"Whatever you say, Allie."

She threw up her hands in frustration. Didn't this man understand English? Talking to him was like conversing with a log. "Mr. Beaudine, I fired you yesterday. Are you aware of that fact?"

"Yes."

"Then what are you doing here?" She barely prevented the question coming out as a shout, barely prevented herself from walking around the desk and shaking him until his teeth rattled.

"Well, I didn't think you really wanted me to go."

"Ooh, but I did. Give me one reason why I shouldn't call the police and have them escort you off the property."

"Trust me, Allie, you don't want to do that."

"Yes, I do. I want to very, very much." She whirled on Chad. "Did you know Mr. Beaudine was in the hotel?"

"Well, I—"

"Did you?"

"Yes, but—" he stammered, his cheeks flushing red, his Adam's apple bobbing up and down.

"Now, Allie," Beau interjected, "don't go blaming this on poor Chad, here."

"Butt out, Mr. Beaudine."

"I won't. Not when it's my fault that he's caught in the middle."

"In the middle? What's he in the middle of?" She

turned her furious glare to Chad again, causing him to squirm uncomfortably. "Well, Chad? I'm waiting."

The silence was a long one. Beau looked about to break it, but Chad held up his hand, stopping anything Beau might say.

"Your father wants him to stay."

"My father?" she asked, confused. What did her father have to do with any of this? Then she saw the guilty look in Chad's eyes, and everything became crystal clear. It took every bit of inner strength she had not to fall into her chair. "You called my father after I fired Mr. Beaudine?"

"Yes," he said, hanging his head like a whipped dog.

"Why?"

"Before you came, he told me I was to call him twice a day while you were here."

"Why?" she asked again.

"To tell him how you're doing, I guess. And I'm supposed to call more than that if anything happens that I think he should know about."

"Ah . . . I see." She did see. She really, really did. "And you felt my firing of Mr. Beaudine would be information which would interest him?"

"Well, he did get personally involved in some of the contract negotiations."

She nodded, looking unruffled even though she was dying inside. "And my father . . . he'd like Mr. Beaudine to stay?"

"Yes."

"He countermanded my decision?" Chad nodded as she continued. "So, you called Mr. Beaudine and asked him to return?"

Knowing how much of a personal blow the answer was going to be, Beau offered quietly, "Actually, Allie, your father called me."

Wow! Wasn't that something? The great and powerful Randolph Masters had called Beau himself!

"Isn't that special?" she murmured. "When were you two going to get around to telling me?"

Chad said, "I wanted to tell you right away, but Beau thought we should wait until you calmed down a little."

"That's so nice," she said sarcastically, "for the two of you to be so concerned about my feelings." She came around the desk until she was mere inches from Chad. She was so upset she was shaking, and to his credit he didn't shrink away. "When you talked to my father, what else did he say?"

Chad looked at Beau, then back at Allison. "Like what?"

"Oh, I don't know . . . maybe something about me, for instance? About how I was doing my job? Something like that?"

"Let it rest, Allie," Beau said, reaching out and resting a hand on her shoulder.

She shook it off. "Shut up, Beau."

"It's just going to hurt."

"Shut! Up! Beau!" she shouted, not looking at him, continuing to wear Chad down with the intensity of her gaze. "What else did my father say?"

"Don't tell her, Chad," Beau said.

"What *else*?" she demanded.

"Lots of stuff."

"Like?"

"Well, he said you'd gone completely off the deep end this time."

"Oh, man," Beau muttered under his breath.

"I see," she said, the comment stabbing like a knife. "Keep going."

"That you never had a lick of sense."

She nodded. "And?"

"He thought this was a simple assignment, but you royally screwed it up on the first day. He obviously couldn't trust you to do anything right." Chad swallowed hard. "Stuff like that."

"It must have been quite a tirade."

"It was," Chad agreed.

The silence was painful, and Allison wished she could simply cease to exist. She took a deep breath, fortifying herself. "Thank you. That will be all."

Chad hesitated for a moment, then finally turned to leave. Beau remained, standing off to the side. She didn't look at him, but continued to stare out the door through which Chad had made his exit. He was watching her, though, and she could feel his heavy scrutiny as if it were a physical touch.

"Are you all right?" he asked once they were alone.

"Of course I'm all right," she answered steadily as she walked around her desk and started sifting through the papers on it. "Why wouldn't I be?"

"Don't pay any attention to those things Chad told you. Your father's a horse's ass."

Eyes lowered, she continued to fuss with her paperwork. "Why don't you go hang your sign, or tune your violin, or do whatever it is you musicians do in the middle of the afternoon?"

He braced his hands on the desktop, leaning across, invading her space so she was forced to look at him. "I'm sorry you found out like this," he said. "I didn't know the best way to tell you."

His eyes searched hers for any sign of distress, but she'd carefully veiled it. Having grown up in a home where showing emotion was strictly frowned upon, it was a trick she'd learned early. Pretending a detachment she didn't feel at all, she said, "It's over. Don't worry about it."

"It's not over."

She wasn't sure what he meant by that, so she didn't respond.

They stood close, his beautiful face only inches from hers, and even though she hated him, even though he'd caused this entire mess, even though she wished the earth would open and swallow him whole, she could feel her entire being drawn toward him as though he were a magnet designed to attract only her. If she wasn't careful, she was going to be in his arms and blubbering like a baby.

She took a step back, forcing some space between them. "If you don't mind, I'd like to be alone now."

"Sure," he said, and Allison could read understanding in his eyes. Concern, too, although for the life of her she couldn't imagine why self-centered, arrogant, egotistical Harley Beaudine would be worried about her for even an instant.

"I'm sorry," he said again, and he reached for her, holding the back of her neck just long enough to press his lips to hers. He kissed her forehead, too, then snuggled her against the crook of his neck while he placed a third kiss in her hair.

For an instant, just the briefest one, she accepted the comfort, inhaled his calming scent, welcomed the solace of his embrace. Just as quickly, she put an end to it, moving away, out of his reach.

He grabbed a pen and a piece of paper and jotted down his home phone number. "Would you call me later?"

"I don't think so."

"Take it, please. You never know how you might be feeling—"

"Okay," she said, reaching for it. Anything to get him out of there. "Thank you."

That seemed to satisfy him. He left, closing the door softly behind him, and she could finally ease herself into her chair. She couldn't have said how long she sat there—perhaps two or three hours. And, even though her entire body felt numb, her brain managed to work just fine.

She thought about so many things. About growing up without a family, her mother deceased and her father absent. About all those lonely years she'd spent away at boarding school. About how deeply she'd yearned for some small show of affection, some tiny hint that her father was proud she was his daughter. She couldn't remember a single instance when she'd felt loved or wanted.

Tolerated. That was what she'd been all these years. Tolerated because she was family, but never loved. Never even liked, really, by any of them.

God, but she was a pathetic creature. Thirty-two years old, sitting in a strange office, thousands of miles from home, pining for her father's love. That was really why she had come to Wyoming. It had been one more futile attempt on her part to prove to him that she was worthy of love. But the trip had been foolish. There wasn't anything she could ever do that would be good enough. She'd never be pretty enough, or smart enough, or capable enough.

Why keep trying?

One thing became clear: she had to get out of there. Immediately. She was a grown woman. She had money. She'd find a place, a place where she belonged, where she was wanted. There had to be a place like that. She'd find it, and to hell with her father, her family, Richard, Harley Beaudine, and all the rest of them.

She grabbed her bag and left the hotel without saying good-bye to anyone. Not that anyone noticed her departure, or would care if they had. It was the story of her life that she wouldn't be missed.

Her past behind, her future ahead, she stepped onto the sidewalk, into the July sunshine.

Where to go? That was the question.

With no destination in mind, she started walking down the street.

Chapter 5

Beau raised his ax and swiftly brought it down against a log, and it neatly split into two pieces. He grabbed another piece of the firewood, set it on edge, swung, and stepped back as the two pieces fell to the ground.

Swing. Crack. Thunk.

The rhythm felt good, took his mind off his troubles. And, for once, he seemed to have plenty. He couldn't get the Masters family out of his head. Randolph Masters, as he'd sounded when he'd called to apologize about Allison. Allison, and how she'd looked when she realized the implications of what her father had done behind her back.

The hurt look in her eyes had been heart-wrenching.

From the moment he'd hung up the phone after talking to Randolph, when the man had advised him that he wasn't fired after all, Beau had been deeply troubled about how Allison might take the news. Better than anyone, he knew all about what had happened to her the past few months, how she was hurting, how she needed support and reassurance. For the bastard to pull the rug out from under her like that was unconscionable.

He didn't know Randolph personally, and, now that they'd spoken he didn't want to ever meet the guy. He could still hear that smooth voice over the phone line, coming from New York, and the words he'd used to describe Allison had made Beau good and mad for a change. *Flighty . . . off the deep end . . . hysterical . . .*

What kind of man said those kinds of things about his only daughter? Even if they were true, even if he really believed them, what kind of man would say those things to another man he didn't even know?

"Bastard," Beau said, spitting into the dirt.

Man, he hated that he'd left Allison sitting there in her office all by herself. Hurt. Alone. Sad. Betrayed. On the verge of tears, but too proud and stubborn to let them fall—just as she'd been in Patty's office, when she'd poured her heart out about all the earlier hurts Randolph and Richard had inflicted.

He should have stayed with her! Even though she'd insisted she wanted to be alone, he should have stayed. He felt responsible for what had happened, that he should fix it somehow, but he wasn't sure what to do. On one level, he hardly knew her, but on another, it was as if he'd known her forever. Weird! He could feel the anguish and heartache she was experiencing, and he wanted to do something to make her better.

Now, that was definitely a switch! Harley Beaudine wanting to do something for someone else! He had no illusions about what kind of man he was. After all, his sister couldn't help analyzing him constantly. Even though he pretended never to listen, he always did, and, even though he'd never admit it to her face, he agreed with her.

He was the king of selfishness. He had it down to a science, doing only what was good for Harley Beaudine. For four decades, he'd lived that way, and it was hard to change.

So, this was a new feeling. Amazingly, it was a good one. He was hurting for Allison, and wanting to help her if he could.

Damn, he should have waited around at the hotel, even if she could have cared less that he was there. He'd called several times now, talked to Chad. Allison had split sometime after all the unpleasantness. No one was sure when. Nobody saw her leave the hotel, and nobody seemed to know where she'd gone.

Foolishly, he'd actually thought she might call, and had even gone so far as to bring the phone outside while he was chopping wood, expecting it to ring, to answer and hear Allison's husky voice on the other end of the line, asking for . . . for what he wasn't certain.

Only she hadn't called. What had he expected?

Tomorrow, he'd track her down, and they'd have it out. He didn't know why he felt so determined to talk it all to death. He never explained or made excuses; he always just lived his life however he pleased.

Right now, he was feeling terribly guilty because his show was starting at the hotel on Saturday night, and he was going to go through with it. He'd spent the entire day obsessing about Randolph and

Allison Masters, and he'd considered canceling, letting the lawyers fight it out after, but better sense had eventually prevailed, and he'd decided he was going to perform.

For some reason, the decision made him feel he was betraying Allison. He was desperate to explain why he would continue to play at the hotel, how it didn't have anything to do with her, that it wasn't personal, that he wasn't doing it to spite her or hurt her. He wanted, needed, her to understand.

That was something else that was new—his giving two hoots about what somebody else thought. The woman was making him turn over a new leaf every minute or so.

Movement out on the road caught his eye. In the quiet dusk of the Wyoming summer evening, someone was walking down the center of the country lane, right toward his house. That was odd, since the bumpy gravel didn't go anywhere except into the national park, where it meandered for miles through the woods until it hit one of the park's main roads. Few cars ever came that way, and no one ever walked by. He couldn't help staring until the person got closer, and he could make out form and figure.

"Well, now, there's a sight you don't see every day." He laughed in the cool night air.

As though he'd conjured her up by simply thinking about her nonstop for the past few hours, here she came. Allison Masters, in all her glory, still dressed in her red power suit with her matching heels, was walking straight toward him. A tiny speck, gradually growing closer and closer, she had a bag slung over her shoulder and a . . . wine bottle in her hand.

Squinting, he saw what she was carrying, laughing again when she raised the thing to her lips and took a big swig.

Drunk. Depressed. And lost, from the looks of things.

He walked around the side of the house, down the short driveway and out to the road, standing in the middle and watching her come. Eyes downcast, kicking rocks, she nearly ran into him before she noticed he was blocking her way.

"What do you want?" she asked sullenly, as though they were meeting on a busy sidewalk in downtown Jackson instead of out in the middle of nowhere.

Her jacket was buttoned wrong. Most of her hair was still pulled back, but many of the pins had fallen out, and several strands were loose and falling around her shoulders. A heel was broken. There were holes in her nylons, a scraped knee that was oozing blood, and another scrape on her hand oozing blood, too. She must have fallen, trying to maneuver in those treacherous shoes of hers.

"I was just wondering where you're going," he responded, trying to keep a straight face.

"To the airport."

"Well, you're heading the wrong way."

"Are you sure?"

"I've lived on this road off and on for almost twenty years now. So, yeah. I'm sure."

"Oh." She turned and started off in the direction from which she'd come.

He stood perfectly still for her first ten steps, wondering what to do. The woman obviously couldn't take care of herself. Sober, she was lousy at it. Drunk, she was even worse. He couldn't let her walk off into the quickly approaching night. Loping after her, he stepped in front of her again, halting her progress.

"Are you still here?" she asked, taking another long swig of the wine.

"How come you're walking?"

"I called that stupid cab company three times! They never came, and I got tired of waiting."

"Wasn't anybody at the house who could give you a ride?"

"I didn't want anybody to give me a ride. They all work for Father."

"I see."

"No, you don't. You don't see anything, Mr. Smarty-Pants-I-Know-Everything-About-Women." Stepping around him, she wobbled a little, and he steadied her by taking her arm. She didn't appear to notice.

"Why don't you tell me, then?" he asked gently.

"I'm not taking anything from him ever again. I'm not working at his stupid hotel. And I'm not living in his stupid house. And I'm not marrying his stupid senior vice president. And I'm not having one of his stupid employees take me to the airport." She took another drink. "Do you get it?"

"I think so." They were walking side by side, and he was surprised at how fast she could move with a broken shoe and such a teeter in her gait. She was drunk, and furious, and upset, and she was about the cutest thing he'd ever seen. "So, what are you going to do when you get to the airport?"

"Get on a plane. What do you think I'm going to do?"

"Where are you going to go?"

That brought her up short. She stopped in her tracks, and he stopped with her. "What?"

"Where are you going?"

"Why? Do you want to go with me?"

"No, I don't ride on airplanes."

"Not ever?"

"Nope."

"Then why do you want to come with me?"

"I don't," he said calmly, smiling. It had been a long time since he'd so thoroughly enjoyed talking to a drunk. "I just thought maybe you should tell me where you're going. Folks might panic if you just disappear."

"Don't worry. There isn't anybody who'll miss me."

"Nobody?"

"Nobody."

She said it with such heartfelt sorrow and longing that it was all he could do to keep from wrapping her in a tight hug. Instead, he stuffed his hands in his pockets, rocking on the balls of his boots. "I'd miss you."

"You would?"

His small declaration brought such a hopeful look to her eye that it settled the question of what he should do with her. The woman was a danger to herself and others, walking around in the dusk, alone and sad and lost. She desperately needed someone to look out for her. Astonishing as it seemed, he wanted to be the one.

"Of course, I would, honey." He stepped closer, resting a hand on her waist. "Let's go inside, okay?"

"Inside where?"

"My house."

He pointed behind them, and she looked back at the lovely, two-story, log home perched on a slope and surrounded by a dark stand of Ponderosa pines. Sounding surprised, she said, "It's a real house."

"That it is," he said, taking her bag off her shoulder and pulling the strap over his own.

"I know why you want me to go in there," she said, eyeing him suspiciously.

"Why is that?"

"You want to have your way with me."

"You're probably right about that." He laughed, thinking this was going to be a lot easier and happen a lot faster than he'd imagined.

"I'm drunk."

"I see that."

"Don't gentlemen have some sort of rule about taking advantage of women who are intoxicated?"

"Well, I never did say I was a gentleman."

"You're not?" she asked, sounding completely taken off guard.

"No. Besides, there's nothing wrong with putting a little alcohol in the mix. Loosens inhibitions." In Allison's case, he thought that might be a very, very, good notion.

She seemed to ponder the idea, then shrugged. "I guess I'll let you sleep with me. You're a good kisser."

"We aim to please." He reached for the wine bottle, which was nearly empty, and she gave it up without a fight. "How many of these have you had?"

"That's the first one." Her brow wrinkled prettily as she counted. "I think."

"Didn't anybody warn you about the effects of alcohol at high altitudes?"

"No. What about it?"

She wobbled precariously, and he could just imagine how bad she was going to feel in the morning. Surprisingly, he liked the idea that he'd be there to take care of her. "I think maybe you should stay away from the booze when you're upset."

"Why?"

"I don't think you handle it very well."

"Huh! I'm doing just fine!"

"You sure are, honey," he said, biting his tongue about the fact that she was walking down his road drunk and lost, and it was going to be dark soon.

"I think maybe you should mind your own business."

"But it's so much more fun to mind yours. Up you go," he said, scooping her up and tossing her over his shoulder like a sack of flour. She was light as a feather, her cute ass wiggling right next to his ear, and he gave her a swat for good measure.

"Don't spill my wine," she cautioned, apparently barely aware that she was hanging upside down. Her face brushed the small of his back with each step.

"I'll try to be careful."

"You have a cute butt."

"Thank you."

"I bet women tell you that all the time."

Even with her drunk, he wasn't about to touch that comment with a ten-foot pole. "What's in your bag?"

A long hesitation. "I don't remember."

He hoped there weren't any clothes. He liked the idea of having her in his house and at his mercy, with nothing to wear but what he gave her. It seemed as if she might not know how to drive, either, so she wouldn't be able to leave until he was ready to take her somewhere. And, it didn't sound as if she had to be anywhere anytime soon. She could just stay. For as long as he felt like keeping her.

The possibilities were growing by the moment.

As he reached the front door and stepped across the threshold, he realized that he was hard just from thinking about having her all to himself.

"You've got nice floors," she said, still hanging over his shoulder where all she could see were hardwood planks passing by.

"Thanks, darlin'," he answered, starting up the stairs. For a nanosecond, he thought about taking her into one of the guest bedrooms, but he quickly changed his mind. He wasn't about to give her a choice.

Walking into the master bedroom, he deposited her on the center of his bed, nimbly steadying the wine, which nearly spilled all over the coverings. He raised the bottle to his lips and took a long sip. It was very good, and he took another and another.

Allison saw him drinking and held out her hand. "I want some more."

"You've had enough."

"What are you? My baby-sitter?"

"Looks like it."

"Oh." She flopped back onto the pillows, her arms flung to the sides, apparently in no mood to argue the point. "I'm ready."

"For what?"

"You know." She eyed him up and down, lingering a long moment at the uncomfortable bulge pushing against the crotch of his jeans. "You *do* know *how*, don't you?"

"I do," he answered, chuckling, thinking she

looked good in his bed, as if she belonged there. For two decades, he'd lived in this house, and had never had another woman where she currently rested. When he'd wanted a partner, he always visited the woman, because he liked to be able to leave when the time was right. He hadn't wanted or needed any of his numerous sexual partners hanging around, eyeing his things, and conjuring up reasons to overstay their welcome.

For the first time, a woman was here, and he was glad she was. The longer she stayed, the better.

"Okay, then," she said, her fingers going to the front of her jacket and, despite her intoxication, deftly unbuttoning it. "I'm ready."

"For what?" There wasn't a blouse under the jacket, just a red lacy bra, the same shade as her suit. The lace was sheer, and barely restrained a beautiful swell of cleavage.

"For you! Just do whatever . . ."

She motioned a hand over her body, as though he was supposed to jump on and ride. Not a bad idea, but he hesitated nonetheless. Considering her state of inebriation, a gentleman would reject her blatant offer. Hell, a gentleman wouldn't have brought her up there in the first place.

So why was he wavering? The woman wanted it, and wanted it now, and he was only human. Who was he to refuse her? He knew he could make sure she didn't regret it in the morning. But still, the idea of taking advantage of her didn't sit well at all. The other men in her life had used her badly, and he didn't care to be lumped on the same pile with any of them.

"I think I should probably take a shower first."

Before she came stumbling down his road, he'd been chopping wood for over an hour and he was covered with sweat and dust. Maybe if he stayed in the bathroom long enough, she'd fall asleep before he came back.

"I don't want you to wash up," she insisted. In a quick move, she came up on her knees and faced him, one arm going around his neck, making her nipples press tightly against his chest. The other hand grabbed the waist of his jeans and pulled him close. "I want you just like this."

"Okay, honey, you can have me just like this," he said, willing to humor her until he could get her settled. He buried his face in her neck, deeply inhaling the fresh scent of her skin, the hint of perfume. Taking a long slow kiss against her nape, he gently bit and teased while his fingers were busy, pushing her jacket off her shoulders and down her arms, baring the creamy white skin. His fingers circled her wrists, and he was pleased to feel the goosebumps he'd caused to pop out all over. At the small of her back, he worked the button and zipper of her skirt, pushing it down off her hips. He was going to control himself for once in his worthless life. He'd just slip a clean T-shirt on her, wash her up a bit and get her into bed—by herself.

Pleased with his new attempt at self-sacrifice, he saw his carefully laid plan instantly go askew when Allison reached to his waist and yanked his sweat-stained T-shirt up his chest, baring his upper torso. She shrieked with delight, "Hair! You've got hair on your chest! Get this thing off!" she commanded, not waiting for his assistance but pulling it off by herself and tossing it over her shoulder.

Her fingers went to his pecs, working through the springy stuff as she burrowed her pert little nose across one of his nipples and then the other. He wasn't sure if she realized how good it felt, or how erotic she looked, mostly naked, pressed against him.

"Oh, you smell good, too," she added wistfully.

The comment reinforced for him just how drunk she really was, but he wanted to make love to her just the same. The thought of having his scent all over her was too enticing. He'd have her marked as completely his own by the time they finished. If that was a strange urge for him, so be it. He refused to look at any of the reasons why he might want to do such a thing.

It's just sex, he reminded himself. *Just sex.* That was all he wanted from her, now and later. Though, with his newfound touch of chivalry, it looked as if it would definitely be later.

He let her nuzzle for as long as he could stand it, then eased her back onto the pillows. When she grabbed for his waistband again and tried to wrestle him down with her, he took both her hands in his and held on to keep them out of trouble. "Hold your horses a minute."

Placing his mouth on hers, he kissed her long and slow until her entire body relaxed, and when he pulled away, she sighed with pleasure. Knowing he'd calmed her down enough so she'd stay put, he walked into the bathroom, found a pan in one of the cupboards, and filled it.

At the sound of running water, Allison yelled, "You're not bathing in there, are you?"

"No, honey, I'm not." He chuckled as he gazed into the mirror, wondering what he was doing.

"Good. Don't make me come in there."

He returned to the bedroom, glad to find that she hadn't moved except to kick her skirt away from her ankles. She'd raised a knee, exposing a delicious expanse of thigh. With a hand tucked behind her head, she painted an alluring picture. He had a sudden flash of how Adam must have felt when Eve dangled that apple in front of him.

"Give me your hand," he said, placing the pan of warm water on the nightstand and rinsing out a washcloth. She did so without argument, and he tenderly wiped away the traces of dirt and blood embedded in her scraped palm. "What happened?"

She stared at her injury for a long time, as though the hand belonged to someone else. "I fell. On the road."

"Better?" he asked, bringing it to his lips and kissing the hurt.

"Yes."

"Let's get these off." He reached for the ruined pantyhose and carefully pulled them down past her scraped knee and blistered heel, revealing a pair of dark red panties, the same shade as the lace of her bra. The swatch covering her mound was so small that it could barely be called a panty. Little tufts of her blond curls poked around the edges.

The discovery gave him pause. Putting her to bed without having a piece of her was going to be much more difficult than he imagined. Man, oh, man, did he want a little taste! Even the nasty red rash marring her skin didn't cool his desire.

With the same gentle attention, he bathed both spots. She was pliable, accepting his ministrations without comment, as though his care of her was the most normal thing in the world, something they had done a thousand times before.

Finished, he tossed the washcloth into the pan and dried his hand on his jeans. Then he went to his dresser and pulled out an old T-shirt.

"Sit up," he ordered, holding her wrist and shifting her up to the edge of the bed, where he pulled the remaining pins from her hair so it dangled free and curly around her shoulders.

Her bra hooked in the front, and with a grimace very much like pain he expertly worked the snap. The cups fell free, the straps slipping down her arms, exposing her full round breasts. He hadn't meant to look, thinking he'd stare at the wall behind her. But, much as he was acting like a martyr, he was only a man, and he couldn't help himself.

The tips were golden, the color of ripe peaches, the nipples hard and extended. It took every bit of resolve he possessed to remain standing, refusing to bend down and close his mouth around one of them, as his body was screaming for him to do.

Just as he thought he'd won the battle, Allison cupped the firm mounds in both her hands and looked down at them as though they were some new body parts that had just been added. His mouth went dry at the picture of her hands exactly where he wanted his to be. "Lord, have mercy," he groaned toward the ceiling, biting hard against his lip and taking several deep breaths before he found the strength to return his gaze to hers.

"Richard says they're too small. He wants me to have implants."

How any man could think they weren't perfect was a mystery. She raised her soulful gaze to his, apparently seeking his opinion, which he gave. "I already told you, honey. Richard is an ass."

"You're right about that," she agreed, the words muffled as he slipped the T-shirt over her head, covering what he so desperately wanted to see, touch, and taste.

Her head popped through the opening, and he reached his fingers under her hair, pulling it through and fluffing it about her shoulders, loving the chance to run his fingers through it. He tapped his finger against the tip of her nose. "You're a mess, baby girl."

"We're not going to have sex, are we?"

"No."

"I *am* kind of tired."

"I thought you might be." He pulled the covers back and tucked her in, kicking himself for being a fool, for not taking what she'd offered. Chances were good that she'd not offer it again in the morning. Still, he loved having this opportunity to take care of her, to know that he could come up during the evening and find her sleeping in his bed, to anticipate the moment later on when he could snuggle next to her and hold her in his arms all night long.

For the first time in a long time, he was glad he wouldn't be sleeping alone. "You close your eyes. I'll check on you in a while."

Their gazes met and held—two pairs of blue eyes, knowing, thinking, assessing. Allison apparently decided she liked what she saw.

"Thank you," she said.

"You're welcome." He leaned down, stole a light kiss—just enough of a one to last for a few hours—

then turned off the light. "You rest now. I'll be right here."

In a chair next to the bed, he waited until her breathing was slow and even. Knowing she slept, he sat there even longer, watching and enjoying how young and unworried she looked.

Moved by emotions he didn't understand or want to examine, he did the only thing he knew how to do at a time like that. He headed downstairs, grabbed his fiddle, and went outside into the backyard. It was fully dark, and the temperature had dropped, so it was cold, fresh, and quiet.

As he tightened the bow and worked the rosin back and forth across the hairs, he searched the woods, looking for some of the night animals who would soon begin to prowl, but no glowing eyes stared back from the shadows.

He raised the violin under his chin and began to play.

Chapter 6

When Allison opened her eyes and found herself in Beau's bed, cradled in his arms and with his splendid, naked, aroused body spooned behind hers, she didn't have to spend frantic moments wondering where she was, or how she got there. Unfortunately, despite the amount of wine she'd drunk, she remembered every shameful detail of the prior afternoon and evening.

From her furtive escape out of the hotel, to her wandering—alone, dejected, defeated—through the tourist crowds of downtown Jackson. From her solitary cab ride out to the summerhouse, to her phone conversation with her father. From the packing and waiting for the taxi to take her to the airport, to the long walk she'd started, hoping to get there on her own two feet. From running into Beau in front of his house, to falling asleep in his bed.

It was all crystal clear. Every humiliating, degrading, humbling moment of it.

Her father's angry words still rang in her ears. Usually, his display of temper would have been a catalyst, would have had her hopping out of bed at sunrise, ready to take on the world. Throughout her life, she'd suffered through much the same diatribes, but she'd always managed to shake off his hurled insults, telling herself that she'd simply do better next time, that she'd use his low opinion as the fuel she needed to push herself to excel. In the past, she'd believed that there had to be some way to win his approval, and she'd continued on. Facing every obstacle. Trying harder. Working more. Assuming extra responsibilities. Always waiting. Always hoping.

It was hard to discern what was different this morning. But everything seemed so clear for a change. All that hard work, and she'd simply been banging her head against the proverbial wall. No amount of effort on her part, no matter how great, was ever going to win her the approval of Randolph Masters. He was never going to accept her. He was never going to love her.

She winced at that. For that's what it had all been about, really. Winning his love.

Impossible.

For some reason, facing this new reality was not the wrenching, soul-shattering event it might have been. At another time in her life, she might have been devastated by the realization that her father would never love her—no matter what she did. Now, the knowledge barely caused her to blink an eye.

It was as if she was finally . . . empty. Yes, that was it. She felt as though her spirit had developed a crack, somehow, and all her fire and energy had slowly leaked out while she wasn't paying attention.

There was nothing left. Strangely, that thought didn't upset her, either. Nothing did.

She was a thirty-two-year-old woman, with no close family, no job, no place to go, no place to be. Nobody would be looking for her, or wondering where she was. No one would be impatiently waiting for her to arrive back home.

Home . . . where was that, anyway? The apartment in New York she'd shared with Richard? One of her father's houses?

She could jump out of Beau's bed right this very second, rush to the airport, buy a ticket and go . . . where?

Nowhere. The thought was not an unpleasant one.

She felt nothing. Not a sense of loss. Not anger. Not loneliness. Not sadness. Zip. Zilch. Nada. It was as if some cord that tethered her to the earth had been severed in the past twenty-four hours. She was floating free. The person she used to be had disappeared, and she hadn't turned into anybody else yet, so she was just . . . here. As she rolled over, the move bringing her body into full contact with Beau's, she decided that there were worse places she could have ended up.

Sunlight streamed in the east window, casting a golden halo around his hair. A lock had fallen across his forehead, and it made him appear young and vulnerable, and she imagined how cute he must have looked as a boy.

His skin was healthy and tanned by the summer sun, his arms muscled and smooth. He smelled clean and fresh, with his special musky scent. Even in his sleep he appeared larger than life, a vision of male virility, and his personality filled the room. A hint of a smile curved his lips, as if he were in the middle of a delicious dream, and she couldn't help hoping it might be about her.

She knew she should be shocked and embarrassed by the predicament in which she'd landed herself. After all, she was lying in the man's bed, wearing only her panties and one of his T-shirts. If he hadn't graciously offered it to her, she wouldn't even have that on. She should exit quickly and quietly before he had a chance to awaken, but she wasn't going to. Along with all the other changes she'd undergone in the past twenty-four hours, she couldn't seem to muster any outrage, and she'd need some to hustle out of the room.

She was supposed to hate him, but her loathing was another thing that had vanished during the night. Such intense dislike simply required too much energy—energy which she no longer possessed.

Besides, despite the fact that he was an overbearing egotist, how could she be angry with someone who had been so kind to her—bringing her inside, washing her scrapes, kissing away the hurt, undressing her, and tucking her in, sitting with her until she fell asleep? He could have had sex with her with no effort at all, but he hadn't. He could have sent her down the road, but he didn't. He'd seen that she was struggling, that she was dispirited, beaten down, and alone, and he'd been the only one in the world who realized that she could use somebody to carry the load for a while.

His actions made her suspect that maybe there were some redeeming attributes which he kept carefully hidden behind the exuberant facade he

showed to the world. There was more here than
met the eye, she knew, for she remembered hearing him in the night, playing his violin. He'd been
outside, the notes drifting up through the open
windows. The sound of it was so sad and poignant
that even now the memory brought a sting of tears
to her eyes. Maybe, just maybe, he felt as lost as she
did sometimes.

So, she wasn't going to sneak out of his bed, rush
to the bathroom, hastily dress, and run away before
he could wake. She was going to stay just where she
was. And she wasn't going to think about the next
month or the next week or the next day, or even
the next hour. She was only going to think about
this moment, because it required too much energy
to look beyond it.

It was a reckless decision, but she didn't care. It
was wild and crazy and impetuous, and so completely foreign to the person she'd been before that
she'd never have considered it. All her life she'd
done the right thing, acted appropriately, tried to
be the person her father expected her to be, and
look where all that had gotten her!

This was a new day in her life. If she felt like
having sex with a man she hardly knew and wasn't
sure she even liked very much, then that's what she
was going to do. With a confidence she'd never possessed, she began to play with him, hoping to wake
him up slowly, just so she could see what would
happen.

She leaned forward and started licking his
nipple. It instantly pebbled into a hard nub, and
she sucked it into her mouth. He tasted so good—
sweat and salt, and man. She raised her leg and

rested it over his hip. The move brought her sex into light contact with his, causing him to spring to attention, and she was surprised how the merest touch sent heat cascading from her center out to the tips of her fingers and toes.

"Ooh, that feels good," he purred, slowly coming awake but not opening his eyes. "Stop that in an hour or two."

"You like that, do you?" she asked, thoroughly encouraged.

"Honey, you feel so good," he said, wrapping his arm around her and pulling her close.

"I think I've figured out why you call me 'honey' all the time." She shifted to find his other nipple.

"Why is that?" he asked in a sleepy drawl.

"Because you have so many women that it's hard to remember everyone's name." She nuzzled her nose in the downy hair matted on his chest. "You don't make any embarrassing mistakes that way."

One corner of his mouth lifted in a smile she couldn't see. "How could I forget your name . . . *Beth*?"

"Beth!" She froze for one second. Then she pulled back, saw his sleepy grin, and chuckled. "Very funny." She liked the fact that he cared about her enough to tease her. Suspicious, she asked, "How long have you been awake?"

"Awhile," he said. He'd never admit that he'd spent most of the night aroused and alert, dozing only occasionally, choosing instead to pass the time watching her, worrying about her, holding her.

"Bounder," she said, but it definitely sounded like a compliment.

"You are so pretty," he said, placing a chaste kiss on her lips.

Just as she had in his sister's office, she couldn't help reacting. Something happened when he looked at her like that, when he touched her like that, and she was beyond the point where she wanted to prevent a response.

He took one of her hands in his own, leaned back to provide some space between their bodies, then placed it on his erection. Her eyes widened in surprise when he admitted, "I've known you for two days, and I feel like I've been this hard the whole time."

A flurry of butterflies cascaded through her stomach. Could it be true? Had this walking sex symbol been lusting after her? She didn't know. She didn't *want* to know. For that one moment in time, she'd let it be. Brazenly, she asked, "What are you going to do about it?"

"I have a few ideas."

"Show me."

"With pleasure," he said. Moving over her, he completely covered her, his body hair causing a delicious friction all the way down her smooth waxed skin. Her blue eyes blazed with reaction, and he met her gaze with that lazy smile that had always driven women crazy and was now beginning to work its magic on her.

He yanked her panties away, then kneed her legs apart, centered himself, and raised her to meet him so that he was perched at her entrance. "Honey, this has been one of the longest nights of my life," he said, meaning it, "and I need to be inside you right now." He entered just the tiniest bit. "Take me."

It sounded like a question, or perhaps an order. She didn't know what kind of response would be required, so she merely nodded, and he filled her with one deep thrust. Unprepared—for his size, his need, for him—she gasped and bit her bottom lip, and he held himself perfectly still, resting his weight on an elbow as her body stretched and adjusted.

"Are you okay?" he managed.

"You're so big."

"And you're so tight," he forced through his clenched teeth. Beads of sweat popped out on his brow. She moved, trying to adjust her thighs so she could accept him more readily. The shift of her hips brought him so far inside that the tip of him touched her womb. His eyes widened, and his nostrils flared. "Ah . . . I can't wait. I have to come right now."

From the tension in his back and leg muscles, she knew it was true, and she couldn't prevent the sense of wonder that shot through her. *She* had aroused him like this—simply from being so near at hand. She'd never imagined herself as any sort of *femme fatale*, but the evidence of her effect on him couldn't be denied. Her heart smiled—if such a thing was possible—and she felt lighter and freer.

"Yes," she urged, raising her legs to wrap around him and pull him closer.

"Hold me tight," he whispered in her ear. "Don't let go."

"I won't," she said, kissing his cheek. She hugged her arms across his shoulders as he pushed in once, twice, a third time. His body tensed and, with a low growl of pleasure, he emptied himself deep inside.

It was over that quickly, and she had to admit that she was disappointed. She'd expected something different. He seemed to be so experienced, and she'd thought there'd be more to it, that he'd at least take his time with her and she'd finally learn some of the secrets others found so enticing. Still, there was something unbearably sweet about the way he'd whispered in her ear, asking to be held, and in how quickly his desire for her had reached a peak.

As he gradually relaxed, she ran her fingers up and down his back. His weight collapsed onto her, pushing her down into the mattress. For the first time, she enjoyed a man doing such a thing. He didn't feel heavy. He felt . . . welcome. She had no need to rush for the shower, and she was content to enjoy the smells they'd created together, the mingling of their sleep, sweat, and sex.

His breathing slowed, and she wondered if he'd fallen asleep. Oddly, she didn't mind if he had. Still buried deep inside, he was rock hard, and she liked the fact that he hadn't instantly pulled away and rolled over once he was finished. He generated a feeling of closeness whenever he was near, and she couldn't get enough of it. There was a subtle magic to be found by letting her fingers drift wherever they wanted to go without worrying if he liked it or not.

Surprisingly, she didn't want this to be over yet. Her legs were still wrapped around him, and she couldn't resist tightening them just a little, which caused his body to automatically flex against hers once again. The move brought a low chuckle from him, and she could feel him smile and place a kiss against the nape of her neck.

"Hold on, my little dynamo. You'll get yours in a minute."

"Get my what?"

Beau raised his head so he could look at her. On the outside, she often seemed to have her act together so much, but, sometimes, like now, there was such an innocence about her. Her beautiful blue eyes were wide, trusting, and questioning, as though she really didn't know what he'd meant. Perhaps she didn't. If not, was it going to be fun to show her!

He'd given up trying to figure out what it was about her that fascinated him so much, accepting that she did. Watching her sleep, he'd been aching and uncomfortable for hours, so that by the time she woke up he'd been so aroused that he took her like a stallion mounting a mare, with no finesse or skill. He was so ready that he hadn't even bothered with putting on a condom first, and he couldn't remember the last time he'd done that. He didn't know if she was on the pill or not; hell, he didn't even care. Something about her overwhelmed his better sense, and, with a primal urgency he couldn't control or deny, he'd needed to spill his seed inside—which he'd done, and couldn't wait to do again.

God, it was good to have her in his bed, and now that the initial desire was sated, he could take his time and show her just how glad he was.

"Good morning." He smiled, loving the way her eyes lit up, her cheeks blushed a rosy red.

"Good morning."

He tried to capture her lips, but she pulled her mouth away and turned her face to the side.

"What?" he asked.

"I taste so terrible. After all that wine I drank last night."

"You taste great." Not having her mouth to play with, he attacked the side of her neck, which she'd presented delightfully when she'd turned her head.

"I need to go brush my teeth."

"Now?"

"Please?" she asked, fixing him in a stare with those gorgeous blue eyes.

"No."

"It will only take a minute."

"You're not getting out of my bed."

"Why?"

"Because I'm afraid you won't get back in."

"Oh . . ." she mouthed, blushing a deeper, more delightful shade of red. "You mean we're not through?"

"Hell, no, we're not through," he said, wondering how few lovers she'd had in her life and how lame they'd been. Maybe this Richard fellow was the only one. If so, he hadn't taught her much about the ins and outs. Beau already knew Richard was a first-class bastard, and he couldn't help wondering if the guy was inept, as well. "That first time . . . well, let's call it an icebreaker. Just to take the edge off a little."

"You want to do it again?"

"Of course I do." Could she really expect so little? Perhaps she didn't know enough to expect any more.

"But, it's morning," she said, gesturing toward the window. "Shouldn't we be getting up, or something?"

"I am *up*," he said, tensing his hips to let her feel how hard he still was. "Besides, I don't have anything more important to do. Do you?"

Allison laughed, loud and full, the pressure of her lower muscles squeezing around him. "No, I certainly don't."

"Good, because I thought we'd stay in bed all day."

"All day?"

"Sure."

"You can do that?"

"Well, I might need to rest a little in between, but, yeah." He was growing harder just from thinking about all the fun they were going to have. His hips started a new rhythm all on their own. "If you're real nice to me, I might feed you, too."

"Food and sex. Wow! Thanks!"

"You're welcome."

"But . . . could I still brush my teeth?" She lifted her head off the pillow and whispered, "And I need to pee."

"Get going," Beau said, laughing and swatting her bottom as he rolled to the side. She jumped up, ready to run to the bathroom, then her alcoholic indulgence of the previous night caught up with her. The room spun crazily, and she lurched to the side as her feet hit the floor. He was there instantly, kneeling behind her on the mattress, steadying her by easing her down to rest between his thighs. "Take it easy."

"I think I had a little too much to drink last night."

"I *know* you had a little too much to drink last night."

"My head is pounding."

"I bet."

They waited together, Allison safely cradled in his arms until the room stopped spinning. "Better?" he asked once she quit swaying.

"Yes."

"Go slow, now." She stepped away and made her way to the bathroom, and Beau flopped back on the mattress, listening to the sounds she made as she puttered around in the other room.

Even though he never lacked for female companions, it had been years since he woke up next to a woman. He'd forgotten how much he enjoyed snuggling together first thing in the morning.

He wondered what she was thinking in there, because he doubted if she had spent many moments in her life, barely clothed, rummaging around in a strange man's bathroom. Luckily, the room only had one door, or she'd probably hightail it out the back way. He didn't relish the thought of chasing her down, which he would, because he wasn't about to let her go until he'd had his fill.

If Beau could have read Allison's mind at that moment he'd have been surprised, because sneaking away was the farthest thing from her thoughts. She stared at herself in the mirror, her hair a curly mess, her neck and cheeks red from his beard stubble. The woman staring back at her was a stranger, not in the least resembling the woman who'd come walking down his road the night before. This mysterious unknown female was ready for whatever was going to happen next. She wasn't concerned about consequences, or tomorrow, or anything. There was just now.

She heard Beau shift on the mattress in the other room. She peeked out the door and spied on him. The blankets were down around his waist, his bare arms and chest exposed. The covers barely hid the huge erection he sported, an erection that hadn't dissipated in the least after their first go-around, one that he was waiting to ease into her again. No doubt, he could have had any woman of his choice here with him this morning—sexy, beautiful, experienced women—but he'd chosen her.

Well, she decided, he wouldn't be sorry. Allison Masters probably would have been a disappointment to him, but this new woman wouldn't be. Every spontaneous, wild, erotic thing she'd ever imagined was now a possibility.

Her resolve firmly in place, she walked back into the bedroom, her knees weakening at the smile with which he greeted her. He pulled back the covers, giving her her first look at his naked body all the way down to his ankles. He was so beautiful that she wanted to weep, all long and hard and firm.

At the edge of the bed she hesitated, then decided to throw caution to the winds. Grabbing the edge of her T-shirt, she pulled it over her head and tossed it behind her on the floor. Gloriously naked, she waited, letting his eyes drink in their fill, loving the way they caressed her breasts, her stomach, and lower, causing a fire to begin sizzling between her legs.

He reached out a finger and traced a line on the red rash still visible under her breasts. "Does it hurt when I touch you?"

"No. For some reason, it doesn't hurt at all this morning."

"Come here," he said, holding his arms open in welcome.

She jumped onto the mattress, stretching out on top of him, and he enveloped her in a body hug with his arms and legs as she kissed him hard on the mouth with all the unrestrained untapped passion that had resided for so long in the secret part of her heart. As the kiss went on and on, Beau worked his hands up and down her back, across her butt and her thighs, through her hair, across her shoulders.

Gradually the kiss gentled, until—by the time their lips parted—her entire world consisted of the man lying beneath her, and the request was easy to make. "Show me what it can really be like."

"I intend to, honey girl," he vowed, initiating the kiss himself this time and rolling with her until she lay beneath him.

He seemed to kiss her forever, so fully and completely that if she'd died right then she'd have passed on a fully satisfied woman. His mouth took careful complete inventory of hers while his hands were busy, those nimble fingers roaming over her face, hair, shoulders, chest, down her stomach, across her hips, her thighs. Never touching where she truly wanted him to—her nipples, between her legs—he let her desire grow because he left those two spots alone.

By the time his mouth began to trace a path under her chin and down her neck, she was writhing in unrelieved agony. "This is killing me," she groaned.

"Good," he murmured, thinking he wasn't doing so well, either. Her body was so responsive that his

arousal was once again at fever pitch, and it was all
he could do to pace himself so he didn't take her
hard and fast a second time. His need to have her
again was almost frightening in its intensity.

He latched on to a nipple, no longer able to
resist the way they'd been begging for the attention
which he'd refused to give. As he sucked hard and
deep, his tongue working across the rough tip, he
was rewarded by the hiss of pleasure that escaped
Allison's lips. The way her back arched up off the
bed told him the delay had definitely been worth it.

Working in a deliberate rhythm, he continued his
sucking, and his hand drifted to her other breast,
twirling the other nipple between his fingertips,
each squeeze of his fingers causing her to squirm
and beg.

"Beau . . ." she whimpered, "oh God, Beau . . ."
but whatever words she'd meant to add drifted
away as his mouth moved to her other breast, giving
it all the deliberate attention it had given the first.

Between her legs, she throbbed with a sweet distress, each pull of his tongue causing delicious friction. He was planted there, right at her center, the
tip of his erection poised to move inside again, but
he didn't enter. Instinctively, her body knew that if
he did, he'd ease some of the torment that was now
so powerful that she felt she might die from it.

She tried to shift her hips, to urge him on, but
she couldn't maneuver him to where she wanted
him to be. He refused to cooperate, instead leaving
her breasts to the fierce attention of his hands and
letting his mouth once again go to work on hers.

"I need you . . . please, I need to feel you . . ." She
managed to speak the words between his devastating

kisses, not caring that she was pleading, not caring that she sounded as desperate as she felt. For the first time in her life, she was frantic to feel a man deep within her and working his body in time with hers. If he didn't hurry, she wondered if she just might expire from the anticipation.

"Not yet," he insisted, leaving her mouth and whispering kisses across her cheek. "Not quite yet." He worked his way down her neck, to her shoulder, across her chest until he once again took her nipple into his mouth. At the same time, his hand stroked down her stomach and lower, finally, finally reached between her legs where she desperately wanted to feel his touch.

With his thumb he parted her delicate folds and found the center of her sex and circled it gently, the light touch causing her hips to rise off the mattress, seeking relief. He slipped two fingers inside, his thumb still doing its thrilling work, and she felt herself slipping further from reality, moving toward a hot fire as if it were burning out of control, waiting for the moment she would step inside the flames and be consumed.

Nothing like this had ever happened to her, and, much as she welcomed the new experience, she could feel a loss of control coming. It scared her, and she struggled against it, afraid to find out what came next, afraid not to.

"Don't fight it, Allie," Beau encouraged, sensing her tension and her fear, and realizing she'd never come this far down the road of desire before. She was so close to the edge, and he wanted to be the one to send her hurling over it. "Just let yourself go. I'll be right here to catch you."

Those simple words of assurance did the trick, and she let herself spiral off into a free fall. The sensation started between her legs and moved out from there, to her breasts, her arms, her legs. She felt as if every pore, every cell, down to her smallest atom, had come undone, and she was flying through the universe. The feeling went on and on, until, gradually, her pieces began to reassemble, and she found herself back on earth, in Beau's bed, carefully sheltered in his arms.

He was looking at her with such a tender sense of wonder that she fell madly in love on the spot—and started to cry. Huge tears surged out of her eyes and splashed down her cheeks, falling into her hair and dripping onto the pillow.

"Ssh, it's all right," he cooed, snuggling her closer, liking the feel of her tears washing over his chest.

"I didn't think I could do that," she admitted.

"You never did before?"

"No." She took a heavy gulp of air and added, "I always thought there was something wrong with me."

"Allie, honey, I keep telling you, there's nothing wrong with you. I think you're mighty fine," he murmured, placing a kiss on the top of her head, unable to believe the rush of pure pleasure he felt at knowing he'd been the first to show her the true secrets of loving.

He held her tight, relishing the feel of her soft skin, the fresh smell of her hair, the musk of their sex drifting up from under the covers. She was a contradiction—so hot, so passionate, but so innocent at the same time. He felt as if he'd just introduced his virgin bride to her first experience in the marriage bed, and he couldn't believe the heady sense of elation he enjoyed because of it.

All the women over the years, many experienced, some not, and never had any of them been moved to tears. The realization made him feel strong and powerful, and he was overcome by such unfamiliar instincts—to shelter and protect, to cherish, to keep—knowing he'd finally discovered something priceless and rare.

"Better?" he asked as she calmed down, the tears having slowed and ended, and he took the sheet and used the corner to wipe away the remnants of her outburst.

"Yes," she said, embarrassed, staring off to the side and not wanting to look him in the eye. "I'm sorry . . ."

"Ssh," he hushed her again, brushing a kiss across her lips. "Don't ever be sorry for anything that happens between us."

His words gave her the courage she needed to let her gaze return to his. He meant it; she could see that. She reached out a hand, tracing the contours of his face, the hard ridge of cheekbone, the bristle of his mustache and brows, the soft fringe of his lashes. All the way down, his body was pressed against hers, a knee between her thighs, his hard sex pressed against her hip, demanding attention, demanding more. "I want to do it again."

"Well, I certainly hope so," he said, smiling in that lovely way he had, the smile lines around his eyes crinkling as he moved over her, covering her once again with his body. "Come with me this time?"

"Yes," she answered. "I'd like that very much."

When he entered her, she was ready for him. Her

body easily adjusted to accept his large size, and she wrapped her legs around the backs of his thighs, bringing him closer, needing to feel him as far inside as she could. His hips began a slow rhythm, which her own instantly learned and adopted. He stroked against her for a long time, enjoying the mutual flexing, his member going in as far as it could and then retreating, over and over.

His desire growing, he placed his palms on either side of her head, watching, assessing, loving the way her eyes widened when he went particularly deep.

"You are the sweetest thing." He sighed. His mouth dipped to take hers. His hands came off the pillow and moved to her breasts as he increased the tempo.

Allison matched him thrust for thrust, her sex working against his, her legs and feet searching for all the ways they could find to bring him closer. As the rhythm escalated and the tension intensified, she reveled in the sensations, aware of what was coming this time. The fear of the unknown was gone, and in its place was a heady feeling of exultation because her body could fully relish what this man offered.

She let him take her higher, ignite the flame, build the sizzle, holding back as long as she could, wanting the moment to never end. His body tensed, his brow beaded with sweat, his entire being and attention focused on her pleasure as his only goal. When she knew he reached his peak, when he could no longer resist the pull toward release, she reached for his buttocks and pulled him close, holding him just there, and letting herself go.

Her universe shattered for the second time, and

she felt herself flying through time and space. With a low growl of satisfaction, Beau joined her, and they soared together, prolonging the moment, letting the pleasure wash over them again and again.

Gradually, their heartbeats slowed, their sweat cooled, their breathing eased. Beau shifted to the side, keeping her close. She wrapped her arms around his shoulders and nestled him against her bosom.

"Thank you," she whispered, pressing a kiss against his temple.

"My pleasure," he said in return, and she could feel him smile against her breasts.

His breathing slowed more, and she could tell from the steady rhythm that he'd fallen back to sleep. She held him, touching him, tasting him, cherishing him, and—when she knew it was safe— she vowed quietly, "I love you. I always will."

In his sleep, he smiled again.

Chapter 7

Allison woke to the sights and sounds of evening. Dusk colored the light filtering into the room in hues of red, purple, and orange. There were evening birds calling to the setting sun. The fresh smell of pine trees tickled her senses.

She reached a hand to the other side of the bed, knowing without looking that Beau wasn't there. Her body had already developed a second sight where he was concerned. For a moment, she closed her eyes in order to picture where he was in the lovely log house, and she could sense him downstairs in the kitchen. As the scene presented itself in her head, she was greeted by the smell of breakfast cooking. Great aromas were drifting up the stairs—bacon and eggs, coffee.

She stretched out onto her back, groaning with pleasure at all the places that ached and thinking that Beau had been true to his word. They had stayed in bed all day, and he'd made love to her in every way imaginable. Fast and hard, gentle and slow. There were burns from his beard stubble across her chest and arms, a sore throbbing between her legs, a bruised feeling inside from where he'd worked himself in and out so often and so thoroughly.

With delight, she thought of what a fallen woman she had become. In a matter of hours, Beau had completely and thoroughly changed her into someone else. Timid, confused, unsure Allison Masters had vanished. In her place was a new woman who knew exactly where she was, and what she wanted.

She loved Beau. There was no getting around it, and there was no hope for it. Smiling, she shut her eyes tight and tried to think of all the adjectives in the world that might describe him, but there simply weren't enough. The man was gentle, tender, funny, kind, passionate. Certainly, he was maddening, spoiled and overbearing, as well, but now that she cared about him so much, she could deal with those facets of his personality. It would always be worth it simply to have him fix that smile on her, catch her in the assessing gaze of those magnificent blue eyes, to see him hold out his arms and know he was waiting for her to step into them.

She rubbed a hand across the center of her chest, feeling a twinge there. Her heart felt too big all of a sudden, as though it had grown during their day of loving until it no longer fit between her ribs just right.

Like a foolish girl with a crush, she snuggled deeper into the bedding, inhaling the smell of his hair and skin. It made her hungry for more, which was an amazing thing. Even though she'd already had her fill of him throughout the day, she wanted him over and over again.

She felt greedy and selfish, and completely wanton. And she didn't care a bit.

Hugging his pillow against her chest, she looked out the doors to the balcony. She could see forest and evening sky. This was such a quiet special place—a haven, a good place to hide for someone who didn't want to be found—and she wondered how long he would let her stay. The day had been so magical, the interaction between them so incredible, and she wished it could go on forever. If no other good thing ever happened to her for the rest of her life, she'd always feel filled to the brim because of this experience he'd given her.

The thought brought tears prickling behind her eyes. She was madly in love with him now. She couldn't help herself. The sad fact was that she'd never had anything like that happen before, and the emotional pull of it was too overwhelming for her to resist. At the same time, however, she was a grown woman, and she understood how flings between adults were supposed to play out, so she had no illusions.

While she had developed deep feelings for Beau, this was just another tryst for him, and would never be anything more. He'd never develop any kind of feelings for her in return, except perhaps friendship. This caused her to smile again as she imagined herself in the years to come, knowing she'd once been a friend—and lover—of a man like Harley Beaudine. This would only be a quick sexual liaison. That bit of insight caused a little fragment of hurt to push its way to the surface, but she buried it deeply.

Her heart might be telling her to want more, to

expect more, to try for more, but she wouldn't. This was a good place—to think, to plan, to rest. She'd use her time wisely, and when he let her know it was time to leave she would do so with no regrets and no complaints, holding all her tender memories of him close to her heart.

But please, God, she prayed, *don't let it be tonight or tomorrow. Let me have this one good thing for just a while longer.* Until she felt better, stronger. Then, she'd be ready to go with a happy heart.

The smells coming from the kitchen were getting more delicious by the moment, and she decided to head downstairs. She stood and searched around on the floor, looking for the T-shirt Beau had given her the night before. The room looked like a war had been fought in it, and she couldn't find it in the mess they'd made. Boldly, she went to his dresser, searched through one of the drawers, and found another. She pulled it over her head, and, even through the clean laundering she could smell him. Inhaling deeply, she wondered briefly where her own clothes were, thinking she might never get dressed again, wishing she could stay in his house forever, running around half naked in one of his shirts.

Tentatively, she made her way out of the bedroom. Because of her awkward arrival the previous night, she barely remembered the layout of the rooms. Letting her nose lead the way, she found the kitchen and stepped inside, hesitantly wondering what he'd be like now, what he'd say, how he'd act.

Gloriously naked, he stood in front of the stove, wearing only a baker's apron tied around his waist, the perfection of his skin marked in a few dramatic spots along his shoulder, back, buttocks, and thighs. He'd been badly burned once, and still bore the scars, but during the long hours of loving she'd been unable to ask how it had happened. In the evening shadows drifting in through the kitchen windows, the scars were barely visible. He looked sexy and powerful, all muscle and sinew, a country god preparing a feast for his adorers.

The table was set for two, a bouquet of wildflowers filled an old Mason jar, and candles burned in their holders next to the flowers. As though he sensed her approach, he looked over his shoulder just as she entered the room.

"Hello, gorgeous." He smiled, catching her, holding her, hypnotizing her with the brilliance of his presence. "I was just about to come wake you up."

Just that . . . just that much, set her heart to fluttering, and from the look in his eyes she could tell this would not be the day that he would send her on her way. She had more time with him. Relief flooded her.

"I'm starving," she said, suddenly realizing it as she rushed across the room and wrapped her arms around his waist.

"Thought you might be," he said, welcoming her by pulling her close, and she nuzzled her face into the hair on his chest.

"I missed you when I woke up," she confessed. And, because she absolutely refused to be timid around him, she added, "I wanted to do it again."

"I've created a monster." He laughed low and long in that way he had, and placed a tender kiss on the top of her head. "Well, my little sexual dynamo, let me replenish a few calories, and we'll give it another go."

"Don't say it unless you mean it," she teased, her hands working their way down and slipping under the hem of his apron.

"Now, cut that out!" he said, but she didn't stop right away, so he reached for her hand and removed it. "You keep that up for two more seconds, and you won't get any breakfast." He pointed toward the table with his spatula. "Sit. And behave yourself."

"Spoilsport." She pouted, but she did as he asked. She was hungry and wanted to eat, but she couldn't help wondering what it would be like to do something as wicked as make love in the kitchen—right on the counter, or the table. Maybe he'd show her later. She blushed, thinking how much she'd changed in a matter of hours.

Beau started setting platters of food on the table—pancakes, eggs, bacon, hash browns, toast, juice. Everything looked perfect and delicious. She took a bite of the potatoes and cooed with pleasure. "This tastes so good. Makes me wish I'd learned how to cook."

"You don't know how?"

"No," she said, which was a lie. She knew how to cook, and cook well. Her father's chef—an older widow—had taken pity on her as a child, and for years Allison had followed the woman around like a lost puppy. A lonely girl, she'd managed to develop a sense of belonging by watching, helping, stirring, and mixing. Cooking and baking were soothing methods she used to pass the time. But she'd learned early on never to admit such a skill to a man. Let a guy discover that a woman could cook, and, the next thing she knew, that's all he thought she was good for.

"Well, it's a good thing I know how, then," he said, "or we'd probably starve to death." He filled her glass with juice. "How come you never learned such a simple thing?"

"We always had chefs when I was growing up," she said, the lies continuing to roll out easily. "And then, as an adult, I just always ate out in restaurants. Usually at the hotels where I was working."

"What?" he asked as he seated himself and noticed how Allison was staring.

"I just realized that you're the only man I know who knows how to cook."

"Really?" he said, spearing a pancake with his fork. "What *do* they know how to do?"

"Make money, I guess."

"Well, I know how to do that, too."

"Aah, a man of many talents."

"You know it, honey," he said with a lecherous smile, and the drawl was suddenly back in his voice and extremely pronounced.

Because of it, she eyed him suspiciously. "Where does your drawl go when you're not using it?"

He shrugged. "I put it in the closet with my work clothes."

"It's all part of an act, isn't it?"

"What is?"

"The clothes and the talk and the attitude. You want everybody to think you're different from how you truly are."

"Maybe." He smiled and winked.

"*Maybe* nothing. I've found you out. You're nothing like you pretend to be, are you?"

"What makes you say that?" He looked down at his plate, suddenly extremely interested in his food.

"You act all rude and bossy, and you try to pretend that you're completely self-centered, but you're not. You've been so nice to me. And worried about me, too, when you found out about my father. You let me stay here when I wasn't in any condition to go anywhere else. You could have taken advantage of me last night when I was drunk, but you didn't. I think you're kind of gallant, but that wouldn't fit with your image, so you try to hide it."

"You think I'm *gallant*?" he asked, looking embarrassed. "Man, do I have you fooled."

"I don't think so." She reached out and rested her hand on his. "I've got your number, Harley Beaudine."

"No, you don't," he felt forced to insist. He'd worn his egotistical shell for so long that it was irksome to think that somebody might be able to see through the walls he'd built. "Just because I didn't jump your bones last night doesn't mean I haven't taken advantage of you. I hid your clothes, so you couldn't leave—"

"You did?" she asked, laughing. "I was wondering where they were."

"I hid my car keys, too, so you couldn't drive off while I was sleeping."

"You didn't need to do that. I don't know how to drive."

That admission caused him to pause. "You don't?"

"Well, I know *how,* but I just never do. I live in Manhattan, so I don't even own a car."

"How do you get along?" he asked, assessing her and thinking that she definitely needed his help in many, many, more ways than he'd first imagined, and it excited and frightened him at the same time.

"Not very well, I've been thinking lately."

"You're right about that." He took a bite of eggs, muttering under his breath, "I hid the phones, too."

"You what?"

"I hid the phones, so you couldn't call a cab."

"You're funny." She chuckled.

"Why?"

"Because I don't want to leave yet. You didn't have to worry about me making some grand escape."

"But don't you see what I mean? I hid everything, and I've had definite designs on your person from the moment I realized it was you walking down my road. And I've had my way with you pretty good since you woke up, so don't be telling me I'm *gallant,* and all other kinds of nonsense. Don't be trying to read more into this than there is."

Whether he'd intended it as a subtle warning or not, she didn't know, but she received the message loudly and clearly. "I won't," she said softly. "I know exactly what we're doing here."

"Do you?" he asked. "Because you need to always remember that what you see with me is exactly what you get." For once, he was irritated by the fact that it was true. "Nothing more. Nothing less."

She didn't think so at all anymore, but she let the matter rest. He attacked his food with renewed energy, and she watched in silence while he ate,

loving each and every thing about him, taking in
the way he held his fork, the way he chewed, the
way he swallowed. The quiet lingered until she finally said, "Are we having a fight?"

"No." He paused in the vigorous attack on his
food, tossed his fork beside his plate. "Hell, I don't
know what I'm saying." Gruffly, he added, "I'm glad
you're here. I'm glad you stayed."

"Me, too."

"It's just that, well . . ."

She waited for him to finish the sentence, or add
to it, at least, but it became clear that he didn't
know what to say, so she finished it for him. "It's just
that this feels different."

"In what way?" he asked, intrigued, wondering if
she could give voice to exactly what he was feeling.

"It's scary to me," she admitted, wondering if she
was anywhere close to describing his feelings, too.
"Being here feels right. I'm comfortable—like I've
always been here, or something." *Like I belong here,* she
thought, but didn't add. Without a doubt, she knew
that the mention of anything permanent or long-term
might be too terrifying for the man to hear.

"Yeah, I guess that's it."

"We just met, but I feel like I've known you for a
long time."

"I feel the same way, too," he admitted grudgingly, and Allison thought he looked angry from
just admitting it.

"Why do you suppose that is?"

"Beats the hell out of me," he said, refusing to
look at it more deeply. There was a bond there, an
important one, and it scared the hell out of him.
He'd felt it the moment he'd lain down next to her

in his bed. Or maybe it was before that. Maybe it was the first moment he'd set eyes on her.

His sister would say it was destiny or some such drivel, but he didn't believe in that sort of thing. But, if there was no destiny involved, what was going on? Why was she there, and why did he feel so connected to her? And why didn't he want her to go? Maybe it was just that she was fun in bed, hot and passionate and eager to learn. He'd never wanted a woman to be more than that, and he was pretty damn sure he didn't want *her* to be more than that.

She interrupted his reverie. "I really don't know anything about you. I mean, did you grow up here in Jackson, or where?"

"No. Mostly Denver."

"When did you come here?"

"The first time?" She nodded as he closed his eyes for a second, remembering those first heady days. "I was a kid, really. Nineteen, and with a barrel of money. I bought this lot and had the house built. It became my home base. Whenever I had a break from touring, this is where I'd come."

"Is your family still in Denver?"

"No. My daddy is out in New England. My mother lives in Italy." At least, he thought she was still in Italy. Last time he'd heard, that's where she was.

"They're divorced?"

"For a long time now."

"Where did your talent come from?"

"Both of them, I guess. Dad's a music professor. He's about to retire. My mom is—was—a concert violinist when she was younger. She doesn't play much anymore."

It sounded so simple, Beau thought, as though

they were a typical American family, when nothing could have been further from the truth. They'd moved constantly over the years as his lecherous father had been caught in one peccadillo or another with his female students. His mother had been one of the girls he'd seduced. He'd actually married her for a short time, but her ascending career—and both their infidelities—had quickly torn the small family apart.

"Did Patty get any of their talent?"

"Sure. She probably could have been a concert pianist . . ."

There was a long pause, and she asked, "But?"

"She doesn't play much anymore. It's stressful for her."

"Why?"

"Well, it reminds her of . . ." He wouldn't say too much, even liking Allison as much as he did. "Let's just say it wasn't Ozzie and Harriet when we were growing up."

"But you kept at it."

"Just by accident." His eyes gleamed with mischief. "Plus, I was too lazy to get a real job."

"There you go, trying to pull my leg again."

"What makes you say that?"

"I know talent can account for a lot, but your level of ability takes hard work. Years of it."

"You may be right," he offered, refusing to admit that, as a child, exceeding at music had been his only way to get any attention from the two self-centered people who'd raised him.

"How did you get started in your career?"

"Like I said. Just by accident."

"Beau, I already told you I'm not buying that story."

"Well, it's the truth. In high school, I kind of had a garage band with my buddy, J.D." He smiled at the memory of the wild boy who had been his friend, the young man who had been his partner, dead now these ten long years. "The year we were seniors, during the Denver Stock Show, this bar had its country band cancel at the last minute, and all those thousands of cowboys were in town. The owner was desperate, and we'd played there a few times on amateur nights. So we filled in."

He made it sound so simple. With his talent, maybe it had been. "The rest is history?"

"Pretty much."

She liked this side of him. Open and honest, and conversing easily. It felt as if they'd always sat there at his kitchen table, talking, eating and drinking coffee. That made it seem like a good time to ask the deeper questions to which she'd been dying to know the answers. His burn scars bothered her most. Cautiously, she lay one hand on his wrist and let the fingers of the other trace a path across his shoulder and back.

"How did you get these?" she asked.

"In the plane crash."

"What crash?" she couldn't help asking, causing him to laugh loud and long, which was the last thing she'd expected.

"You are so good for my ego."

"Why would you say that?"

"Well, Patty always tells me it's way too inflated. I guess I'll have to keep you around so you can regularly poke holes in it." More quietly, seriously, he added, "I thought everybody knew I'd been in a plane crash."

"Not me." From the way he was squirming in his chair, she could tell it was a difficult subject. She could only imagine. Gently, she prodded, "Want to tell me about it?"

"There's not much to tell," he said, shrugging as though the life-altering event was a matter of no consequence. "We'd done a show in Minneapolis, and we were flying to another one in Sioux Falls. Got caught in a thunderstorm and crashed in a cornfield." For a moment, just one, he let it all come swirling back, remembering the sounds, the smells, the fear, but all he said was, "It was pretty awful."

"It must be difficult for you to ride in an airplane after something like that."

"I've never set foot on one of the blasted things again." He shuddered involuntarily. "I can't even stand to drive by an airport." Hearing the roar of a jet engine raised his anxiety so high that he always felt as if his heart might burst.

Although she thought she probably already knew the answer, she asked delicately, "What happened to the other guys in the band?"

"All died. All but me."

And he felt guilty because of it. She could sense his anguish. "How long ago?"

"Ten years ago this weekend. Tonight and tomorrow." He turned and looked out the window, staring at the red and orange sky, and said softly, "Sometimes, it seems like it was just yesterday."

She got up from her chair and moved to his, snuggling herself on his lap and resting her head on his shoulder. "This is a terrible time for you."

"Yeah," he said, trying to sound unmoved and failing miserably.

"Then I'm doubly glad I'm here."

So was Beau. As the anniversary had approached, he'd suspected that it might be unsettling, and he'd tried to pretend that he was coping well. Perhaps that was why Allison had been dropped into his lap. Maybe one of those guardian angels—in whom he no longer believed—had decided to let her watch over him during these few hard days.

He took the comfort she offered, holding her close, lost in thought and reveling in the companionable silence. That was one of the things that he liked about her so much. When she was near, he felt comfortable, with no need to talk, or be, or do. He felt better just being around her. The only other time he'd felt such a rapport was with his old friend, J.D. He and Patty had been Beau's only constants in a life where there had been few.

Memories of J.D. made him smile into Allison's hair, and for once he could think about the man without all the "what-ifs" that usually assailed him. He could be happy simply to remember. "I've been thinking a lot lately about J.D." Oh, how good it felt to speak his name without all the heartache it usually engendered. He smiled again, saying, "He was such a terror. When I think of some of the trouble he got me into—"

"You loved him."

"Like a brother." Beau swallowed, the words choking him. "We were holding hands . . . in the wreckage. We were trapped, and it took a long time to get us out. He died before . . . well, before . . ." He couldn't say the rest.

"He died holding your hand." Beau nodded into her hair, and Allison was glad he wasn't looking her in the eye. She didn't think he could have spoken about any of it if they'd been looking at each other.

So many things about him were clear now. The heady flash of fame, the joy of young men at their prime doing what they loved. All of it ended in a moment. After, he'd come here to his house, a sanctuary in the mountains, to recover and recuperate. And he'd stayed all these years, alone with his guilt and sorrow and memories.

"I'm glad you were with J.D. at the end," she said, hoping her words offered some small comfort.

"So am I."

He hugged her tight, and they finished their meal with Allison sitting on his lap and feeding him small bites. They talked of many things while they ate. Of Allison's lonely childhood, and Beau's wild one. Of Allison's crazy family, and Beau's crazier one. Of Allison's methodical planning of her career and Beau's instantaneous burst into the limelight and his immediate withdrawal from it a decade later.

By the time they finished, the leftovers were cold, the coffeepot empty, and it was late and dark outside. Beau took her hand and led her back up the stairs. He lit a candle and made quiet love to her in the dim light. There was no need for talk. With his body, he showed her how glad he was to have her by her side. Allison silently accepted the attention he showered on her, gently returning each kiss, touch, embrace, hoping she could do some good in easing his aching heart.

When they finished, both weary and sated, she held him for a long time wrapped by her body, her arms and legs holding him close, wanting to shield him from the battering of retrospection the weekend anniversary would bring. His breathing slowed, and he fell into a deep sleep, and she had the chance to study him, loving the way his golden hair tickled her nose, his breath warmed her skin. He looked younger in his sleep, less alone, much of his inherent cockiness vanished.

She placed a soft kiss on his brow, so glad she was there, that he'd let her stay. With a prayer of thanks to whatever powers might be listening, she closed her eyes and slept, as well.

Sometime late in the night, she awakened to the sound of his violin coming from outside. Her first thought was to let him be, to let him pour out his sorrow to the dark night, but the sound of his music was so unbearably sad that she couldn't bear him being outside and alone. She grabbed a T-shirt and headed downstairs to the back door.

He was dressed only in a pair of jeans, no shirt, no shoes, the violin under his chin, his eyes closed as he played a haunting melody. The bright moonlight shone on his golden hair and sharply defined muscles, making him look like a statue of a god, painstakingly sculpted, his beauty so breathtaking that he was placed on earth for humans to worship and admire.

Patiently, she waited on the stoop until the song ended. As the last sounds reverberated through the forest, he lowered the violin against his leg and looked up at the stars.

"Beau," she said quietly, hating to interrupt the moment. "Are you okay?"

"I just couldn't sleep." Sounding embarrassed, he

admitted, "Sometimes I come out here when that happens."

He pulled his gaze from the sky and focused it on her, and he held out his hand in welcome. She rushed from the doorway and into his arms. His skin was cold, and she wondered how long he'd been outside.

"You're freezing," she said, hugging her arms around his waist and trying to share some of her body heat.

"Am I? I didn't notice."

They stood there for a long time, Beau staring out at the stars as they held each other and listened to the night sounds. Allison rested her cheek against the center of his chest and was lulled by the steady beating of his heart.

Finally, as though he'd reached a major decision, he looked down at her, saying, "I'm going to go through with it."

"With what?"

"My contract to play at the hotel."

"It never occurred to me that you wouldn't," she said. "Is that what brought you out here?"

He nodded, pulling her closer. "I don't like what your daddy did to you, how he treated you, the things he said about you. It just seems wrong to plod along like everything he did is okay with me."

"I'm used to it by now. It doesn't matter to me."

"Well, it matters to *me*," he said with a grim finality, "and it seems like I'm betraying you if I go through with it. I'd never do anything to hurt you."

"It won't hurt me if you play there."

"You're sure?" he said, searching her eyes and

trying to read the truth of her statement in the dim light.

"I'm sure." She chuckled, touched that he'd be so worried about her feelings. "You know, your reputation with me is completely ruined. If you keep this up, I'm going to start thinking you're a dear sweet man."

Beau snorted at that. "Sweet like a rattlesnake, maybe." He looked out at the sky once more. "I need that job, Allie. So much. I need to perform again."

"I know you do."

"I get asked to play all the time, and I thought maybe, if the hotel worked out, I'd stretch out a little. Maybe take something in Bozeman, or down in Salt Lake."

"I think that would be a great idea."

"Or Cheyenne. Every year, they ask me down for Frontier Days."

"But you always say no?"

"I just couldn't do it before," he said, shaking his head, confused by his behavior. "Lately, I don't know . . . it's like there's all this music waiting inside, trying to burst out. I don't know if it's the anniversary of the crash, or what. It just feels like it's time to get back at it. I need to go through with this job."

"Of course you do."

"So you won't be mad?"

"Never at you." She stood on tiptoe and kissed him on the mouth. "It's cold out here. Come back to bed."

His eyes twinkling like diamonds, he nodded toward the house. "You go on. I'll be up in a minute."

"Promise?" As his answer, he gave her a kiss of such sweet assurance that she couldn't do anything but obey his wishes.

"Go on, baby girl. I'll be right there." She turned and went back inside and he watched her go, thinking how comforted he was by her presence, how glad he was that she'd be waiting upstairs.

For the first time in a long time, he felt better.

Chapter 8

"Are you sure you're going to be all right here by yourself?" Beau asked.

"Yes," she responded, exasperated. He'd asked her a different version of that same question over and over during the afternoon, while he prepared to leave for his first show.

"You're positive?"

"I'll be fine. Quit worrying about me." She walked across the living room and straightened the points of his collar, and he fidgeted like a kindergartner in church. "Hold still."

"I can't. I'm too charged up."

"No kidding!" She laughed as he wrapped her in his arms and waltzed her around the room. His excitement level had been building all day. Now, when it was time to head for the hotel, he was a teeming bundle of manic energy.

"Tell me how great I'm going to be."

"I will not," she insisted breathlessly, hardly able to keep up with his frantic pace.

"Tell me how much they're going to love me," he commanded, still twirling her in circles.

"No. If your head swells any more, you won't be able to get through the door."

Stopping suddenly, he decided to try a different tactic by laying her back across his arm and kissing her senseless. He played with her mouth until her blood was throbbing through her veins, her ears ringing, her heart pounding, her knees weak.

"Tell me," he said, his lips warm against her own.

"You'll be fantastic," she vowed, giggling as he tickled the response out of her. "Great. Magnificent. Fabulous. Awesome."

"That's more like it," he said with a nod and a smile, straightening and bringing her up with him.

He looked so fine that she could hardly stand it, dressed all in white, a stark contrast to the fancy black outfit in which she'd first seen him. The shirt had gold-and-silver sequins embroidered across the shoulders and chest. He sparkled and shone, and he wasn't even under a spotlight yet. The light color faded his hair to a white-blond, and he looked like a wicked angel come down to earth to wreak havoc.

Seriously, she said, "You'll be terrific."

"I know," he agreed, swatting her on the butt and making her laugh.

"Get going before you're late."

"I'll be back around midnight. Maybe one."

"Take your time. Have fun."

"I intend to," he said. One final time, he asked, "Are you sure you don't want to come along?"

"Go!" she insisted, practically shoving him out the door. Pausing on the front porch, he grabbed her fast and hard, giving her one last long kiss before he jumped down the steps, his violin case slapping against his thigh. His pickup roared to life, and he peeled out of the driveway. With an arm stuck out the window, he waved once as he veered onto the road, and she stood in the door, watching him until he disappeared.

His departure had created such a whirlwind that she was almost glad to see him go. Almost. As she stepped back into the quiet house, it felt unbearably empty without him. How one man could generate so much intensity was a mystery, but with him gone, everything seemed less bright.

Still, she was surrounded by his things. He'd told her to make herself at home while he was away, and she intended to do just that. She'd spent three days in his house, but hadn't seen much besides the bedroom and the kitchen. This was her chance to snoop and pry, which she was itching to do.

Her first stop was the music room with its incredible stereo system, which took up most of one wall. He had thousands of albums and CDs, and she began methodically searching through them until she found what she was looking for. Copies of his albums, some over twenty years old with worn and faded covers, were discreetly alphabetized with the others, as though they held no special significance.

"They look so young," she murmured as she pulled out the earliest one and then the rest, arranging them by date, looking at the cover photos, the text on the back, reading the names of the songs, the songwriters, the musicians. On each cover Beau and J.D. took center stage, sitting on farmhouse porches, in old cars, on bar stools. J.D. always held a guitar, Beau a fiddle, and the rest of

the band stood behind, outshone by the good looks
and charisma of the two stars.

There were twelve albums in all, plus one solo
album by Beau. She wanted to listen to all of them,
but was almost afraid to touch them. The older
ones, especially, seemed like precious antiques, so
she walked to the shelves holding the CDs and discovered that all of them had been rerecorded onto
discs. She pulled out the first three and put them in
the CD player, turned up the volume, and went ex-
ploring further.

The next stop was his library, or *office*, she supposed it might be called. Here she found photo
albums and scrapbooks. There were speakers which
piped Beau's music into the room, and she let the
sound of his voice and violin fill up the empty
house as she pulled a chair next to the bookshelf
and started through the row.

The scrapbooks were dated from about the time
he entered high school, and they were meticulously
kept, recording every accomplishment, news release, and photo opportunity. Allison wondered
who had done it for him. She couldn't imagine
Beau having the interest or taking the time. His
sister, Patty, came to mind, and the image fit. Allison
could just picture her snipping away over the years
at magazines and newspapers, carefully recording
the small and major events of her big brother's life.

The personal history ended abruptly with the
plane crash. There were a few photos of the wreckage, which caused Allison to flinch. They were ac-
companied by several pages of memorial articles
about the band, the members' funerals. The last
photo, taken by a tabloid photographer, was of

Beau leaving the hospital three months after the date of the crash. He appeared rail-thin, broken down and apart, and there was little that was recognizable of the happy famous man he'd been before the accident.

The rest of the pages were blank, as though Patty had lost the energy that was necessary for the effort. Or, perhaps, there were so few mentions of Beau in the media after he retired to Jackson that there wasn't any reason to continue.

Allison closed the book and sat in silence as one CD cycled to the next. Once the music started again, she moved around the room, studying a scattering of family photos. There was a collection of his mother taken over the years, what looked to be publicity photos, with her dressed in concert blacks and holding a violin. A few playbills were framed and hung, announcing her performances with various world-class orchestras. She was a thin, striking, blond woman who hadn't aged much, and Allison wondered if Beau had gotten his seductiveness from her.

Once she discovered a photo of his father, though, she knew from where his appeal had come. He was ruggedly handsome, one of those men who always looked better with each passing year and never lost the allure that drew women. Beau looked just like him, causing her to imagine how he would look at fifty, sixty, and beyond. His blond hair would turn more white, the smile lines around his eyes and mouth would increase, but, for the most part, he'd stay the superb dynamic male he was.

There were dozens of other photos. Of Patty. Of Beau and J.D. Of Beau with what she thought were probably other famous country stars. She recognized Roy Clark in one, but, she wasn't familiar enough with their industry to be able to name any of the others.

As she ran her fingers over the last of them, she paused just as the music ended. She headed back to the music room and started a new pile of his CDs. Quickly, the house was filled once again with his voice and music. The pulse and rhythm of it pounded through her at a loud volume, and she liked the way it made her tap her toes and smile. And she liked the way that it made him seem as if he were there with her. He had that ability, even through the audio system, to sound near. It occurred to her that she'd have to purchase all of his music, so that after she left she'd always be able to hear his voice whenever she wanted.

One song ended abruptly, the silence lingering much longer than necessary before the next one started, which gave her plenty of time to remember the fact that she'd be leaving one of these days. She tried to shove the thought away, but couldn't. Like a pesky insect, it remained. While Beau was in the house, she'd managed to stave off the future, to pretend there was only now, but with him gone she wasn't so capable of skirting reality.

Sooner or later, she'd have to go, but oh, how she wanted to stay! She loved Beau, worried and cared about him much more than was appropriate or wise. He was a man she could love forever.

She could easily picture herself living in his log house, making love, listening to his music, helping him dress for his shows, calming him after, laughing at his stories, putting up with his ways, stroking his ego when he needed it, bringing him down a peg when he needed that, too.

The things she'd always believed she wanted—the big city life, the corporate position, the whirlwind of travel—were easy to forget when she was here in this quiet spot on the edge of the woods.

She could remain by his side permanently and be perfectly happy. Loving him. Married to him. With a handful of little blond Beaus, running wild and filling up her life.

But it would never happen that way. Beau wasn't a man given to love or fidelity, or settling down with one woman. He was a shining star, his personality so grand, his allure so vast, his appeal so great, that he would always need more and better things to fill up his life.

While she wished it wasn't true, the fact of the matter was that she was a fairly boring person. She worked, she ate, she slept. There was no flash or dash to keep the interest of a man like Beau over an extended period of time, and he'd quickly grow bored.

For the moment, he wanted her around. He needed her—probably through the weekend of the anniversary of the crash, maybe even beyond that for a few weeks. Then, she'd be gone in a heartbeat, because the very last thing she could endure was to see the spark of interest in his eyes begin to fade. To look at him and fail to be caught up in that smile would be the very worst kind of torture.

So, she'd stay while he let her, but she planned to be gone long before he ever had the chance to become apathetic or restless. When she left, the only things she wanted to carry with her were the memories of this hot, glorious, passionate time.

"Reality is highly overrated," she muttered as she left the library and wandered into the hall.

She was itching again. Scratching and miserable, she walked out to the kitchen, knowing she needed to take her mind off the future and put herself back into the void where she blissfully escaped from any thoughts about what would happen next.

Desperately, she needed to do something with her hands, something that would occupy her thoughts for the next few hours until Beau came home, and she knew just the thing—baking. Childhood memories of the hours she'd passed in the kitchen were always comforting, as were the delicious aromas she'd generate. Baking never failed to help her achieve the tranquillity she sought. If Beau said anything, or acted differently because he learned she could cook, she didn't mind. She wouldn't be around long enough for it to matter.

Next to the kitchen was a small pantry. She turned on the light and stepped inside, looking over the assorted canned goods. Beau had said he kept tons of food handy. Many times during the long harsh winters, he was snowed in for weeks at a time before the county crews plowed all the way out to his driveway. It wasn't unusual to go without power, either, during a blizzard. She smiled, wondering what it would be like to be stranded with Beau, the electricity off, the roads closed, the phones out. Just her and Beau in his log house, and the rest of the world far away.

She pulled out two cans of blueberries, found a canister of flour and one of sugar, and headed for

the counter. From memory, she began the simple
pastry recipe, and the mixing and stirring instantly
calmed her troubled mind and heavy heart. With
the first stir of the spoon, the itching of her rash
eased.

Beau arrived home in an odd mood. The show
had been spectacular; he'd played better than ever,
and the crowd had been enthusiastic and responsive, so he was as pumped up as he'd ever been
after a great performance. But, as he mounted the
front steps and opened the door, he hesitated.

In the past, he and J.D. had usually headed for
the bars and partied all night after a show. If they
headed home instead, *home* had been a hotel suite
in a strange city filled with a large group of people
who rocked and rolled till dawn. In all the years,
and all the shows, he'd never had someone who
cared about him waiting with a quiet gentle welcome. For some reason he wanted one now, and he
wanted it from Allison.

But what if she wasn't there? What if she'd left
while he was in town?

His worry over just such an event was all out of
proportion, and he couldn't figure out why it was
so important to find her waiting. It just was. All
evening, his concentration had slipped away as
he'd wondered about her. How was she doing?
What was she doing? Once, between sets, he'd
almost gone to the phone and called home just so
he could hear the sound of her voice, but he'd
stopped himself before doing something so crazy.

The emotions she stirred were certainly curious,

but he'd given up trying to make sense of them. He liked her quirky mixture of competence and innocence; he was wildly attracted to her; the sex was terrific—like no other he could remember—and he felt connected to her in different and powerful ways. Why all this had happened was beyond him, but he'd decided to let it all play out.

He wouldn't go so far as to say they were having some kind of *relationship*. By its very definition, that was something he avoided like the plague. Throughout his life, he'd made it a point never to endure one. But, for now, they were together, and he was glad. He didn't intend to read any more into it than that.

As he stepped up to the house he smiled, his trepidation vanishing as he heard his voice coming through the stereo speakers scattered in various locations around the house. Judging from the smell of things, she was in the kitchen, so he headed in that direction.

Barefoot, dressed in one of his T-shirts, with an apron around her waist, a smudge of flour on her cheek, and her blond hair falling out of the clip on top of her head, she was a sight for sore eyes. In one hand, she held a cookie sheet. In the other, a spatula which she was using to scoop cookies onto the counter. There were baked goods everywhere. Cookies, various kinds of pastries, a cake.

Not wanting to frighten her, he leaned against the doorjamb and observed, unnoticed, as she moved around his room. She'd obviously made herself at home—in his kitchen, anyway—and he liked seeing her there. She looked good, taking up space in his house.

The song coming from the CD player moved into the chorus, and, when he heard her humming along to one of his melodies, he decided they were making some definite progress. Her wall of reserve was crumbling fast, and he couldn't help wondering what kind of woman he'd be left with once it was completely gone.

The song ended, the silence filling up the kitchen, and she sang a bar of the chorus—sort of off-key, and the words not exactly right—and he thought it was about the sweetest thing he'd ever heard.

She looked up just then, not in the least surprised to find him standing there watching so intently.

"Hello, you," she said with a smile.

"Hello, yourself."

"How was the show?"

"Terrific."

"How were you?"

"Terrific."

She chuckled. "I didn't need to ask, did I?"

"Nope. I'm always great." He took a step into the room. "Looks like you've been busy."

"I decided to bake a few things," she said, looking embarrassed, as though realizing for the first time how thoroughly she'd been occupying her time. "I guess I got a little carried away."

"That's all right, honey. I told you to make yourself at home. I'm glad you did."

"I used up a lot of your surplus food in the pantry. I'll pay you back."

"Don't worry about it," he said, shaking his head. "If doing this makes you happy, I'll buy you flour in hundred-pound sacks."

"It was fun," she had to admit, wiping the back of her hand across a hot cheek and smearing even more flour, adding to how adorable she looked.

"I thought you said you didn't know how to cook."

"I might have fibbed about that a little bit," she admitted.

"How come?"

"Habit," she shrugged. "I learned the hard way that if you admit to a man that you know how to cook, next thing you know—"

"You're darning socks and scrubbing toilets?"

"Something like that." She relaxed slightly, relieved that he understood.

He reached out for a cookie, still warm from the oven, and took a bite. It melted in his mouth. "This is really good."

"Thanks." Her cheeks blushed a delightful shade of pink. "I just do it to pass the time when I have a lot on my mind. It helps me think."

"And what were you thinking about"—he waved his hand—"while you were making all this stuff?"

"What I want to do next. Where I want to go. Things like that."

"Did you make any decisions?" He tried to sound casual, but he was suddenly gripped with an overwhelming dread that she might have already made up her mind to leave.

"No, not a single one," she said, shaking her head. He breathed a secret sigh of relief. For now, while he tried to figure out what to do with her, she'd be staying.

Reassured by her failure to reach any conclusions, he couldn't help asking cockily, "Did you miss me?"

"Maybe a little," she said, asking just as cockily in return, "did you miss *me?*"

"Maybe a little," he answered, as well, then held out his arms in invitation. "Come here."

She took quick steps across the room, hugging him around the waist, burying her pretty nose against his chest and saying, "I'm glad you're back."

"So am I." And he was. During and after the show, there had been the typical invitations. To party. To drink. To eat. To bed. He'd passed them all up for this moment, and, he decided, there was definitely something to be said for receiving a warm welcome and a pleasant smile when he walked in his door.

He held her for as long as she'd let him, which wasn't long. She pulled away, making a face. "You stink."

"Yes, ma'am, I do." He smiled down at her, knowing he reeked of cigarette smoke, alcohol, stale bar odors, and sweat. When he finished a performance, he always felt as if he'd run ten miles.

"Come on, you," she said, taking his hand and leading him toward the stairs. "Let's get you cleaned up. Then you can relax and tell me all about your night. I want to hear everything."

He went willingly, and, like a child, he sat on his bed doing very little while she removed his boots, his clothes. She went into the bathroom, turned on the shower, adjusted the water temperature. He followed, standing in only his briefs, watching as she bent over the tub, her delicious ass poking out from under the hem of the T-shirt. Unable to resist, he ran a hand across a smooth expanse of thigh, earning himself a dazzling smile full of temptation.

Then she was in his arms, and he was kissing her, running his hands through her hair, across her back, down her hips. Lifting her, he pressed her back against the bathroom wall, holding her up with his thighs. Her legs were open wide and wrapped around his waist, and her secret place pressed against him where he needed it most. He was hard and aching for her, and, with a start, he realized that this was what he'd really wanted all night long. To be here alone, like this, with her.

With a sudden urgency, he removed her shirt, letting his eyes feast on her glorious breasts. His hands went to work, then his mouth, and he couldn't believe how he loved the little sighs of pleasure she made in the back of her throat, the wriggles and squirms of her hips which brought her into closer contact with his swollen manhood.

He stepped into the shower and took her with him. There was no hesitation on her part, and he couldn't help thinking how much she'd changed in the few short days he'd known her. The Allison he'd first met would never have considered stepping into a shower with a naked man. This Allison, the new one she was becoming, hardly blinked an eye.

Like a blossoming flower, she was opening up a little more each day. All that hot passion he'd initially sensed was gradually working its way to the surface. She was more beautiful for it, the glow in her hair and eyes returning, the color in her cheeks blooming. There was a sweetness about her, too, and it coupled with her sensual flair in ways he found irresistible.

Her confidence was soaring, and he couldn't help wondering again what he was going to do with the woman she was becoming. Who would she be when all this ended?

The warm water sluiced over them, making them hot and slippery, and she did all the work. He reveled in her attention as she took the soap and washed him all over—under his arms, across his chest and back, down his legs, between his thighs. On her knees, she took special care with his privates, her ministrations making him ache with the pleasure of it.

When she took him into her mouth for the very first time, he was so amazed by her boldness that he hardly knew what to say or do. He stood still, letting her learn the way of it, her innocent attempt making it all the more erotic. He watched as long as he could stand it, but those full lips and that wicked tongue were more than he could bear.

Unable to stand the building pressure another second, he grabbed a handful of her hair and moved her mouth away, chuckling when she gazed up at him with those big blue eyes, giving him a pouting look as if she were a child and he'd just deprived her of her favorite candy.

Pulling her to her feet, he grabbed the back of her thighs, and she once again wrapped her legs around his waist. He took her hard and fast, and she let him, holding him close and whispering soft sex words in his ear when he spilled himself deep inside.

Afterward, he washed her, taking his own sweet time, just as she had. When they finished, they dried each other, and he was overcome by the sensation that they'd done this hundreds of times before. It seemed as though he'd played a thousand shows, and she'd been waiting for him after every one. There was nothing new, only a comforting sameness, with Allison instinctively knowing how to care for him as he wound down and let the excitement of his performance slowly ease away.

They sat together in his kitchen, Allie on his lap, feeding him bites of goodies and listening while he talked about the night, the show, the crowd. She knew the exact things to say, the questions to ask. This didn't seem like the first time, either, but a continuation of many many times that had gone before.

The early summer dawn was coming by the time he'd exhausted himself enough to sleep. She held his hand and led him up the stairs one more time, and he welcomed the feel of her next to him in his bed. He took her again, slowly and gently, until he was sated and happy because of it—because of her—and he couldn't help thinking that life didn't get any better than it was at that very moment.

As he rolled onto his side, she snuggled her backside against him, spooned close just the way he liked her. He rested a lazy arm across her hip and fell asleep with a smile on his face.

Chapter 9

Allison stood on the back patio of Beau's house, coffee cup in hand, staring out across the yard. Beau was asleep upstairs, resting peacefully after their late night of talking and loving. It had taken several hours, but she'd finally managed to calm him down enough to relax and sleep. But she'd been too restless to stay in bed with him. The summer day beckoned, and she'd felt compelled to rise.

She smiled, thinking about how hyper he'd been when he arrived home from his show, how he'd talked for hours, unable to relax, the excitement of performing still flowing through his veins.

He was probably always like that, and she couldn't help wondering what he usually did with all that energy, or how many other women had helped him calm down over the years. She didn't dwell on that too long. The reality was that she didn't want to speculate much about how Beau spent his free time.

Even though it was early morning, the temperature was already in the sixties, and she knew it would be hot by afternoon. Wearing one of Beau's shirts, and not caring that she still had nothing else to put on, she surveyed the scenery.

In one direction, past Beau's yard, the mowed green lawn turned into prairie grass. The meadow was dotted with a profusion of wildflowers for as far as she could see. A creek meandered through the length of it, and an early morning mist had settled, hovering just above the riverbed like a mystical cloud. She had a view of all the mansions down the valley. The sun was so bright that it hurt her eyes, and she finally had to turn away.

In the other direction, she saw only dark forest. High above the trees, she could just make out the craggy summit of the Grand Teton. The view held her spellbound for many minutes. There was something magical about it, she realized. Maybe it was the grandeur, or the silent beauty. It exerted an enchanting spell, and she could feel its potent gravity luring her closer. Just staring at it made her wish she were standing at its base, touching some of its rocks and stones, letting the power of the mountain flow through her veins. Never in her life had a natural object held so much power over her, and she couldn't resist its pull.

No sounds of civilization intruded. Only the sounds of nature could be heard. A butterfly flitted past her nose. Morning birds called to one another, and, while the air was blessedly still where she stood, somewhere off in the distance the wind whistled through the high branches of the pines, making the oddest swishing sound. When she closed her eyes and listened, she could pretend it was the sound of the earth turning, or the hum of the universe rumbling in her ears.

At the edge of the trees, to her surprise and delight, a small, shaggy brown bear quietly stepped into the light, skirted the outer edge of the yard, ran across the road, and disappeared in the forest on the other side. It happened so fast that she blinked several times, certain she'd imagined it.

Her immediate reaction was that she couldn't wait for Beau to wake up so she could tell him about it. It was amazing how quickly and easily her world had shrunk to this moment and this house and this man. Nothing else mattered.

There was a sense of serenity, a peacefulness which pervaded everything, and she could easily understand why Beau had chosen this spot when he needed a quiet place, and why he had stayed for so long after. She wouldn't mind staying, herself. All her troubles faded as she stood on his back porch staring out at the valley and the park and the mountains. All that stress and work seemed pointless. All that heartbreak paled to insignificance. She was content to have the rest of the hectic world pass her by.

With a wistful sigh, she turned to go back into the kitchen to refill her coffee cup. Just as she stepped through the door the phone rang, and without thinking she picked it up and answered.

There was a breath of hesitation on the other end, then a familiar female voice—one she couldn't quite place—said, "I'm sorry. I must have the wrong number."

Allison replaced the receiver and reached for the coffeepot, only to have the phone ring again. Irritated that the noise might wake Beau, she reached for it and said hello a second time.

The woman was still there, saying, "Is this Harley Beaudine's?"

"Yes."

"Well, this is his sister, Patty."

"Oh, hi, Patty," Allison said in response, as though talking to her was the most normal thing in the world.

"*Who* is this?"

"Allison."

"Allison?" Patty paused, searching her memory, but she could only manage to conjure up one Allison. Shocked, she inquired, "Allison . . . Masters?"

"In the flesh." Allison could almost hear the wheels turning in Patty's head as she tried to make sense of the situation, but who could? Allison could hardly figure it out herself.

"Put on a pot of coffee," Patty said. "I'll be right over." She hung up before Allison could respond.

Twenty minutes later, Patty pulled into the drive. The front door was open, so Allison didn't get up but waited patiently in her chair at the kitchen table. She listened to the other woman's cautious footsteps, coming over the stoop, crossing the living room. As she neared the kitchen, Allison supposed any normal person would be embarrassed about the coming visit, but she wasn't.

Her previous life and everything that occurred in it, including her disastrous first encounter with Beau and Patty, seemed far removed, as though they had happened to someone else. Not even the fact that she was about to greet her visitor while wearing only an oversized T-shirt could bring her to any state of agitation. Life was just flowing, and she was happy to let it.

"Hi," Patty said, stepping through the door and holding out a white bakery bag. Her astute gaze quickly surveyed the kitchen. "I brought some croissants from the bakery in town, but I guess I didn't need to."

"I went kind of overboard last night," Allison said, glancing over her shoulder to where every inch of counter space was covered with the goodies she'd created during her baking frenzy. "I was trying to keep busy while Beau was doing his show."

"Is he around?" Patty queried, pulling out a chair and sitting across from Allison.

"Still asleep."

"Oh. Hmm," Patty said, watching her carefully. "I'm sorry I called so early. I thought he might be up. He has insomnia a lot, so sometimes I can catch him at weird hours."

"Not this morning." Allison rose, poured Patty a cup of coffee, and sat back down. "Last time I checked, he was sleeping like a baby." She hadn't meant for the statement to sound so intimate, but after the words were out she realized it did. Patty regarded her even more shrewdly.

"How was the show?" Patty finally asked.

"Great. Just great."

"I couldn't be there. I'm going tonight, though." She stopped, assessing, calculating. She leaned forward, taking a deep breath and plunging ahead. "Allison, what are you doing here?"

"I don't know," Allison answered honestly. "I was trying to get to the airport, and I came walking down the road." She shrugged. "Beau was just . . . just . . . standing there waiting for me."

"How long ago?"

"Five days, I guess." The days had run together in her mind. Her brow wrinkled, and she counted back and decided she was correct. She couldn't help chuckling over the fact that she—punctual, obsessed, reliable Allison Masters—was living in a time warp. If she hadn't known that Beau's first show was on Saturday night, she'd have had no idea that it was now Sunday morning.

"You've been here all this time?"

"Yes." She nodded.

"Doing what?" Patty asked. Then, seeing the blush that quickly colored Allison's cheeks, she held up a hand. "Don't answer that. I know my brother better than anybody. I shouldn't have even had to ask." She relaxed back in her chair, sipping on the hot coffee. "I'm intrigued."

"By what?"

"By you. That he brought you inside. That he let you stay."

"Well, I sort of didn't have anywhere else to go. I guess he felt sorry for me."

"Felt sorry for you? My brother? Are we talking about the same Harley Beaudine?"

"The very one."

"I wonder if he's coming down with something."

"Why would you say that?" Allison asked, unable to keep from laughing.

"This is just so out of character for him. I mean, I've had my practice here in Jackson for six years now, and in all that time I can't remember a single occasion when he had a woman stay overnight here at the house. He just doesn't do it."

"Really? Not one?"

"No."

Allison took a moment to digest that information, and the implications of what it meant. "But he hasn't been . . . I mean, all this time, he certainly hasn't been . . ." She blushed furiously. She might be turning into a new woman, but she had no idea how to discuss Beau's sexual proclivities with his sister. Finally, she settled on an inane comment. "I imagine he has any number of female friends."

"Sure. He always has. That's just his way," Patty agreed, "but they never stay here."

The two women stared at each other across the table, considering, thinking, wondering. Allison finally shrugged again, not able to make sense of things any better while talking to Patty than she could while sitting and stewing on her own. "It just seemed like a natural thing to have happen. Everything's been so easy."

"Well, I'm certainly amazed. Are you guys getting along okay? I mean, when you first met, you clashed pretty hard."

"We clash pretty hard now, too, but it's no big deal. Since I got him figured out, he's been fairly easy to handle."

"You think you've got him figured out?" Patty raised a brow very high. "Now I know we're talking about two different men."

"He's not so hard to understand," Allison insisted.

"He's not?"

"Not once I realized what he needed."

"What he needed?"

She laughed. "Patty, you keep repeating everything I say."

"That's because I can't believe what I'm hearing. I'm just trying to be sure that I haven't completely lost my mind."

"You haven't." Distracted, Allison ran a hand through her hair. "Look, don't try to read too much into my being here. I don't think it's so much that *I'm* here, specifically. I think it could have been anybody. With this weekend being the anniversary of the plane crash, he's having a hard time."

"He talked to you about the plane crash?"

"Yes, and J.D. has been on his mind a lot lately, and—"

"Whoa!" Patty said, cutting her off. "He talked to you about J.D?"

"Patty!"

"What?"

"You're doing it again. Repeating everything I say. I have to tell you, you're kind of driving me nuts."

"Sorry," Patty said, not looking the least bit apologetic. Silently, they stared at each other for the longest time. Eventually, Patty said, "As far as I know, Beau has never talked about the crash with anybody. He tried once, right after it happened, with a therapist, but I think it was too soon, and he never went back. And he's never mentioned J.D. Not in all these years."

"Maybe it's time he started."

"I've always thought so."

"He needs to let some of it go."

"I agree," Patty said as footsteps sounded on the stairs. A moment later, Beau stomped into the room, wearing only a faded pair of sweatpants.

Looking grumpy and sleepy, he rubbed a hand across his chest and yawned.

"What are you doing out of bed?" Allison asked.

"I heard voices," he said testily. "Woke me up." He didn't admit that he'd been afraid Allison's father or ex had finally caught up with her and he didn't want her to face either one of them alone. The very idea had him dragging himself out of bed long before his body wanted him to rise.

"I'm sorry we were loud," Allison said. "Now, go back upstairs."

He looked at Patty, apparently noticing her for the first time, and grumbled, "What are you doing here?"

"Good morning to you, too." Patty smiled pleasantly, evidently used to his morning temperament.

Allison answered with, "She came to have some coffee and say hello."

"Right!" Beau scoffed. "Butt her nose in my business, more like."

"Somebody needs to," Patty said. "It might as well be me."

"Damned busybody," he said, riffling through a plate of pastries. "That's what you are."

"Come on," Allison chided, "don't bark at your sister. You're growling like an old bear." He walked across the room and reached for the coffeepot, ready to pour himself a cup. Allison stopped him with a smile. "And the last thing you need is a big dose of caffeine."

Like a chastised child, he replaced the pot on the burner, griping, "A man can't even have a cup of coffee in his own damn house!" He snorted and started to leave the room, but he stopped next to her chair and whispered in her ear. "Come join me as soon as she leaves."

"I'll think about it," she whispered back. "Now, you go get some more sleep. You're too grouchy to be awake."

He stomped away without saying another word to her or his sister. As he started up the stairs, they heard him complain, "Women!" The rest of his comments were indecipherable, and ended with the sound of the bedroom door closing.

Patty's eyes were wide with surprise, delight, and amazement. "How did you do that?"

"Do what?"

"You ordered him around like you guys are an old married couple. And he just obeyed!"

"Is that strange?"

"Strange?" Patty shook her head. "I've been trying to make him do what I say for thirty-six years. I haven't been able to make him listen yet. My mother tried. My father tried. His old manager tried. Everyone who's ever known him has tried, but he's pretty much done what he wanted to do— no matter how irritating his behavior or how upsetting he is to those around him."

"I don't think it's a matter of him not caring. I think he just knows what he wants with more certainty than others, and he's not willing to settle for less. In my book, that's a good thing."

"This is so . . . *weird.*"

"What is?"

"To hear you defending him. You know better than anyone how he behaves sometimes."

"It's all an act."

"Really? Is that what you think?"

"Sure. He likes to make everyone think he's different than he really is."

"Different how?"

"I don't know." Allison paused, thinking. "Maybe tougher or colder. It's all defensive, to keep him from having to show how he really feels about things. When you get right down to it, he's pretty bighearted."

"Wow," Patty said, thoroughly intrigued to receive this view of Beau through Allison's eyes. "You really care about him, don't you?"

"How could I not?"

"Well, considering the way he acted the day you guys met, I'd have bet anything that you'd never be civil to each other, let alone become friends."

"Friends, huh?" Allison said, thinking about the word and all it entailed. From the new perspective she used when reviewing her own life, she realized she didn't have any. Was Beau her first? Her only? "Is that what you think we are?"

"Well, it seems to describe what's happening between you better than anything else I can think of. There's definitely more going on here than a quick tumble between the sheets." *Which is his usual style,* Patty thought, but she was reluctant to say so.

She couldn't help noticing the fire in Allison's eyes as she talked about Beau. Or the way she'd looked at him during his brief visit to the kitchen a few minutes earlier. Beau had looked back at her with the same affection shining in his eyes. But the sad fact was that it didn't mean anything! He looked at every woman that way—particularly the ones with whom he was sleeping. That was why women found him so irresistible. They all felt unique at just a look, a word, a touch. Allison was in way over her head, and Patty couldn't help but worry.

"You love him, don't you?" she asked quietly.

"Beau?" Allison asked. "No," she scoffed, suddenly stirring her coffee with more force than necessary. "Whatever makes you think such a thing?"

"The way you were looking at him when he came downstairs."

"How was that?"

"Like he walks on water."

"You're being silly," Allison insisted.

"Am I?" Patty asked, letting the question linger.

"Yes," Allison finally said, not sounding nearly as sure as she wanted to. What did it matter if she loved Beau, silently and unseen, for a few days in the privacy of his home? It was her own affair, and it irritated her that Patty was forcing her to look more closely at her behavior. She wasn't ready for any deeper assessment.

"We're friends, as you said," she admitted, adding testily, "but what if it was more than that? If I did have strong feelings for him? That wouldn't be a crime. I'm a grown woman. I'm allowed."

"Of course you are. That's not what I'm saying."

"Then, what are you saying?"

"I guess I'm just worried about you," Patty offered, leaning forward and resting her chin on her hand.

"Worried? About me? Why?"

"Because I've seen hundreds of women look at him that same way over the years. And I've seen him look back. It doesn't mean anything. Not to him."

"I know that," Allison said, but it hurt to have Patty say it aloud. She wanted her illusion—where she loved Beau and he eventually loved her in return, and they lived happily ever after. It didn't have to become a reality, but she wanted it to stay that way for a few more days, maybe even a few more weeks, if she could make it last that long. "I know who I am, and what I am. I'm not so stupid that I would think I could mean anything to a man like him."

"That's not what I meant at all."

"It sure sounded like it."

"Well, I didn't. I didn't mean it personally, and I don't want you to take it that way. It's just that . . ." Patty paused, wondering how to phrase her concern so it wouldn't hurt Allison more than necessary. The woman had to be made to realize the truth.

For whatever reason, Beau had let her get so close that they'd developed an odd sort of relationship. That, in and of itself, was worth something, because Patty was glad about any attachments Beau made. But just being around the man made women start imagining all sorts of possibilities. To someone in Allison's precarious emotional state, an association with Beau would be the worst sort of mistake.

For lack of any better way to say what she wanted, she asked, "Do you know very much about him?"

"More than you'd suspect, I think."

"Well then, do you understand that he doesn't believe in marriage, or fidelity, or any of the things that go along with a long-term relationship? He learned it early, from our parents. They were two very self-centered, egotistical people who never should have had any children. But they did, and Beau and I were caught in the middle of all of it.

They were extremely successful at the example they set, because he doesn't even accept the *possibility* that love exists."

"I know some of that, and I figured out the rest."

"I realize that you understand in your *head* what he's like. What I'm worried about is your *heart*. I hope it doesn't make you angry, but after that first day at my office, Beau told me some of what you're going through. I know you're vulnerable right now."

"I've been worse. I've been better." Allison shrugged, refusing to let Patty know how her jabs were damaging Allison's carefully constructed fantasy bubble.

"You're having a hard time, and I'm afraid that you're going to grow too attached to him. I just don't want to see you hurt." Patty would have needed a calculator to tabulate the number of women over the years who thought they were establishing some kind of connection with Beau, only to find that a relationship had been the furthest thing from his mind. He didn't hurt women deliberately; they just always placed more importance on his intentions than they should.

"Patty, listen!" Allison said, knowing she couldn't stand to talk about any of this much longer. Patty's reality treatment was so unnerving that Allison felt as if there wasn't enough oxygen in the kitchen for breathing. She needed the subject dropped—and dropped fast. "I know what he's like, okay? You don't need to lecture me or worry about me. I realize that this is temporary. I'm helping him through a rough couple of days, and he's doing the same thing for me. I'm not expecting anything more. To tell you the truth, I don't want anything more right now." The lie was a small one, but she felt it was forgivable. "Don't worry. Once we're both feeling a little stronger, I'll be down the road so fast you won't even remember I was here."

"I doubt that," Patty said, smiling and thinking that she'd feel Allison's presence well into the future. If the only purpose she served was to pull Beau a few feet out of the rut he was in, she'd have done more for him than anyone had been able to in a very very long time.

Once Patty had voiced her concerns about Allison's interest in Beau, their conversation moved to friendly banter, so that by the time she left, loaded down with a bag of pastries, Allison was sorry to see her go. She was an interesting amiable person who was easy to like. Plus, she loved Beau. That counted for everything with Allison, because the more she grew to know Beau, the more she suspected that, for all the fame and glory, he'd had few people in his life who had truly cared about him. Patty was one; Allison intended to be another, even if it was from afar. She would always find a way to remain Beau's friend after she left Jackson.

She stood on the front porch, watching Patty pull out of the drive and motor down the road toward town. Long after the taillights had disappeared and the dust stirred by her tires had settled, she remained in her spot. Then, surrounded once again by the quiet sounds of the country, she went back inside and climbed the stairs. On tiptoe, she headed into the bedroom.

The windows were open, and the door out to the balcony, as well, and a warm July breeze rustled the curtains. For a long while, she stood at the foot of

the bed watching Beau, who was sleeping soundly.
His glorious blond hair was scattered across the
pillow. The covers were down around his waist, his
chest languidly rising and falling with his deep
breathing.

The sweatpants he'd worn downstairs were tossed
on the floor, so she knew he was naked underneath. The sheet outlined his sex, the bulge and
swell moving slightly with each intake of breath.
Every inch of his body was familiar—the pleasure
points, the way he smelled and tasted, the ways he
moved as he took her, soft and slow, hard and
rough. She loved them all. She loved *him*.

As she watched, an encompassing wave of love
swept over her, and she never ceased to be amazed
at how quickly or thoroughly it occurred. This hot,
all-consuming, desire for Beau—the need to be
connected with him physically, mentally, emotionally, spiritually—was so overpowering that it completely eclipsed everything in its path, making it
hard to imagine why she'd ever thought herself in
love with Richard. The feelings he'd engendered
were so lame in comparison that she could barely
remember harboring any tender emotions for him
at all.

Now, for the first time, she knew what love was,
and she'd never settle for less again. At least she'd
managed this bit of insight during her stay. If nothing else came of her sojourn at Beau's house, she'd
carry this knowledge into her new life. If she was
ever lucky enough to fall in love again, she'd know
what she wanted.

She wanted that hot sizzle she felt every time
Beau looked at her. She wanted that feeling of com-

pletion she received just from knowing he was nearby. She wanted that heightened sense of awareness that told her when he was close, when he'd entered a room, without her having to even look.

While she knew her relationship with him would never go anywhere—her conversation with Patty had only confirmed what she already sensed to be true—he had given her this understanding of love. Of what it meant, how it felt, how it happened, worked, and grew, and she'd never again be contented with less than the real thing.

She had to seriously consider, though, that it might never happen again. How many times did a woman meet a man like Harley Beaudine? He was one of a kind, which made her feelings for him all the more potent. In a strange way she was glad he believed that people couldn't fall in love, because she didn't want him to feel for another woman what she, herself, felt for him.

It was bad enough to think of another woman in his arms, in his bed, doing the physical things she did with Beau, sharing the intimacies they had shared. But she could handle that. He was a physical man, and he'd have many lovers throughout his life. As time passed, she knew the hurtful prick of that knowledge would fade. But she didn't think she could ever stand to learn that he'd been consumed by love. *That* would be too hard to bear.

He shifted slightly, rubbing a hand across his chest, and she continued to observe. He looked so beautiful, so young and unencumbered, and tears wet her eyes as she thought about how much she cared for him.

There were many small chores she could do to

pass the time while she waited for him to wake, but none of them attracted her like the chance to be with him while he slept. She loved the sound of his breathing, the warmth of his skin pressed against hers, the peaceful sense of fulfillment she received from lying next to him.

Shedding her T-shirt, she glided to the edge of the bed, slipped under the covers, snuggled close. She was rewarded with a hint of a smile springing to his lips, as though in his sleep he had realized she'd joined him. Without waking, he pulled her into his arms, kissed the top of her head.

He mumbled something that sounded like, "About time."

She decided to pretend that was what he'd said. With a smile of her own, she rested against his chest, happy and content to be in his bed and nowhere else.

Chapter 10

Beau reached out and rang the bell. Inside Randolph Masters's country mansion, they could hear it reverberating through the large rooms. To Allison, it sounded like a bell announcing her doom.

That very afternoon, with no fanfare, Beau had announced that her father was in Jackson and that they were going to the summerhouse to have dinner with him. No warning. No discussion. Just the decision, already made.

At the mention of Randolph Masters, Allison had panicked, and her stress level had been running on overdrive ever since. She didn't want to see her father or talk to him. He'd insist on her returning home and assuming her desk at MasterCorp once again so that he could keep an eye on her, and she simply wasn't ready to return to her former life.

He had a way of pressuring her into doing things she didn't want to do, and if she wasn't careful she'd find herself on the next plane to the East Coast, with her future completely mapped out by her father. While she didn't know exactly what he intended for

her, she had a pretty good idea, and she wasn't
interested in any of the choices he'd make.

The problem was that she couldn't say no to him;
she'd never been able to. What he wanted, he got,
and she was terrified about how quickly he would
overwhelm her, substituting his plans for her
own—especially since she didn't have any plans of
her own. While she'd spent most of the past three
weeks thinking about how she was going to make a
break from him and the family, now that it was time
to face him, she didn't know if she could.

Oh, if only she'd had more time to prepare herself!

"Stop fussin', would you?" Beau scolded as she
ran a nervous hand across her stomach, smoothing
the front of her new dress.

"I can't help it. I never wear clothes like this."

"About damn time you started to, then, I'd say,"
he responded gruffly. Then he leaned down and
kissed her on the cheek. "You look nice."

She *did* look nice, but different. Not Allison Masters at all, but someone changed, the person she
was becoming, leaving no trace of the original
stuffy Allison he hadn't liked very much. Beau
seemed to know this. Because she hadn't had anything else to put on, she hadn't had much choice
about what to wear to this meeting with her father,
and she wasn't wearing anything of her own. Even
her underwear had been in the bag Beau had
handed her—all purchased at one of the tourist
shops on the Square in town.

The dress was a frilly thing by her standards,
though probably not by anyone else's. She'd call it
country style—usually her worst nightmare—and
she looked good in it. It was a black cotton calico

with small white and pink flowers in the print.
There were ruffles along the bodice and hem. The
skirt was full and calf-length, and just brushed the
tops of the black, silver-tipped cowboy boots he'd
brought to go with it. They were fancier than a
man's boots, but cowboy boots just the same. To
her surprise, they were extremely comfortable and
looked good with the dress.

For jewelry, he'd given her turquoise and silver,
Native-American stuff—a ring, wrist bangles, and
dangling earrings which she'd never have chosen
for herself. Beau had insisted on them. He'd made
her wear her hair down and curled around her
shoulders, too, brushing it out himself until she
had the exact look he wanted.

With the clothes and jewelry on, her hair just
right, Beau had made her take a few twirls in front
of the mirror. She looked pretty! Like someone totally altered, as though she had been a lump of clay
when she'd arrived at his house and, over the inter-
vening days, he'd molded her into someone else.
After he left the room, she'd continued to stare at
her reflection, unable to believe the transforma-
tion. Standing in Beau's bedroom, she'd thought
her outfit seemed perfect for the occasion, a statement about her new life.

On her father's steps, though, it was all wrong—
too soft, too feminine. She felt exposed, and lacking in power because of it.

"I should have worn something different," she
muttered.

"Like what?" he asked, eyeing her up and down.
"One of those red or blue suits you're so proud of?"

"Well, I would feel more comfortable—"

"When you go out to dinner with me, you're gonna look like a danged girl! You ain't dressin' like some Wall Street lawyer."

Allison couldn't help noticing that his drawl had increased the closer they got to her father's summerhouse. Now, as they stood on the front porch, his full western act had returned. The cocky, irritating, overbearing cowboy she'd first encountered was back in full force.

It was bad enough to have to dine with her father after the debacle at the hotel, but the thought of him butting heads with Beau at the same time, while Beau was acting like this, had her nerves screaming.

Footsteps sounded inside, and she winced. "This is a really bad idea."

"Why?"

"It's never going to work out. Maybe we should go . . ." She let the thought trail off, hoping Beau would agree, but he stood like a statue as the door swung open, unyielding and unflappable. A Rocky Mountain earthquake couldn't have moved him.

The buxom blond housekeeper greeted them. Allison couldn't remember her name, because she hadn't spent enough time at the place to learn who worked there. As the woman's eyes lit on Beau, Allison realized there was no need. She was suddenly and completely irrelevant.

"Hey, Beau," the woman said, taking a quick step forward as though to embrace him. She stopped herself at seeing how he had a hand balanced on Allison's waist.

Allison wanted the ground to swallow her up.

"Hi, Becky," Beau greeted her, that predatory

look he focused on every woman now present in his eye. "I didn't know you worked here."

"Yeah, for a couple of months. Are you here for dinner?"

"Sure am."

"I don't think Mr. Masters is expecting you?" The sentence came out sounding like a question, and, as she eyed Allison for the first time Allison felt unsure of herself—not pretty, but plain, and out of her element.

Becky added, "He's just expecting Miss Masters."

"I know," Beau said, "but you tell old Randy that there's another guest. He'll need to set an extra place."

"I'll do that," she said with a wink and a naughty smile. "You wait over there." She pointed to a group of small couches off to the right. "I'll tell him you're here." She turned and sauntered away, her hips swaying provocatively.

With a sinking heart, Allison realized that in her cocoon at Beau's house she'd managed to forget the standard come-on he made to every woman he met. He was so different behind the closed doors of his home that she'd obliterated any memory of what he was like out in the real world.

What was she doing with him? What had she been thinking?

They stepped across the threshold together, into the elaborate expanse of pine and glass and high ceilings, and she began to itch. It took every bit of self-control she possessed to keep from scratching.

Beau looked over at Allison, who was pale as a ghost, and he couldn't help wondering for the hundredth time if this had been a good idea. Once he'd hooked up with Daddy Masters, though, Beau's feeling had been that they might as well get the meeting over with. Allie could say what she wanted to the old bastard, and he could stew in his own juice if he didn't like it.

He hadn't foreseen that Allie would be so unprepared for the visit. He thought she'd gotten stronger over the past few weeks, but, looking at her now as she seemed ready to crumble, he had to wonder if it had all been a facade.

When Randolph Masters had finally phoned with the grand pronouncement that he'd be in Jackson on Tuesday night, he hadn't asked about Allison at all. He'd simply ordered Beau to produce her at the summerhouse for supper. Beau wasn't ever one to obey an order he didn't feel like following, but he had in this instance, because he knew Allie would have to face her daddy sooner or later. Better for it to be sooner, to his way of thinking.

So, he hadn't given her a chance to think about the coming encounter. He was fairly sure she'd have refused to attend, and he wanted the visit to occur while he was standing by her side and holding her hand. Looking at her now, though, he realized that this was going to be much more difficult for her than he'd imagined, and he was getting a pretty interesting picture of why.

What kind of father would make his daughter knock at the front door, be greeted by the housekeeper, then wait in the front room to be presented? Hell, it had taken the man a week to realize that she hadn't arrived home after she'd walked out of his hotel, that she hadn't called or checked in. If Beau hadn't had the foresight to whisper her whereabouts to Chad Hastings, Masters still wouldn't know where she'd gone. His lack of concern was frightening. No wonder Allie was upset.

What she didn't realize was that Beau was there to help her. His presence was meant to be calming and reassuring. Apparently, she didn't see it that way at all. As far as she was concerned, he might as well have been invisible, which was a definite prick at his enlarged ego. Did she think he'd let something bad happen to her at the hands of her father? Didn't she think he could protect her?

She had moved away from him so that she could look out the front windows toward the mountains, and, as she gazed she was surreptitiously scratching the inside of her elbow.

He asked, "What's the matter, darlin'?"

"You know her, don't you?"

"Who?"

"The housekeeper." She turned to face him. "What's her name? Becky?"

"Yeah. Becky. I know her."

"I mean you know her really well."

"Sure, I do." His response caused her to swirl back so she was facing the window once again. He wasn't certain, but he thought there were tears in her eyes. Coming up behind her, he rested his hands on her shoulders. "Hey, it's a small town."

"You know that's not what I mean."

"Are you jealous?" Liking the thought that she might be, he smiled and kissed her hair.

"What if I am?"

"I guess I'm flattered."

"They're everywhere, aren't they? All the women you've been with?"

"There's definitely a bunch." His answer earned him a jab in the ribs with her elbow. "Ow—"

"Couldn't you at least pretend for my benefit?"

"Nope," he said. "What you see with me is what you get, remember?"

"No, I didn't remember. That's the problem." She added something else that might have been, "God, I am so stupid."

Gently, he turned her around, his hands at her waist, but she wouldn't look him in the eye. "How come you're mad?"

"I'm not mad."

"Sure you are. How come?"

She hated it that he could read her so well, and the fact that he could made her even angrier, causing her to complain sharply, "I don't want to be here, okay? You shouldn't have made me come."

"You're a big girl, honey. You could have said no."

"You're absolutely right about that. I shouldn't have *let* you make me come."

"I'd say you're mad at yourself."

"So what if I am?"

"Then quit barkin' at me." He wrapped his arms around her and nuzzled a kiss against the nape of her neck. "What are you so stressed-out about?"

"I'm not stressed-out!" she insisted with much more strain in her voice than she wanted.

"Right! And I'm not Harley Beaudine." He reached for her wrist and pushed up the sleeve of her dress, revealing her rash, which was already quickly reappearing. "Look at you."

Allison didn't want to talk about her rash or let him know how high her anxiety was running, so she changed the subject. "You weren't even invited!"

"So?"

"Don't you see? He wanted me here all alone, so he could wear me down."

"Wear you down how?"

"He'll want me to go back to New York. To go back to the office." *To go back to Richard,* she thought, but didn't say. "I don't want to do those things."

"And you don't have to."

"You don't understand what kind of pressure he can put on me."

"Well, he can apply any pressure he wants, but it won't work. I'm on your side in this. I'm here, and I'm stayin'."

"But he's going to be so upset!"

"So?"

"Quit saying that! Quit being so flip about this!" She shook her head, running a weary hand through her hair. "You don't know what he's like, what he can be like when he's angry."

"I've got a pretty good idea," he said, although he was unwilling to reveal the fact that he and Randolph had now had quite a few chats in which she had been the main topic of conversation. "I know how to deal with crazy fathers."

"Not mine."

"Wanna bet?" He rested his thumbs under her chin, trying to force her to meet his gaze. "Look at me."

"No," she said, turning her face away.

"Don't be like that, honey," he coaxed, easing her body closer until she stood in the safe circle of his arms. He kissed the side of her neck, all he could reach, saying softly, "He doesn't walk on water, Allie."

"Sometimes it seems like he does."

"He doesn't," Beau persisted. "And I'll tell you what—I'm here because he is not going to treat you bad. If he says one thing to upset you, we're out of here."

"You make it sound so simple."

"It will be." He kissed her cheek, worked closer, found her mouth for a quick taste. Pulling away, he asked, "You trust me, don't you?"

"No farther than I could throw you!"

"That's my girl." He chuckled, then grew serious. His blue eyes dark and intent, he vowed, "I won't let him hurt you. I won't let anybody hurt you ever again."

Becky, the housekeeper, took that moment to poke her nose back in the room and tell them that they would be dining on the back terrace, and that Allison's father awaited them there. They followed her to the rear of the house, and Beau held Allison's hand, giving it a reassuring squeeze as they stepped outside.

Beau took one look at Randolph Masters and decided he was just as he had expected him to be. In his sixties, he was a handsome man who had aged gracefully in the way of successful well-bred men, with blond hair that had turned to silver, a deep tan, and age lines that only added to his good looks. He was about Beau's height, with the lean hungry look of a runner. His blue eyes were the same shade as Allison's, but shrewd and predatory.

He was dressed in khaki-colored tailored trousers, and a yellow golf shirt that had a fancy doodad on the breast pocket. From the perfect cut of each hair on his head and the tips of his manicured fingernails to the tops of his highly polished shoes, he was the picture of wealth and sophistication.

Beau was glad he'd chosen to wear jeans and boots.

Masters had positioned his chair on the far side of the round patio table, the other two chairs directly across, so that he was centered to command all their attention—like a king in his throne room, overlooking his lowly subjects.

Beau could barely keep from rolling his eyes. He'd met this guy's type before on numerous occasions, and he liked nothing more than to bring them down a peg or two. In this case, he had a double mission: to challenge Randolph Masters as much as possible, and to make Allison see that her father wasn't a fire-breathing dragon capable of consuming everything in his path.

Masters waited just a rude moment too long before rising to greet his guests, giving them both a visual dressing-down, obviously meant to instill fear. The look was probably practiced, and no doubt worked often and well, Beau thought. As though they were a pair of naughty schoolchildren who needed chastising, it was clear that he wanted to impress on them that he wasn't happy with their behavior.

The move worked on Allison, and Beau felt her stiffen in dismay. However, the intimidation was wasted on him. He couldn't have cared less about the man's opinion.

Apparently, Masters decided he'd gotten his message across, because he finally stood, saying, "Hello, Allison."

"Hello, Father," she answered dutifully. She sounded to Beau like a whipped dog, and the meeting hadn't even started yet. Beau held her hand tighter.

"Introduce me to your . . . friend," her father said, pronouncing the word *friend* as if it were something he'd just stepped in and wanted to wipe off his shoe.

"Father, this is Harley Beaudine. He was kind enough to drive me over, and I hope you won't mind if he joins us for dinner."

"Not at all," Masters said tightly, the lie thoroughly apparent.

Allison glanced quickly at Beau, not meeting his eye, and said, "Beau, this is my father, Randolph Masters."

Beau stepped away from Allison and extended his hand across the table, giving the man a hardy shake and saying, "Hello, Randy."

"It's Randolph," he corrected tersely.

"Right, *Randy*," Beau said. Allison winced, and Masters shot him a glare that could have set a log on fire. "I gotta tell you, it's a pleasure to finally meet Allie's daddy. She and I have grown pretty darn close over the past month, haven't we, honey? Why . . . I feel almost like family."

"Really?" Masters muttered, fuming. "How nice."

Allison glared at Beau, then pursed her mouth in dismay when he draped an arm over her shoulder and pulled her into a hug, kissing her on the temple. She pinched him hard, whispering, "Stop it."

Beau ignored her. "What's a fella gotta do to get a beer around here?"

Masters snapped his fingers at a server they hadn't noticed when they first walked onto the terrace, and the twenty-year-old boy, dressed in a black suit and bow tie, stepped forward.

Beau smiled at the young man, whom he knew from town—a budding rock musician and ski bum—and said, "Hello, Jason."

"Hey, Beau!" the boy said in return, a huge welcoming smile on his face.

"When did you land this gravy job?"

"This is my first night."

"Well, you're doin' great. And don't you look sportin' in that suit!" Beau ran his hands along the lapels, adjusted the kid's bow tie.

"Isn't it cool?" Jason said, proud.

"Get Mr. Beaudine a beer!" Randolph said curtly, his tone suggesting that it would be the boy's first and last night if he didn't remember his place.

"Yes, sir," Jason said. Making a face which Randolph didn't catch, he walked to a small bar on the edge of the patio and returned with a tray that held three different bottles.

Beau perused his choices, all of them microbrews from some Massachusetts brewery, then looked over at Masters. "You got any real beer? I sure could go for a Budweiser."

"I'm afraid that's all we have right now," Masters explained, obviously hating the fact that he was expected to. "That beer is from an extremely popular East Coast brewery."

"Isn't that special?"

"I'm sure if you try it, you'll find it acceptable."

"All right." Beau shrugged, picking one off the tray. "I guess I can make do in a crisis."

"How nice of you to suffer on our account," Masters said hotly. He turned his full attention to

Allison, studying her new style of clothes. "You've changed. What have you done to yourself?" he asked, making it obvious that he disapproved.

With her father's displeasure so obvious, she decided she loved her western outfit and jewelry more than anything she'd ever worn. Defensively, she said, "I just thought I'd try something a little different."

"And isn't she lookin' pretty?" said Beau, stepping close to Allison again, resting his hand on the small of her back, daring Masters to do anything but agree. Beau was about at the point where if the man said one bad thing, he'd come across the table— father or no.

Obviously, the meeting wasn't going as Masters had envisioned it. He eyed the two of them, trying to determine how to proceed, and finally chose a new plan of attack. "Would you wait inside, Mr. Beaudine?"

"Nope."

The refusal obviously stunned Masters. Beau assumed that there weren't many times when he'd had to deal with such an eventuality. Sputtering for a recovery, he said, "I want to talk to my daughter." In case Beau didn't get it, he added, "Alone!"

"Well, she doesn't want to talk to you alone. So I'm stayin'."

"I want to discuss her fiancé," Masters said, smirking as though he'd just dropped a huge bombshell.

"That's funny," Beau said casually. "Last I heard, she wasn't engaged."

Both men turned their angry gazes on Allison who stood still as a statue. Then as though showing his trump card, Randolph said, "Richard sends his regards."

"How about it, Allie?" Beau asked. "Are you engaged, or not?"

The silence extended much longer than it should have, and Allison knew both men were fuming, waiting to hear whether she still considered herself to be in a relationship with Richard.

In all actuality, Richard was the farthest thing from her mind.

The last few minutes had been a revelation to her. Beau was being his usual obnoxious self, and she might have laughed at his antics if she hadn't been so stunned.

Basically, he'd told her father to go screw himself—several times—and nothing had happened. The sun was still hanging in the sky, the earth was still rotating on its axis, time was still ticking away. Her father's face was so red that he looked like he was about to suffer a stroke, but no earth-shattering event had occurred.

No one talked back to Randolph Masters. He was fawned over with sickening deference at all times, no matter how insulting he was, no matter how overbearing. No one sassed him or made fun of him. But Beau was doing it with ease, and getting away with it. Allison had never seen anything like it. She suddenly had an entirely new view of her world, as if she'd needed glasses all these years and had finally found a pair that corrected her vision.

She turned to Beau and asked, "Would you wait inside for me? Just for a few minutes?"

"No," Beau answered. "I'm not leaving you out here by yourself."

"Wait inside, Beaudine," Masters added, nearly

shouting, "or your days of playing music at my hotel have just ended."

"Ooh, Randy, now don't you have me shakin' in my boots?"

With that comment, her father nearly came around the table, and Allison couldn't help wondering what he'd do if he could get his hands on Beau. Randolph Masters wasn't a brawler. Would the two of them go at it, fists and bare knuckles?

"Calm down! Both of you!" she ordered, holding up a hand to stop her father. Like magic, it worked. He didn't move. Looking at Beau, she stepped closer, begging with her eyes for understanding. "Just a few minutes, please? I'll be all right."

"Don't let him do this to you, darlin'," Beau pleaded. "Let's you and me hightail it out of here. I'll take you into town for a fancy dinner. This old bastard," he said, tossing a rude thumb in Masters's direction, "can sit out here all alone in his big expensive house and eat his chef's cookin', with only the servants to keep him company."

For once, Allison saw her father through Beau's eyes, and the sight wasn't pretty. He was an aging, dictatorial, arrogant man. Acquaintances tolerated him because of his wealth, but he had no true friends. He'd never remarried after Allison's mother died. Though Allison was his only child, he'd never treated her with an ounce of kindness or respect. Then again, he'd never had to, because Allison had let him be cruel all her life.

Well, his insufferable behavior was about to end, or he was going to have a very lonely old age.

She stepped closer to Beau, resting her hands on his waist, inhaling the clean smell of his clothes and skin, staying near longer than necessary, letting his presence help to build her courage.

"I can handle this," she insisted. "You go inside now."

"Allie, honey . . ." Beau paused.

He wasn't sure why he was so afraid for her. If she remained, Masters would thoroughly insult her, which she seemed to be used to. The thought of the man hurting her further was offensive to Beau, and just thinking about it made him angry. He was growing more furious by the moment.

He was mad at Randolph Masters for his behavior. Mad at Allison for the way she accepted it. Mad at her for refusing to let him help, for refusing to rely on him or use the support he wanted to give her. Mad at himself for caring one way or the other.

What was the worst that could happen after they talked? The very worst was that her daddy would pressure her to return to New York, and she'd go. What did he care, one way or the other? He wasn't looking for anything more than a few weeks of good sex, was he? And he'd already had those.

So, to hell with Allison and her daddy. He took hold of her hands and removed them from his waist, putting space between them. More than anything, he wanted to stomp away in a huff, but, much as the idea appealed, he couldn't abandon her completely.

"I'll wait for fifteen minutes. If you need a ride out of here, be in my truck before I drive away." He took a step back. "If not, you and Randy"—he nodded to her father—"and *Richard* have a real nice life together."

The last thing he heard as he entered the house

was Randolph snarling, "That man is a Neanderthal!"

"Better a caveman than a tyrant and a fool," he gave back, not looking around to see if Masters had heard.

None of the hired help was in the oversize, extravagant living room, and he needed something to occupy his attention for the next quarter of an hour. Why he'd agreed to stay that long was a mystery, but he'd made the offer, so he'd wait it out.

On the far wall was an expensive stereo system. He walked over, opened a cabinet door, and was faced with an entire wall of CDs, alphabetized by artist. There were thousands of them. He shook his head at the weirdness of life when he saw some of his, right next to a few of his mother's. While he was egotistical enough to want to hear one of his own rocking through the monstrous house, he picked out one of his mother's instead, one she'd recorded years earlier. He pushed the POWER button and hit PLAY, turning up the volume as loud as he could stand it, and the sweet sound of her classical violin filled the room.

He crossed to the front of the house and stared at the Grand Teton, remaining rooted in his spot so he wouldn't be tempted to peek out at the goings-on on the terrace. The time passed in slow motion. After an eternity, the second hand on his watch ticked to the end, and he looked over his shoulder to the large windows that showcased the backyard and valley beyond.

Through the glass he could see Allison talking animatedly and gesturing with her hands. Her father sat listening impassively, sipping his wine, as though bored by the entire affair.

"Adios, amigos," he muttered, walking outside and shutting the heavy carved oak front door with a determined click. "And good riddance," he added as he climbed into his truck. He certainly didn't feel happy about what was happening, though, and he couldn't understand why. Her daddy was right. That girl was flighty as a mockingbird, and he wasn't about to sit around cooling his heels, waiting for her to make up her mind about what she wanted to do with her life.

If he didn't see Allison Masters again for the next twenty years, he decided, that would be about one minute too soon, and he didn't care if she *was* great in the sack, kind, and smart, and funny, and all the other things he liked in a woman. To hell with her, and the whole shebang.

But, as he started the motor, ready to head toward his house, the pitch of his roof just visible at the end of the long valley, he couldn't quite muster any enthusiasm for the moment when he'd enter his empty home, which would once again be barren and silent.

Just as he shifted the truck into drive, the passenger door flew open, and Allison stood there. He slammed on the brakes and glared at her, but with the way she was smiling at him he couldn't maintain the scowl.

"Hey, cowboy," she said saucily, "going my way?"

"Git yer ass in here!" he said. Smiling now, too, he reached across the front seat, grabbed for her hand, and pulled her into the cab, and she came up in a swirl of skirts.

"You were going to leave me behind!"

"Damn straight," he said roughly, realizing that a rush of gladness had left him feeling weak in the knees, and he was awfully happy to be sitting down. To cover some of his foreign surging emotions, he tried to sound stern. Failing, he said, "I've got better things to do with my time than wait for some danged woman to make up her mind. I'd never get anything done that way."

"I'm sorry I made you upset," she said, and she was, although she could tell from the gleam in his eye that he hadn't really been mad.

"What did you say to your daddy?"

She climbed up on her knees, slowly working her way across the seat. "Well, I didn't say much of anything at first, until he told me he'd talked *everything* over with Richard, and that my dearest fiancé"— she batted her eyes at this—"would forgive *me* if I would just come back home. And we'd go on like nothing had happened."

"He'd forgive you? For what?"

"For my *indiscretions* with you!" She burst out laughing.

"Do you want to be forgiven?"

"Heck, no!" She wrapped an arm around his neck, pulling him close. "So I told Father that I didn't know what my future held, but that he'd be the first to know once I made up my mind. And that whatever it is, it won't include him or New York or MasterCorp. And as for Richard, they both needed to get it through their thick heads, once and for all, that I'm not going to marry Mr. Stupid Senior Vice President!"

"Bravo, honey. I'm real proud of you."

"Are you?"

"You know I am."

Allison shifted her weight and pushed him until he was wedged tight between the seat and the steering wheel, the driver's side door pressed against his back. "Randy?" she asked, chuckling. "You had to call him *Randy?*"

"He pissed me off . . . bad-mouthin' you all the time."

"Harley Beaudine, you are some piece of work."

"I know, honey."

When they'd arrived, she couldn't have imagined how she'd stand up to her father. Now that she had, she felt strong, invincible, ready to take on the world. She couldn't remember ever feeling this way about anything, and in celebration she closed the distance between them, kissing him with all the love, happiness, and passion that pounded through her veins.

The embrace went on and on, and, when their lips finally parted they were both breathless.

"Take me to town," she ordered. "You promised me a fancy dinner, and I'm starving."

She always managed to arouse him beyond his limits of toleration, and he was hard and aching. A quick tumble before dinner would be just the thing to ease the pounding between his legs. "Are you sure you don't want to stop by the house first?" he asked hopefully. "Just for a few minutes?"

"Down, boy." She laughed, patting the front of his jeans. "I'll deal with you later. Feed me first."

"You got it," he said, disappointed but not overly so. He knew what would come later, and it would definitely be worth the wait.

He pulled down the short driveway and turned toward Jackson. Instead of scooting back to the passenger seat, Allison remained snuggled by his side, her warm breath tickling his neck, his arm wrapped tightly around her shoulders. He was, he decided then and there, a very happy man.

As his truck slowly motored past on the gravel country road, neither looked back toward her father's mansion. If they had, they'd have seen Randolph Masters staring out at them from one of the upstairs windows, an isolated solitary figure, all alone in his big empty house, watching with curious detached interest as they drove away.

Chapter 11

Richard Farnsworth slowed his rented luxury car and leaned across the seat in order to read the letters printed on the rural mailbox, grimacing when he recognized the name. Behind it, he could see Beaudine's house, and he braked and studied it with a critical eye.

The log home was classy looking in a rural sort of way, with its big windows, rock chimneys, and porch that ran across the front and around the side. Randolph had said that Allison seemed smitten with the place, but Richard had a hard time understanding why. It was just a house, for pity's sake, set out in the middle of nowhere. Compared to the other domiciles he'd passed on the road leading up to it, it was absolutely quaint.

He turned into the yard, the tires sounding overly loud as they crunched across the gravel, and pulled to a stop next to the front steps. The locale was so isolated that he was certain anyone inside must have heard his approach, but, as far as he could see no one peeked out from any of the windows. They were open, and curtains fluttered inside with the slight breeze, but there were no cars in the drive, no activity in the yard.

Wondering what to do, he rolled down the window to the sound of country quiet. His engine pinged, a few insects hummed, and an irritating wind blew through the trees, unceasing in its rattle of leaves and branches. How anyone stood living out there was a complete mystery. The silence, alone, would drive him batty in a matter of hours. This reinforced his opinion that Allison had gone completely off the deep end.

That she'd had the audacity to involve herself with another man—a country-western singer, of all things—was the absolute limit as far as Richard was concerned. It was time for all the nonsense to end, and he was thoroughly irritated that he'd had to come all this way to make it happen.

He'd wanted to just pick up the phone and order her back—Beaudine's phone number was easy enough to find through the hotel paperwork—but Randolph had insisted that Allison wouldn't return on her own, and he'd ordered Richard to personally retrieve her.

Randolph hadn't come right out and said it, but Richard wasn't stupid. He knew that if he didn't marry Allison, his job and his future at MasterCorp were on the line. So here he was, prepared to grovel, ready to mend fences, geared up to do whatever it took to convince Allison to return to New York and resume their relationship. His entire life was hanging in the balance.

With so much riding on a marriage to Allison, he hadn't minded chasing after the gullible female. All he'd had to do was wed the plain introverted woman, sire a few children with her, and his position as the eventual leader of one of the wealthiest corporations in the country was assured. What could be easier?

Of course, he hadn't counted on the fact that Allison would turn out to be so opinionated. Or so stuffy. Or so moral and righteous. Or that she'd be up on such a high horse so often. When she got on it, there was no getting her off.

After the way she'd acted at the board meeting the previous month, throwing his engagement ring in his face, and calling him names he didn't even realize she knew, *he* was the injured party, not her, and he was sick and tired of the perpetual snit into which she'd worked herself. He had to admit she was probably entitled to tweak his nose a bit after catching him with Cindy, especially since he and Cindy had been carrying on for over a year right under her nose and she hadn't suspected.

But enough was enough.

Somehow, word had circulated through the corporate offices that Allison had taken up living with the Jackson country singer. Whenever Richard walked down the halls, he could hear people tittering behind his back and whispering about her goings-on. She might think she could behave in any shameful way she wanted, but not when his reputation was the one suffering for it. It was time she learned that she wasn't going to be allowed to embarrass him. Not ever!

Most of all, Allison had to realize that he was not going to tolerate her jeopardizing his prospects at MasterCorp. He had spent years plotting, planning, and scheming to get where he was, and he wasn't prepared to lose what he'd worked for so vigorously simply because Allison wanted to make a point— when he didn't even know what the point was.

Fun was fun, and she'd certainly enjoyed her bit of it, but she was coming home. She was going back to work, where he and Randolph could keep an eye on her. They were getting married. Her shenanigans were over. And that's all there was to it.

Confidently, he took a final quick glance in the rearview mirror, opened the door, and stood on the gravel driveway. As usual, he looked impeccable, wearing a dark blue knit shirt and tailored trousers which hung perfectly, just brushing the tops of his tasseled loafers. He was tall and lean, and, except for the fact that his hair was brunette while Randolph's was blond, he appeared to be a close copy of Randolph Masters, thirty years younger.

In fact, people had often commented that they looked enough alike to be father and son, and Richard had taken the statements to heart. He knew on which side his bread was buttered, and if that meant he had to look and dress like Randolph, so be it.

Allison was not going to screw this up!

His determination restored, he squared his shoulders and, in case anyone was watching, bounded confidently up the steps and gave a brisk knock at the door. No one answered. He knocked again and again, his burst of energy waning as he waited impatiently. He tried the door, surprised to find it unlocked, and poked his head into the front room.

The stereo was going full blast, playing some sort of country tune, and he decided that someone must be home but unable to hear his knocking. For a moment, he thought about entering and searching for Allison, but he quickly nixed that as a bad idea. From numerous sources, he'd heard that Harley Beaudine was a loose cannon, crazy as a loon, and the last thing Richard wanted to do was encounter him in the confines of his home. He'd heard stories about life in the West. Out here in the country, Beaudine was just as likely to greet him with a shotgun as a hello.

The song on the stereo ended, and he called to the empty rooms, receiving no answer. Off to his left, he could see the kitchen, and the back door was open. He pulled the front door closed and walked around the porch and into the backyard, where he found the object of his pursuit.

Allison was stretched out on a lounger, her eyes closed, wearing only a man's T-shirt and—he was fairly certain—nothing else. She looked completely different—tanned and healthy, and she had gained a few pounds which made her body appear softer, more rounded. Her hair was longer, curled around her shoulders, and streaked with highlights from the sun, as though she spent a great deal of time doing nothing but reclining outdoors.

Granted, he hadn't seen her in almost five weeks, but it seemed impossible for one woman to be transformed so much in such a short period of time. If he hadn't been expecting to find her in this exact location, he might have mistaken her for someone else. The changes unnerved him, and he was overcome with a sudden awareness that he was approaching a stranger. Irritated by the thought, he shook off any trepidation. This was Allison. He knew her inside and out, knew how to play her exactly right to get what he wanted.

He moved across the back patio until his shadow covered her torso. She stirred and smiled, but didn't open her eyes, murmuring sleepily, "Hi, baby. I didn't hear you drive up."

She had never called him *baby* in all the years he'd known her. His well-laid plans for wooing and cajoling her flew out the window. Hearing the endearment shook loose his temper, and he pulled himself up to his full six-foot height. With every ounce of outrage, disdain and moral indignation he could muster, he said caustically, "Allison, cover yourself immediately."

The strength of his Boston accent came ringing through, the word *cover* sounding like *cuvuh*. Allison's entire body tensed, and her brow furled, as though she was trying to scrutinize the sound of the voice she'd just heard. She lay completely still for the longest time. Eventually, one eye opened, then the other. She squinted hard against the sun at his back, and, after a moment of silent assessment, her eyes widened with glaring recognition.

"Richard! What are you doing here?"

"I might ask you the same question."

Jumping to her feet, she tugged at the hem of her T-shirt, which seemed way, way, way too short for their encounter, and leaped behind the lounge chair, gripping the back with both hands, looking ready to wield it as a weapon if necessary.

"I was taking an afternoon nap," she said, her mind frantically searching for calm while she decided what to say and how to act. She hadn't meant to doze off, but the summer sun and the lazy afternoon, when she had nothing to do but wait for Beau to return from rehearsal, had lulled her to sleep. Groggy and unprepared for meeting her ex, she quickly tried to gather her wits. A man like Richard preyed daily on the innocent and unsuspecting. She couldn't show a bit of weakness, or he'd gobble her up like yesterday's leftovers.

"A nap, Allison?" He gestured up and down her body. "With nothing on?"

The condescending tone of his voice made her angry, which was a good thing. It stirred her awake like nothing else could have. "I have clothes on." With a wicked gleam in her eye, she added, "Just not very many!"

"I see that! Your sense of appropriate behavior has flown out the window."

"Yes, and I'm so glad it has." The back door to the house was only a few steps away, and she had the lounger between him and her. She didn't think he'd try to grab her or hurt her—he'd never been that kind of man around her—but she wasn't taking any chances. In three quick leaps, she reached the door and hid behind it, using it for shelter. "Wait there, would you? I'll put something on and be right back out."

"I will not stand here cooling my heels," she heard him say haughtily. She slammed the door and locked it, then rushed to the front door and locked that one, as well.

Feeling safe, at least for the moment, she hurried up the stairs to Beau's bedroom, pondering what to do. In all the weeks she'd been in Jackson, Richard hadn't called her a single time. Not that she'd missed the contact. His existence was now so far removed from her own that it was hard to remember that they'd once been a couple. There had been no flash of emotion when she'd opened her eyes and seen him, no welling of unrealized regard, no sense of regret for what might have been. The only thing she'd felt was a great deal of annoyance that he'd come to bother her.

She sneaked to the bedroom window and looked down onto the patio. Richard's back was to her, and he stood gazing out across the valley. From the stiff set of his shoulders, she could tell he was fit to be tied. His fists were clenched and resting angrily on his hips. His foot tapped impatiently against the wooden planking.

He had probably assumed that he'd just come to Jackson, order her home, and she'd obey. That was the way their relationship had gone from the very first day, and he obviously expected it to continue. She'd grown up accommodating her father's wishes, and had always treated Richard in the same manner. Whatever he'd wanted her to do, she did. Whatever he'd asked for, she gave. Whatever made him happy, she was willing to try. All that made his life with her disgustingly easy, and he took advantage of her at every turn. No wonder he'd been so eager to marry her. She'd been his doormat for two long years.

Oddly, she almost felt sorry for him. She wasn't the woman to whom he'd become engaged, and he was in for a shock when he finally realized how much she'd changed.

As she continued to secretly watch him pacing back and forth below, she could see that he was seething. The thought occurred to her that she should simply stay up in Beau's bedroom until he got tired of waiting and left, but she quickly discarded the idea. They were both grown-ups, and could and should talk about this reasonably.

Besides, she wanted him gone before Beau came home from town. His feelings about the Randolph Masters and Richard Farnsworths of the world were exceedingly clear, and she didn't want the two men to meet. She could imagine what Beau might do.

Quickly, she looked around the room, trying to decide how to dress. She had a few things to wear now, mostly shorts and sandals and other casual summer clothes, but she wasn't about to select any of those. When she faced him again, she wanted to make a statement Richard couldn't fail to understand, so she wasn't going to put on anything the old Allison might have worn.

In Beau's closet, she found one of his sequined western shirts. It was satiny and bright red, and hung to her knees. She pulled it over her head, rolled back the long sleeves, looped her waist with one of his fancy belts, and, with a few quick adjustments she was decked out in a hot red minidress. She added the silver-tipped cowboy boots Beau had bought for her, and the turquoise jewelry.

Her hair, she quickly scooped to the top of her head so it fell from her crown in a funky ponytail, and she did a fast application of makeup, ending up by painting her lips bright red to match her dress. The brilliant shade was one she would never have selected before she met Beau, but it had been in the bag he'd brought home from the drugstore. When she'd first seen it, she'd laughed, thinking she'd never apply such a drastic color, but now she was glad she had it.

After an appraising twirl in the mirror, she headed downstairs to meet her old flame. She looked pretty, sexy, and completely different from the somber demure Allison Masters to whom he'd been engaged, and she hoped he'd spend long hours when he returned to New York wondering what he'd missed.

She stepped out on the patio, outwardly calm, but inwardly as nervous as could be. The sound of the door opening brought him spinning around. At first, he didn't say a word. The expressions that moved across his handsome features as he assessed her appearance almost caused her to laugh, but she didn't. She truly didn't want to hurt his feelings, make him angrier, or anything else. She just wanted him to say his piece. She would say hers. And then she wanted him to leave.

Eventually, after a few sputtering beginnings during which he couldn't give voice to what he was thinking, he asked, "What have you done to yourself?"

"What do you mean?" she replied, all innocence.

"I mean . . ." He took a deep breath, and Allison could see he was struggling to remain calm. "I mean . . . that you're wearing a man's shirt! And your legs show practically all the way up to your navel!"

"It's cute, don't you think?" she asked, running a hand across her hip and gaining courage from the feel of Beau's shirt caressing her.

"No, I don't." He looked at her mouth in distaste. "Red lipstick, Allison?"

"It adds great color, doesn't it?"

"No. It looks cheap," he said, shaking his head in

dismay. "I must say that when your father advised me of how you behaved when he was here in Jackson, I hardly believed the things I was hearing. I see now that he definitely should have taken a firmer hand."

"A firmer hand? What does that mean? Do you think he should have given me a spanking?"

"Perhaps he should have," he responded, sounding superior and righteous.

"For heaven's sake, Richard." She laughed now. She couldn't help herself. "I'm thirty-two years old. I think I'm a little past spankings."

"You may be thirty-two, but you're acting like a crazy woman, and I, for one, have had enough of it." He motioned toward the door. "Go inside and put on something appropriate. Then grab your things, because we're leaving."

"I'm not going anywhere with you."

"Yes, you are! I've had enough of your nonsense. My God, Allison, people are talking. About you! About us! I won't stand for it, I tell you. Now, get your things. You're coming back to New York, where your father and I can keep an eye on you."

His voice was rising, his temper coming to the fore. If he didn't relax, they'd never be able to hash this all out. "Richard, I'm not going—"

"You are! You've had your fun. Your little *fling*." He spat the word at her. "But enough is enough. As my future wife, you will not continue to display yourself in this disgusting manner. Come!" he ordered, holding out his hand, expecting her to take it. "We're leaving right now."

Beau took that moment to step around the corner of the house, and Allison had never been so glad to see another person. In his usual style, he sauntered slowly across the patio, keeping a bored assessing eye on Richard the entire time. He came to her side, rested a hand on the small of her back, and kissed her on the cheek.

"Hello, darlin'," he said, giving her a sweet smile. "I see you've got yourself some company. Why don't you introduce me?"

Allison slipped her hand into his, reassured when he gave it a tight squeeze. "Beau, this is Richard Farnsworth. He works for my father in New York. We *used* to be engaged." She added the emphasis for Richard's benefit, since he seemed so certain that their betrothal was still a reality.

Beau squeezed her hand tighter, asking quietly, "Are you all right?"

"Yes, I am."

He leaned down and kissed her on the mouth— just a quick brush of his lips against hers, but something about the way he did it made it an entirely possessive gesture.

"I say!" Richard huffed.

Beau straightened and turned to face him, stepping in front of Allison so that she was shielded protectively from Richard's gaze and his wrath. In a deadly tone, he asked, "You say what, Richie?"

Richard was momentarily flustered by the nickname, but quickly regrouped. "I've had just about enough of you, Beaudine."

"Is that right?" Beau asked. "Well, I'd say you ain't seen nothin' yet." Without taking his angry glare from Richard, he asked, "Allie, honey, did this guy upset you?"

"No," she said quietly.

"Did you have something you wanted to say to him?"

"I do." She snuggled closer to Beau, hugging him around his waist, and she faced Richard from the shelter of Beau's arms. Feeling safe and secure, she said, "Richard, we are *not* engaged anymore. I've told you several times now, and I don't know how to say it so that you understand. It's over."

"We'll see about that!" he vowed, gulping for air. "I'm calling your father."

"That won't do any good! I told him the same thing. I'm not coming back to New York. I'm not working at MasterCorp. And I'm not marrying you." She shook her head for emphasis. "I'm not!"

"There you have it, Richie," Beau said. "Now, why don't you mosey on back to your car and head out?"

Unconvinced, Richard didn't move, saying, "If you're still upset about Cindy, you don't need to be. It's over between us, and has been for some time."

"I couldn't care less about Cindy." Allison smiled. "In fact, I'm glad I found out about her. The two of you kept me from making a dreadful mistake." The moment she spoke, she could see that had been the wrong thing to say. His rage hit flash point, and she realized she'd jabbed too hard at his male ego.

"Marrying me would have been a mistake?" he hissed. "I suppose you think this is a better idea, flaunting yourself for this two-bit cowboy." Beau bristled but kept silent as Richard sneered, "You can't seriously expect that he'd have any real interest in a woman like you?"

"Easy there, Richie," Beau said lethally, taking a step away from Allison and closer to the other man. "I don't care what you say about me, but if you speak one bad word about her, you're askin' for a pack of trouble."

Allison watched nervously as Beau's threat caused Richard to take a reflexive step back, knowing instinctively that they were not evenly matched. Although they were close to the same height, Beau weighed thirty more pounds, and there was an aura of a street brawler about the way he carried himself. Stirred into the volatile mix was the fact that Richard was stupid enough to think he could say any offensive thing and get away with it.

Desperately wanting to defuse the situation, she said, "I'm sorry about this, Richard. I really am. But we would have made each other miserable. Surely, you realize that?"

"And I suppose you think you'll be happier with a man like *him?*" Richard laughed scathingly. "He eats stupid little girls like you for lunch. I know all about him. He screwed you a few times, and you're just idiotic enough to think that means that he really cares about you."

Beau took another step forward, Richard another step back, as Beau threatened, "This is your final warning, Richie. You've got some real pretty dental work, and if you make one more remark your smile's going to be rearranged."

"This is your last chance, Allison," Richard snapped. "I won't beg you, and I won't ask you again. If you want to throw your life away over the likes of him, that's your business. Just don't expect to come crying to me after he tosses you out."

"Richard," Allison said, "I just want to be happy. That's all I've ever wanted. I *don't* know what part Beau will play in my future, but I *do* know what part you'll play. You're not in it, okay? Please get this through your head."

As Richard looked at Allison, standing serenely at Beaudine's side, he realized what it was that had concerned him when he'd first walked onto the patio: this was not the woman to whom he'd been engaged the past few years. She was someone completely different. There was a confidence in her posture, a sparkle in her eye, that hadn't been there before. He didn't know this woman; he'd never known this woman. Somehow, Beaudine had lured her to the surface, and she'd completely usurped the old Allison's personality.

This woman, this new person, wasn't ever going to marry him.

He saw his life crumbling into a heap of ashes. The job was gone. The corner office, with the full windows looking out at the Manhattan skyline, was lost, as were the perks, the bonuses, the salary, and most of all, the assured future running MasterCorp.

With the terror of a drowning man surging through his veins, all he could do was lash out, wishing for a safe harbor when there was none. "I don't know why I didn't realize it before," he said, "but you're a whore. I'm glad to be rid of you."

"That's it!" Beau said, lunging for him and grabbing him by the front of his shirt.

Richard shrieked in dismay, as though it hadn't occurred to him that Beau would actually do something physical. "You're a whore, Allison!" he shouted, unable to stop the frantic flow of words that spewed forth. "That's all you are. I can't believe I've been engaged to a whore. You hopped into bed with the first man who acted the least bit interested."

Beau held Richard tightly with one hand and reared back with the other, ready to punch Richard's lights out. Before he could swing his arm forward, Allison grabbed it and held on, using her entire body weight to keep him from landing a blow.

"Let go of me," Beau barked, trying to shake her off.

"I won't!" she declared as he looked down at her, furious. "Don't hit him, Beau. You'll hurt your hand."

"I don't care!"

"Well, I do," she said, pressing harder. "You have to perform tonight, and I'm not letting you break any fingers." His body relaxed a little as she maintained, "He's not worth injuring your hand over."

Beau stood there for a few moments looking at Allison, who was begging so prettily with her eyes, at Richard who was cowering in fear. Her entreaty that he not hit the man was the first true request she'd ever made of him, and he couldn't refuse her.

"All right, honey." He nodded in agreement. "I won't hit him." With that, he gave Richard a rough shove, tossing him across the wooden planking. Richard fell in a heap, sniveling in fear as Beau reached for a piece of firewood and waved it menacingly. "You've got ten seconds to get off my porch and out of my yard."

Finally, Richard got the message. On hands and knees, he scampered away. Searching for and finding his legs, he took off, running around the side of the house toward the safety of his car. Beau hurled the piece of firewood after him, intentionally aiming to miss, and it whizzed by his head, causing him to run faster. They stood in place, listening as Richard jumped in the car, slammed the door, and roared out of the driveway. When they saw his taillights in the dust Beau turned to her. "Are you okay?"

"Yes. Shaken up a bit, that's all."

"I can imagine. Whew, am I glad I came home when I did!"

"So am I. I don't know what might have happened. He was so upset."

"You've got that right," he said, opening his arms in welcome, and she gladly stepped into them. She was shaking slightly, and she rested a cheek against his steadily beating heart while he ran a calming hand up and down her back, gentling her until the trembling slowed. Once it had, he placed a kiss on the top of her head, chuckling as he said, "I can't believe you were ever engaged to that guy."

"Neither can I. All the time we were talking, I couldn't help thinking that he was a stranger. That I'd never really known him at all. I feel so different these days from the woman I was when I first came here."

"You're not different, honey. I keep telling you that. The *real* you is finally coming out. You've just been hiding from everybody." He pulled back, looking down at her outfit. "And I have to say, it's definitely been a change for the better."

"You like it?" she asked, encouraged by the speculative gleam that had come into his eye.

"I more than *like* it, darlin'," he answered, scooping her up into his arms and heading for the house, his lips already warm and attentive against her neck and shoulder. "My, oh, my, but I think you look good in red!"

Chapter 12

"No peeking!" Beau warned, his hand along the small of Allison's back as he guided her to the front door of the empty building. The keys he'd snagged from the realtor jingled loudly as he pulled them from his pocket and inserted them in the lock.

"Where are you taking me?" Allison asked, hearing the sound. Her eyelids fluttered as she desperately tried to get a glimpse of their location.

"Close 'em," he growled. "Tighter!" She obediently did.

He pushed the door open and took her hand, ushering her over the threshold.

"Now?" she asked.

"Not quite yet," he said, depositing her in a chair in the center of the room. The shades across the picture window were drawn, and he wanted her first view to be perfect. He pulled them open, flooding the room with September sunshine and an unobstructed view of Snow King, the ski mountain which towered over the south side of town.

"Now?" she asked again.

"Yeah, now," he said, coming to stand by her side.

"Oh, my," she said, as she opened her eyes, her first sight the masses of wildflowers covering the bright green slopes of the mountain. The aspen trees between the ski trails had already changed color with the early approach of autumn in the high country, and they added splashes of yellow, orange, and red to the hillside. "Where are we?"

"Well, it *was* a café," Beau said, gesturing behind her. "More of a sandwich and deli kind of place, I guess. I never came in here when it was open."

Allison turned from the front window and looked around, viewing the remnants of the former business that had been located behind the small storefront. There were a half-dozen tables, chairs stacked along one wall, a counter with a work area behind it, soda dispenser, coffeemaker, and espresso machine, all sitting forlorn and abandoned by the previous owners. Through a door behind the counter, she could see an industrial kitchen. The lights were off, but she could make out shiny refrigerators, stovetops, and ovens.

"We're only a block from the town square," Beau said, "so there's plenty of foot traffic, and there're a bunch of shops along here where people stop to browse." He went on, highlighting the features of the property—the view, the intimate size, the motivated sellers—sounding like a realtor, but he wanted her to see it as he did.

When he paused in his recitation, she asked, "And you brought me here because?"

"Well." He hesitated, suddenly embarrassed. "You've been trying to figure out what you should do next. You don't want to go back to New York, and you don't want to work for your family anymore. You hardly seem the type to sit and twiddle your thumbs all day, so I just thought—"

"Thought what?" she asked when he didn't finish his sentence, intrigued by the flustered look in his eye.

"Ah, hell, I don't know," he admitted, tipping his hat back on his head. When he'd first laid eyes on the café, he'd had an instant vision of Allison standing in it, baking pastries, selling them over the counter, looking cute and harried with flour on her apron. The image had been so vivid that he'd immediately parked his truck, called the real estate agent from his cell phone, and she had come right over to show it to him.

But now, seeing Allison in the dusty rundown room, he didn't know what had possessed him to fantasize such a moment. Beautiful classy Allison Masters had better things to do with her life than sitting around in Jackson, baking cakes. "I do not know what I was thinking. Let's hit the road, okay?"

"No. Tell me," Allison coaxed.

"Oh, I just had this silly idea that maybe we could buy this place, and you could have a little bakery. Sell espresso and cookies, and all that danged stuff that the snooty tourists like. It was stupid." He turned toward the door. "Let's go."

"What made you think of something like that?"

"Temporary insanity," he said, impatient to leave now that he'd made a fool of himself. He opened the front door and held it for Allison, but the blasted woman went in the wrong direction.

"Is the power on?" she asked, stepping behind the counter and searching for a light switch.

"Yes," he answered just as she found one and the fluorescents in the back kitchen hummed to life.

She disappeared out of sight, and he felt obliged to follow. He found her inside the walk-in freezer. As if he weren't there, she looked at everything— poking her nose in the ovens, checking the shelf space in the pantry, snooping out the parking behind the store.

"There are three spaces," he pointed out, parroting the real estate agent, "which is important, because it's hard to find parking downtown. Plus, the alley's big enough for delivery trucks."

Without responding, she shut the back door and turned the lock, returning to the front of the store and stepping out on the sidewalk. Although it was the beginning of September, the tourist rush had hardly slacked off at all, and there were people strolling up and down, window-shopping while they enjoyed the autumn sunshine. On one side was a funky jewelry store, on the other a used bookstore. Both were small, like the café, and both were packed with customers.

The sidewalk was wide, and there was enough space for two or three outdoor tables when the weather was good. Allison could just picture the little round coffee tables, with red-checkered tablecloths and umbrellas, the chairs facing out toward Snow King, the customers sipping their hot drinks and chatting comfortably.

She stepped back inside, to where Beau was leaning against the counter.

"It's pretty filthy in here. It would take a lot of work to get it ready."

He shrugged. "You'd need to hire some counter

help. I figured you could just hire them early, and they could help with the cleanup and setup."

Allison looked around, completely surprised and amazed that Beau would picture this future for her—one she'd never have imagined for herself. The longer she stood in the small room, the clearer she could see what Beau had visualized. She could be happy here. Baking was something she loved. Working with the public, finding new and better ways to please people, were things she was good at.

With growing enthusiasm, she said, "I could put tables in here and out front. Maybe some pastry display cases along this wall." She indicated with her hand exactly where they would go.

"Sure," he agreed, warming to the idea again now that she seemed to actually be considering it. "A couple of fancy prints for the walls, some hanging plants. You could have yourself a cute little place without too much trouble."

"When do the skiers come?"

"Things are rolling pretty good by Thanksgiving."

"So I'd have through November to get ready."

"Plenty of time."

"I could shoot for a December first opening date." Walking to the front window, she stared out, imagining the winter scene. The town would be magically changed into a winter wonderland, the snow piled high along the curbs by the plows. Customers, bundled in bulky sweaters, would be sipping her special coffees while watching the skiers swish down the mountain in a silent graceful dance.

She could picture every delicious bit of it so clearly that her heart ached with how much she suddenly wanted it to become a reality. However, much as her heart desired making the scene come true, her head was sitting on firmer shoulders these days. Money wasn't a problem for her, so buying the store wasn't the issue. Committing to owning and running a small business wasn't the issue, either.

The major obstacle to any such plan was right behind her, trying to be silent and unobtrusive, which was impossible. No matter where Beau stood, he simply took up too much space.

"I think it would be a great idea for me," she said, turning to face him, "but I have a few questions first."

"Shoot."

"When we first came in here, you said *we* could buy this place. Were you thinking we'd be partners, or what?"

"No. I just didn't know what your finances were like, and I thought if you liked the idea I'd spring for the purchase price. I have all kinds of money rattling around in the bank, and I don't have anything to do with it."

"You'd buy this place for me?"

"I like making you happy, darlin'. You know that."

Allison had no idea what the going price was for commercial property in downtown Jackson, but, even for such a small amount of square footage, she thought a million dollars wouldn't be out of line. Beau was offering to spend that kind of money with little thought, the same way he'd taken her out to dinner or bought her new clothes. Pocket change. The man was a mystery.

"You don't have to spend money on me to make me happy."

"I know, but I'd be glad to."

"You wouldn't have to," she said, shaking her head. "If I decided to go through with it, I'd have enough of my own money."

"Really? So your daddy isn't going to make you go begging for your supper?"

"No."

"Well, good," he said, but for some reason he wasn't happy about her financial security at all. To his great surprise, it occurred to him that he'd wanted her to have to rely on him. Deep down, he'd wanted to do this for her, to give her this gift which would settle her future. *Why* he'd want to do such a thing was a good question, but one he wasn't going to answer—one he wasn't even going to ask.

"What made you think of this place for me?" she wondered aloud.

"It was the weirdest thing," he admitted. "I was driving by, and I noticed the For Sale sign in the front window, and I could just picture you, plain as day, in here working and happy."

"Starting a small business would be a big undertaking for me."

"You bet it would."

"I'm not a quitter. I mean, if I started this up, I'd be here for the long haul."

"Well, I certainly hope so," he said, apparently not getting what she was driving at, "it would cost a pretty penny to get it going."

"I realize that. So, if I did it, I'd be committed. For a long time."

"You sure would, but that's the great part of this," he said, smiling. "You've needed something to give you a direction."

"I'd have to move here. To Jackson. Find a place to live."

"Yup."

"Rentals are impossible to locate, which means I'd probably have to buy something. That would cost an arm and a leg, too. Another major commitment."

"Yup," he said again.

She crossed her arms over her chest, biting at the inside of her cheek as she assessed him. It was so hard to know what he was thinking sometimes, but she had to. The answer was too important, and they both needed to be clear, so there was no use beating around the bush.

"Are you asking me to stay, Harley Beaudine?"

"Well, of course I'm asking you to stay."

"You know that's not what I mean." She chuckled. "I swear, you can be so thick sometimes." She stepped closer, until the tips of her loafers were touching the tips of his boots. "If I stay in Jackson, what do you envision happening between us?"

"What do you mean?"

"Well, you seem to have thought out the business end of this, but I don't think you took it much farther than that."

"Where should I take it?"

"I've grown kind of partial to having you around. I like spending time with you. Would we still see each other if I lived here full-time?"

"Sure."

"Would we still be lovers?"

"If that's what you want."

"When would that be? Maybe Saturday nights after your show?"

"Or maybe more than that," he answered, suddenly looking nervous.

"What about a few months from now, when some of the excitement of the sex wears off? Then what?"

Beau realized she was exactly right. He hadn't thought any of this through. From the very beginning, he'd wanted Allison close and available, but he'd never been able to picture what that meant in the long-term. When he'd first met her, he'd thought to bed her through the summer, maybe take it into the autumn, but Labor Day had come and gone, and he hadn't tired of her in the slightest. In fact, he'd gotten to the point where he couldn't imagine what his house would be like without her in it.

Slowly and gradually, with his hardly being aware it was happening, she'd settled into his world, and it now seemed as if she'd always been there. He liked coming home late at night from a performance and having her waiting up to hear how it went. He liked waking up the next morning, lying in his bed and hearing her puttering around downstairs. He liked the way she filled up the empty spaces of his life until he felt whole and happy again.

Much to his consternation, she'd been living with him for two months, and he hadn't found anything about her that he didn't like. He couldn't imagine what she could possibly do to make his interest start to wane. If anything, it continued to grow. How long their current association would last was anybody's guess, but he knew it would end eventually.

She'd asked: *Then what?*

He gave the only truthful response he could. "Damned if I know."

"Do you picture us being together?"

"Well . . ." He hesitated, and she laughed right out loud at the obvious impossibility of his honestly answering the question.

"Do you think we'll get *married* someday?" she asked, laughing anew as his knees buckled. She pulled over a chair and eased him down into it. "Sit down before you fall down."

"I'm not the marrying kind, darlin'," he insisted, sweat popping out on his brow just from hearing her say the word.

"I know you're not. That's why I'm so curious. I just don't know exactly what it is you see for me if I stay here. Would I classify as being your *girlfriend*?"

"Well," he tried once more, unable to say *no*. What woman wanted to hear a thing like that? And he liked Allison too much to hurt her feelings that way.

"Okay, okay," she said, knowing he needed rescuing from his continued vacillations. "I know you don't have *girlfriends*. That would indicate some kind of continuing *relationship*. How about this? Would we still be friends?"

"Always," he vowed, feeling that they'd finally stepped onto firmer ground. "Of course."

"So the sex would gradually trickle out, and we'd see each other less and less frequently, until we didn't see each other at all. Then, *maybe, sometimes,* you'd stop in here at the café to have a cup of coffee, and we could talk about your show or the weather, or whatever tickled your fancy."

He frowned, not liking the way that sounded at all. Sensing that he was about to walk into a verbal trap, he said cautiously, "I'd check up on you from time to time. I'd want to know how you were doing."

"And maybe you could bring some of your new

female acquaintances around once in a while? Like . . . after a night on the town, you could treat them to a quick breakfast before you headed home."

"What?" he asked, growing angry. "What in the hell would make you say something like that?"

"Or maybe I'd go out to dinner some night, and I'd see you with one of those twenty-year-old blondes you're so fond of."

"Now hold it just a darn minute—" he started, feeling the need to defend his lifestyle so it didn't sound quite so cheap and tawdry.

She placed a finger against his lips so he wouldn't say anything silly, then stepped between his legs and perched herself on his thigh. "You don't want me to stay here."

"I do, too!"

"For how long? Another week? Two? A month? Till winter comes?"

"I don't think that's something you can put a time limit on," he said, uneasy.

"That's because you really don't want me here. Don't you see how it would be if I stayed?"

"I guess I don't," he lied, because he really did. Now that she'd pointed it out so definitely, he realized they were destined to head down a long miserable road with no good ending.

"Well, I see it clearly enough for both of us." She gave a sigh, long and slow. "Let me tell you something, Harley Beaudine."

"What?" he asked, disheartened. He couldn't take much more of this.

"I love you." She hadn't meant ever to tell him, but it suddenly seemed important that he know. From the look of panic the admission brought to his eye, she knew she'd been wise to keep it a secret. "So, what do you say to that?"

He swallowed hard. The powerful emotional state was one in which he did not believe, one he would never experience. Sure, with Allison, he'd wondered sometimes if the giddy feelings she inspired were something close, but he refused to speculate too deeply.

He gave a lame response, one which he hoped would suffice, but doubted it would, with the way she was poking and prodding. "I'm flattered."

"You can't say the words back to me, though, can you?"

"I wish I could, honey."

"But?" she asked, waited, and waited some more. When he didn't fill in the blank, she finally continued with, "You don't love me? You can't love me?"

"It's just not something that's possible for me."

"I don't believe that," she said, taking his hand and lacing her fingers through his, "but *you* believe it, so that's all that counts."

"I don't mean to hurt you. I just don't want to lie about it. I think it's important to tell the truth in these situations, so there aren't any misunderstandings."

"Well, here's one truth I want out on the table. I love you, and I always will. And I'm so glad I came here, because now I know what I want."

"What's that?" he asked, glum and worn out.

"I want what I feel for you. This neverending happiness, where my world is brighter just because you're in it. Now that I've experienced it, I'm not willing to settle for anything less. I want it all, Beau. I deserve to have it all."

"You sure do, honey."

"You can't give it to me, but then, I never imagined that you could. But I'll find it somewhere. I know I will," she said wistfully. "And now that we've had this talk, I realize that it's time for me to get on with my life."

"What do you mean by that?" All of a sudden, his heart was pounding too hard.

"It's time for me to leave."

"Leave?" he asked, his mouth falling open in shock. How had this happened? The visit to the empty café had started out as such fun, so full of joy and possibilities, and now she was talking about leaving? He didn't know what he'd do with her if she stayed, but he sure as hell wasn't ready for her to go. "Why would you want to go and do that?"

"It just feels like it's time." Her announcement had put such a scowl on his face that she couldn't resist leaning forward and kissing him between his eyebrows, trying to wipe out some of the creases. When her kiss didn't help, she added, "Don't look so put out. You always knew I wouldn't stay here."

"Yeah, I knew, but one minute you're sitting here telling me that you love me, and the next, you're telling me you're movin' on. What kind of decision is that?"

"It's for the best." When he looked ready to argue the point, she persisted. "You know it is!"

"I don't know any such a thing."

"Oh, Harley, you are the sweetest man."

"And *you* are one crazy woman."

"No, I'm not. For a change, I'm feeling very very wise." She kissed him on the nose, both cheeks, his mouth, then said, "When you look at me from across a room, there's this gleam in your eye—this fire—and I love seeing it. I want to leave while it's still there, before it has time to fade. That's what I want to remember most about you," she said, tears suddenly filling her eyes as she thought about how much she'd miss him. "Nobody ever looked at me like that in my whole life—like I'm the center of the entire universe. And I want to always remember that—that fire in your eye that you always had just for me."

Unable to say more, emotion choking her, she stood and walked across the room, staring out the big window at the ski mountain. For just a moment, she closed her eyes and pretended it came true, that she really did get it all in the end—the man. The café. The small town life. The beautiful house in the country—but just for a moment, because if she knew anything at all, she knew that some wishes just weren't meant to be fulfilled. A life with Harley Beaudine was one of them.

"Could we go home now?" she asked softly, afraid that if she stayed one more second she'd burst into a flood of foolish tears over what could never be. And wouldn't that be a waste of a good cry?

"Sure," he said sullenly, not understanding what had gone wrong or why he felt so bad about it. There was a fierce ache in the center of his chest, in the area of his heart, and, for the briefest instant he wondered if it might be breaking. Which was silly all the way around.

She was making this as easy as pie. He'd grown close to her over the past few weeks, much closer than he'd ever come to any other woman, but that kind of connection only led to a miserable parting with angry words and hurt feelings. He should be glad that she was taking the simple way out. Making a clean clear break was the only way to end these things. He knew it to be true! But, somehow, this time, it just didn't seem for the best.

There had to be a better conclusion. As they drove to his house in uncomfortable silence, he tried and tried to think of what that could be, but he couldn't come up with any ideas. The only viable alternative was to ask her to stay and to mean it, but he couldn't do that.

If there was one thing they agreed about a hundred percent, it was the fact that Allison deserved to have it all—a man who loved her, who'd give her a stable home life and a family. If it hurt to think about some other guy being the one to provide those things, so be it. He couldn't be the one! No matter how much he wished it was possible, he truly believed that he could not make her happy.

So he didn't ask her to stay. Not during the lazy afternoon at the house. Not during the phone call she made to the airline, booking a last-minute connection to New York. Not during the intimate dinner that they cooked together and ate out on the back patio, sipping wine and staring out at the Grand Teton as the sun slowly sank behind it.

Not during the long night of slow tender love-making. Not during the hours of talk about what the future would hold for both of them—separately. Not over breakfast the next morning as they sipped coffee and shared a final plate of Allison's pastries.

And, especially, not two hours later, when they stood on the front porch, Allison's bag resting between them, the taxi in the yard ready to whisk her to the airport in plenty of time to catch her flight.

"Are you sure you don't want me to drive you?" he asked.

"You don't need the extra stress of being around all those planes," she said, mindful of his phobia.

"I don't mind. I really don't."

"It's sweet of you to offer, Beau, but you don't have to."

The silence stretched as they stared at each other, drinking in their fill and memorizing with their eyes, each hoping they wouldn't forget too soon.

Beau swallowed his pride for once, a real mouthful, and asked, "Do you want me to call or to write?"

She gazed into his beautiful face for the longest time, finally saying, "No. Let's just let it go. Just like this."

"You're sure?"

"Yes. I swear. If I thought you might call, I'd spend the rest of my life waiting for the phone to ring." Tears flooded to her eyes, but she refused to let them fall. She wanted this to be a happy good-bye. "I couldn't live like that. I'd make myself crazy."

"I won't, then," he said, tamping down the hurt that flared with her admission that she didn't want to hear from him again. He could live with that, he kept telling himself. All this was for the best! He took her hands in his, running his thumbs across the center of her palms. "If you ever need anything, you call me first."

"Oh, Beau—"

"Promise me."

"I promise," she said, though she knew she never would. Seeing him again sometime in the future was the worst possible thing she could imagine.

The cab driver subtly stepped on the gas, urging

them to get a move on, and she knew it was pointless to prolong their parting one more moment. She stepped forward, welcomed instantly into his open arms, and hugged him tightly. When she pulled away, a few tears had managed to dribble down her cheeks despite her good intentions. "I'll miss you every day."

"And I'll miss you, honey girl." With his thumbs, he wiped at them, then cradled her face in his palms, gently kissing away the remainder. His mouth touched hers, light and brief, his mustache just a quick tickle against her upper lip. "Bye-bye, Allie."

"Good-bye, Beau."

"You knock 'em dead in New York."

"I will."

"Get going now," he said, setting her away, "or you're going to miss your plane." He carried her bag to the car and helped settle her in the backseat. He'd meant to close the door immediately, but he couldn't seem to make his hand push it shut. For the longest time, he stared at her, finally leaning down for one last kiss, one last tight hug.

Then he managed to force himself to return to the porch. The cab pulled away slowly, and he remained on the steps, watching her go. She was turned around in her seat, waving out the window, and he stood there, unable to move, long after she was out of sight.

Chapter 13

Beau leaned back in his chair, surveying the empty bar and working a packet of rosin across the hairs of his violin bow. The guys in his small band had already left after their afternoon rehearsal, although there hadn't been much to it. After playing the same show four nights a week for six months, there wasn't a lot that needed going over.

Chad sat across from him, yammering on about one thing and another. Beau was only half paying attention. The young man was like an adoring puppy, so it was hard to get mad about his hanging around. Besides, he was one of the handful of people who had known Allison during the short time she'd been in Jackson, and, sometimes, if Beau worked the conversation just right, Chad would offer some small tidbit he'd heard about her through the office grapevine.

The blasted woman had been gone for three months, and he couldn't get her out of his head. She was always there. When he practiced. During rehearsals. In the middle of a show. The worst was at home when the phone rang, and he rushed to answer it like a lovesick fool, or when someone knocked on his door and he nearly yanked it off the hinges in his haste to open it and see if she was standing on the other side.

She never was, though.

The fickle female had said she was going, and she'd meant it. With a snap of her fingers, she'd vanished like a magician, heading back to New York and her life there, and he'd never heard from her again. She'd asked him not to call, so he hadn't, but could she waste a little of her precious time to pick up a telephone? No way!

There'd been no calls. No letters. No *Happy Fortieth* birthday card—although why he imagined she should have remembered such a date was a question that had kept him tossing and turning more than one night. No *congratulations* over the mention in *People* about his return to the stage. They'd even put his picture in with the story, but did she notice? Hell, no.

He cut off the thought, refusing to continue down that road. It happened this way all the time; he'd get on some tangent about her and couldn't get off. The woman was like a prickly thorn that had implanted itself in the center of his brain, where she continually jabbed and prodded until the memories he carried of her were like to drive him batty.

"Crazy as a bedbug," he muttered, thinking—as he often did these days—that he'd completely lost his mind since meeting Allison Masters.

"What did you say?" Chad asked.

"Nothing important. I was just remembering some stuff I have to do today."

"So, what do you think?"

MOUNTAIN DREAMS   241

"About what?" Beau asked, realizing the boy had been talking for a good fifteen minutes. Beau had been so obsessed with chasing Allie out of his head that he couldn't remember a single topic of the conversation.

"The new contract terms!" Chad said.

Any other person would probably have been completely exasperated by Beau's continued lack of interest in the subject, but not Chad. He was so fixated on getting Beau to sign for another six months that he was willing to endure any personal hardship in order to get Beau's signature on the dotted line. It had become his personal mission in life.

Unfortunately, Beau didn't know if he wanted to sign or not, so everything Chad talked about was just so much chatter. Things were happening since he'd made his brief foray into public performing by doing his nightly shows at the Masters Inn in Jackson. He had other options to consider. His phone was ringing again, with his business manager calling to say he was creating a buzz. There were possibilities arising quickly. His old record company was interested in talking about a new album. Another company was interested, as well.

Concerts were available in various spots around the country—one nighters, or longer. While he knew he wasn't ready to head to Nashville, a few nights in Salt Lake or Denver were certainly worth considering.

Some Hollywood type was even interested in shooting country music videos, using some of his old songs. Having left the business before videos became so popular, he'd never made one, but his ego was certainly big enough to enjoy the idea of

seeing himself splashed across television screens
around the country.

For a change, Beau was intrigued by all the offers
and wanted to seriously consider some of them
before tying himself to another six-month stint at
the hotel. He needed advice about what to do, but,
if he'd learned anything at his first go-round with
success, it was that there were few people you could
really trust to give it. His sister, Patty, was one of
them, but he didn't even need to ask her opinion.
It was always an unqualified do it, do it all! Talking
to her was like getting no opinion whatsoever.

Allison Masters was another person he trusted,
but do you think he could ask her? Miss High-and-
Mighty New York had made her choice, running
back to the city at the first opportunity without even
a glance over her shoulder to see what kind of car-
nage she'd left in her wake.

"Some *friend* she turned out to be," he muttered,
thinking about how knowing her had turned him
into a dottering fool, one who rambled around in
his empty house, reminiscing and talking to himself.

"Beau, you're not listening!" Chad cut through
his reverie like an annoying insect.

"Nah, I'm not, Chad. I've just got a few other
things on my mind." *Like deranged women, old age,
and insanity.*

"No problem," Chad said agreeably. "We can talk
about it again tomorrow."

"Sure thing," Beau said, just wanting the kid to go
away.

His next comment had Beau's head whipping
around, though. "Oh, my God!" Chad hissed, his
eyes growing wide as saucers.

Beau looked over his shoulder to see Randolph Masters standing in the doorway of the small bar. Out of the corner of his mouth, Beau whispered, "What the hell is he doing here?"

"I don't know!" Chad whispered back. "I had no idea he was coming to town." He jumped to his feet, smoothing his trousers and heading for the door with his hand extended in greeting. "Mr. Masters . . . Welcome to Jackson."

Masters looked at him as if he were some sort of alien being, and didn't accept the offered hand. "Hastings, isn't it?"

"Yes, sir."

"Beat it!" he ordered.

"Yes, sir!" Chad said like a dutiful private, scurrying away down the hall, sending Beau a frantic questioning look, then disappearing from sight.

Beau rose to his feet, taking stock of the older man, wondering what he wanted and knowing none of it could be good.

"Beaudine." Masters nodded in acknowledgment.

"Call me Beau. Everybody does," Beau said, giving his standard opening line. Enjoying the opportunity to tweak Masters's nose, he added, "How's it goin', *Randy?*"

"The name is *Randolph*," he said tightly, walking through the bar to face Beau across the table.

"Whatever you say, *Randy.*" Just for spite, he'd repeated the name. He couldn't help himself.

Masters ignored the insult and looked behind Beau to the open violin case sitting on the edge of the stage. Nodding toward the instrument, he said, "I understand that you're quite good."

"I am," Beau admitted with no trace of humility.

"I heard somewhere that you studied with your mother when you were younger." With a feral smile, he pulled up a chair and asked, "How about doing something of hers for me?"

"You heard wrong. I don't do classical," Beau said shortly. He didn't feel that he owed Masters any special favors. He sat, as well, blocking the instrument from Masters's view. "My show starts tonight at nine. Come back then, and you can decide if you're getting your money's worth or not."

"You're a cocky bastard, Beaudine," Masters said, eyeing him as though looking for flaws and finding too many to mention.

"I had to be," Beau answered, "or I'd never have gotten where I am today."

"I suppose you're right." Masters snapped his fingers at the bartender and ordered a Scotch, and they sat in silence until the woman set the glass in front of him then retreated. Sipping the amber liquid, he assessed Beau over the rim of the glass. "If you weren't so good at what you do, I'd have run you off months ago."

"Like I give a hoot." Beau chuckled, his lack of concern extremely irritating to Masters. No longer able to conceal his curiosity, he couldn't prevent himself from asking, "What are you doing here?"

"Have you heard from Allison lately?" Masters inquired, much too casually for Beau's liking.

"Nope," he responded. His senses suddenly on full alert, he asked, "Should I have?"

"I just thought she might have talked to you."

"Is she pregnant?" Beau could hardly believe the joyous flare of hope which surged through his veins. Quickly, he counted the months back, thinking that she'd be between three and four months, probably just starting to show, her abdomen slightly rounded, her gorgeous breasts fuller and heavier. Was she sick? This would be the time for morning sickness. Was it bad? *Jeez*, he thought, *I should be with her if she isn't feeling well.*

"No, she's not pregnant," Masters said flatly.

Just like that, Beau's bubble of happiness burst as though Masters had stuck it with a pin, and he couldn't believe how it hurt. How could the idea of having a baby with Allie be so alluring? How could it be so shattering to find out a pregnancy hadn't occurred? He hadn't ever wanted children, had he?

A more disturbing thought crossed his mind— this one a thousand times more painful than the first. "What, then? Is she finally going to make you a happy man by marrying your buddy Richard?"

The question tasted like ashes in his mouth, but he asked it, anyway, trying to appear as if he could have cared less though the possible answer had him dying inside. He'd never wanted to get married, had he? He didn't care if Allie married somebody else, did he? So where the hell was this feeling of dread coming from?

Masters scoffed as though the idea—one he'd pushed to the extreme—was preposterous. "She hasn't seen him in months. He no longer works at MasterCorp. It seems he wasn't quite what we were looking for, after all."

The wicked gleam in Masters's eye actually made Beau feel sorry for Richard. While he didn't like anything about Allison's ex, he could definitely imagine what it would be like to be on the bad side of a powerful man like Randolph Masters. The poor guy probably never knew what hit him. Having crossed the powerful magnate, Richard was probably now washing cars for a living somewhere in New Jersey.

"So, what are you doing here?" Beau asked, too stirred up emotionally to play Twenty Questions over the cause of Masters's sudden appearance. "And cut to the chase, would you? I know you didn't come all the way to Wyoming to talk about my fiddle playin'."

"She's buying a hotel," Masters said without preamble.

"A hotel?" Beau repeated, sounding like an imbecile.

"Not a *hotel*, really. Some old house. One of those bed-and-breakfast places. In Vermont." He wrinkled his nose in disdain. "It seems she's discovered a sudden fondness for ski towns."

"Hmm." Beau's non-comment provided him a few moments to try to assess what Masters was really saying, but he couldn't figure that out. Giving up, he finally said, "Well, good for her. I hope she's happy."

"Do you think she will be?"

"Why wouldn't she?"

"You tell me," Masters said, fixing him in a stare that made Beau squirm like a grade-schooler. Allison had looked at him exactly that way sometimes when he was doing something that particularly irritated her. He missed that look coming from her. Coming from her daddy, he couldn't say that he cared for it at all.

"I don't have any idea," Beau responded truthfully.

"You are thickheaded, aren't you?" Masters asked

rhetorically, relaxing back in his chair and tapping a finger against the table. "You know, Beaudine, I see a lot of myself in you. I was much the same when I was younger. The talent, the single-minded determination, the arrogance. But I can tell you, if you keep this up you're going to be a lonely old man."

Was that a hint of wistfulness he heard in Masters's voice? Resignation? Sadness? Beau shrugged it off, not wanting to feel any sympathy for the man who had caused Allie so much unnecessary grief over the years. Masters's life was one of his own making.

Refusing to see any similarities, Beau said, "Don't be comparing my life to yours."

"It's hard not to," Masters said, suddenly looking and sounding much older than his sixty-five years, but it only lasted a moment before he shook off the touch of melancholy, appearing once again to be self-assured and confident of his life choices. "Much as you probably doubt it, I love Allison. She's my only child, and all I've ever wanted is for her to be happy. For some reason—only God knows why—I think *you* would make her happy."

"Me? She said she didn't ever want to hear from me again after she left here."

"Harley," Masters began, as though explaining something to a simpleton, "you're supposed to be some kind of expert with women. Have you ever met one who knows what she really wants?"

"Well, no."

"Then get your head out of your ass and stop her before she goes through with this." Showing much more emotion than he'd intended, he added, "When I sent her here to Jackson last summer to cool off, I knew there were company people who'd keep an eye on her for me, so I wasn't worried. But I don't like this new idea she has at all. She doesn't know anybody where she's going in Vermont. Neither do I, and I don't want her moving off to that strange town where she'll be all by herself. Where there's nobody to watch out for her or take care of her." He stood up, apparently deciding his mission had been accomplished. "She signs the papers tomorrow. If she buys that place, she'll be locking herself in for years. Knowing her bullheadedness, maybe decades."

"You think I could stop her?"

"If you wanted to." He turned to leave, a taunt in his voice. "Funny, but I thought you might be able to offer her something better. But maybe you're not man enough to realize what that is."

He walked out of the bar, leaving Beau to fuss and stew in the encompassing silence.

Allison stared out the window of her Manhattan apartment at the snow drifting past—the first measurable amounts of the season. Everyone complained about the white stuff when it fell, but not her. With all the lights twinkling through the heavy flakes, she thought it made the city look like a fairyland, especially from higher up, where she didn't have to see the pedestrians or the traffic trying to manipulate the slippery pavement.

As she continued to watch, she couldn't help thinking that there was probably a lot of snow on the ground in Jackson Hole, her mind easily drifting to the spot where it wanted to perpetually linger. With Christmas just around the corner, the hotels would be full, the ski trails perfectly groomed, the skiers enjoying the cold winter air, beautiful scenery, and exotic ambiance of the mountain community.

For a minute or two, she closed her eyes, imagining that she was standing in the small bakery Beau had found for her. The smells of her cooking permeated the air—yeast, rising dough, and fresh baked bread—with the aroma of fresh brewed coffee hanging over all. Sounds soothed her ears—of cups clinking against saucers, of teaspoons slowly stirring, of conversation humming.

Outside, the stores would have their Christmas lights hung. Hers would be up, as well, blinking on and off in an odd rhythm as she stood looking out at the skiers as they silently swished their paths back and forth down the mountain.

Just then, the door would open, the bell jingling lightly. Beau would step through, bringing with him all that charm and presence, bundled up in his sheepskin coat, wearing one of his Stetsons. His ears would be red with the cold.

Several of her customers would recognize him and say, "Hey, Beau," and he'd smile and wave in return, then take her in his arms and kiss her in front of everybody. His mustache would tickle, and be moist and icy from the frosty air. She'd laugh as he pulled away, embarrassed to have others watching, but unable to be upset.

He'd say, "Hello, darlin'," in that way he had, with a welcoming smile on his face and gleam in his eye that showed he burned just for her. . . .

With a sigh, she opened her eyes and turned away from the window, glancing over at her briefcase. The last of the papers she'd requested from her attorney were in there. Everything appeared to be in order. Now, all she had to do was put on her coat, go downstairs, get in a cab, and head for the lawyers' offices, where she'd sign her life away on the dotted line.

She had to be there in less than an hour, and she knew she should get going. With all the snow, it was going to take forever to get across town, but, for some reason, she couldn't move. There was such a finality about this decision that it was weighing on her more heavily than it should.

Part of that, she knew, came from the heated conversations she'd had with her father. The questions he'd asked had nearly driven her crazy. What was there for her in Vermont? Why go up there where she'd be all alone? Why not stay at MasterCorp? Why a small bed-and-breakfast? If she wanted a hotel, why not let him buy her one?

Those were the easy questions, the ones she could answer. She wanted a place of her own, where she could do things her own way and have some control over her life, where she could feel she was needed and necessary. Her father had seemed to accept that.

It had been the personal questions she couldn't answer, the ones he wouldn't quit asking, the ones that made her decision about Vermont seem all wrong.

What about Jackson? he'd asked repeatedly. She had seemed to be happy there. Would she like to go back and live there? She wanted to own a hotel; what about the Inn? How about if he gave it to her? Which always ended with the final question: What about Harley Beaudine?

And, of course, she had no answer to that one.

What about Harley Beaudine? That arrogant, self-centered, talented, cocky, funny, kind, tender, and loving man who had quietly and carefully helped her to find pieces of herself she'd managed to lose somewhere along the way. Who had helped her to grow confident, content, astute, and ready to take on the world.

What about him?

She wanted to explain to her father about Beau, but could never quite find the words to describe what had blossomed between them. It was more than just a few weeks of sex. Something had happened to her while he'd sheltered her in his country house. Something wonderful. And she loved Beau for it every second, but, just as it had been on the day she left Jackson, it didn't matter. Loving Beau was not enough to change anything.

His solitary life was the one he'd built for himself, but he was a grown man who didn't have to continue down the road he'd originally selected. By returning to New York, she'd given him the perfect opportunity to alter his direction. Foolishly, she'd believed that his picture of his future might come into focus after she departed, when he'd had time to think about what he wanted. She'd thought he might come to his senses and realize that he loved her as much as she loved him.

But, he hadn't. He hadn't come to New York. He hadn't called. He hadn't written. Yes, she'd asked him not to do any of those things. But, like a silly junior-high schoolgirl, she'd hoped that he wouldn't listen, that he'd take some initiative.

Once she'd arrived home, overwhelmed and lonely but determined to build a new life, she'd halfheartedly gone through the motions of finding a future of her own that didn't include him. Quickly, she found that she couldn't muster much enthusiasm over any of her choices, because she kept expecting him to show up on her doorstep.

The days of waiting became a week, then two, then four. As one month passed, then another, she'd had to face the fact that he wasn't coming. What she'd known to be true about him hadn't changed. He was a confirmed bachelor, a *single* man in every sense of the word, and, while they'd shared an intense few weeks, that's all it was and would ever be for him.

Which meant there wasn't any reason to keep her from buying her place in Vermont.

Shaking off the melancholy that had never quite gone away since her return from Wyoming, she went to the hall closet and retrieved her coat, thinking of how much work she'd have to do in the coming weeks. Packing and moving would definitely keep her mind off her troubles.

With another sigh, she started to put her arms into the sleeves just as the bell rang at her door. No one had called from downstairs to say that she had a visitor, so, cautiously, she went to answer it, wondering who it could be.

On tiptoe, she stuck an eye to the peephole, and her heart skipped a beat. All she could see was a cowboy hat. Her pulse suddenly soaring, she rested her forehead against the wood, hoping—trying *not* to hope—as she asked, "Who is it?"

"Who the hell do you think it is?" came the gruff drawled response. "Open the damned door."

Beau! Beau was here! Right outside in the hall!

What could possibly have brought him to New York after all this time?

With trembling fingers, she fiddled with the locks, taking a few deep breaths, struggling to calm herself. Striving for composure, she turned the knob and pasted a controlled smile on her face as she caught her first glimpse of him in three and a half months.

Dressed all in black, he wore one of his fancy hats, jeans, and boots. For a coat, he had on a cream-colored, canvas, wrangler's duster. His shoulders and the brim of his hat were wet from the snow, his nose, ears, and hands red from the cold. His blond hair was longer, curled around his shoulders, his eyes shielded by expensive sunglasses. A duffel bag was slung over his shoulder, and he held his violin case in his hand.

As always, he looked handsome, sexy, commanding, noticeable. What a swath he must have cut out on the streets of Manhattan! How she wished she'd been a little bird, watching him turn heads. Even jaded New York pedestrians, who'd seen it all, would have had to take a second look.

"Hello, Beau," she greeted, trying to sound casual though she was dying inside. "What a nice surprise."

She hesitated, wondering if she should hug him, shake hands, kiss him on the cheek. What kind of welcome did you give to a man who had once meant everything in the world to you? His sunglasses shielded his eyes, so she couldn't begin to guess at his emotional state.

For lack of anything better, she stepped aside and gestured into the room. "Won't you come in?"

"You're dressin' like a lawyer again," he said, taking in her blue suit and low heels with a quick glance as he stepped across the threshold. "I thought I got you out of that habit."

"Well, some habits are hard to break."

He paused, taking in the sterile room, the white walls, the black furniture. "So . . . this is where you live, huh?"

From the disdain evident in his voice, she could tell he hated it as much as she did. She'd let a friend of Richard's decorate it, thinking the stark lines and austere furnishings looked chic and fashionable. Since returning from her trip to Wyoming, she'd found them drab and colorless. She shrugged. "Home sweet home."

He dropped his duffel on the floor, carefully laid his violin on the coffee table. Walking to the window, he gazed past the ten stories down to the street. In silence, he stared at the miniature people and cars below. She was too intrigued by his presence to interrupt the moment. The unexpected sight of him was too much like a dream, and she was afraid if she said the wrong thing he'd vanish, and she'd wake up to find that it had been.

Finally, glancing over his shoulder, he asked, "Do you like living like this?"

"I thought I did." She shrugged again. At that, he made a derisive sound and returned to looking out the window, another prolonged silence ensuing.

Over the past few months, she'd had numerous flights of fancy over how their next meeting would go—if she was ever lucky enough to see him again. In her vivid imagination, their encounters certainly hadn't been anything like this. She'd always pictured soft words of remembrance, hot looks of undisguised longing, followed by torrid embraces, not this uncomfortable quiet. It had never been that way between them, and she couldn't help but wonder what it meant. It didn't seem to bode well.

Gathering her courage, she commented, "You seem kind of . . ." What was the word for which she was searching? Different? Distracted? Angry? She settled for, "Upset. Is everything okay?"

"No, everything's *not* okay," he said, turning back to face her and finally taking off his shades so she could see those remarkable blue eyes. "In the past twenty-four hours, I have been insulted by your daddy. Yelled at by my sister. Up all night. In airports. On airplanes. Just now, I caught a ride from the airport in a taxi with a driver who hardly spoke English, except enough to tell me he'd grown up in the desert and didn't know how to drive in the snow. Which was fairly obvious, since we'd just had an accident! I got out of the car and walked the rest of the way, through the slush and cold and crowds. I hate the city, which is why I don't live in a place like this, but I am not leaving until you come with me. And you're not buying any damned bed-and-breakfast in Vermont, so just get it out of your head."

He stood there, taking up all the space in her living room, a bright, shining star in a universe of one, hands on hips, totally pissed-off, and she'd never seen anything quite so wonderful in her entire life. "Anything else?"

"No. That about covers it." He shrugged out of his duster, tossed it and his hat on the couch as if he'd been inside her apartment a thousand times.

"Now, I'm hungry. Have you got anything to eat in this high-rise fandango?"

She blinked, then blinked again. Did he really think that was all there was to it? He'd just show up unannounced after nearly four months, say his piece, and everything would be settled? Boy, was he in for a rude awakening!

Needing time to collect her thoughts before responding, she decided that feeding him was a good idea.

"Sure," she said to his request for food, heading for the kitchen.

"I could use some hot coffee, too," he said behind her. "It's colder than Christmas out there."

"I have some of that, too," she said, as she pulled out a chair and motioned him into it. Glad for something to do with her hands, she busied herself around the stove, taking occasional glances over her shoulder only to find him staring at her intently. His little speech had raised a million questions. He'd talked to her father? He'd flown on an airplane? Her mind was whirling as she tried to figure it all out.

The coffeemaker began to gurgle as the water dripped through, the sound taking away some of the tension in the room. Grabbing a plate, she quickly built a sandwich and handed it to him before sitting across from him at the small table.

For a few minutes, she contained her curiosity, content simply to watch while he ate with his usual hearty appetite. Eventually, she was no longer able to stifle her need to know, and she blurted out, "When did you talk to my father?"

"He came to Jackson yesterday."

"He did?"

"Yes," Beau said, taking a final bite of his sandwich. "And I gotta tell you true, honey, I know he's your daddy, but I don't imagine he and I are ever going to get along very well."

"No, I don't imagine you ever will," she agreed with a wry smile, thinking of how the two of them had butted heads the first time they'd met at the summerhouse in Jackson. Which brought images of the rest of that long-ago evening springing to mind. The leisurely romantic dinner in downtown Jackson. The unhurried moonlit drive home on a park back road. The slow tender lovemaking once they arrived. All of that now seemed like something that had happened in another life.

Getting a grip on her unruly imaginings, she asked, "What did he want?"

"He wanted me to get my butt here so I could stop you from throwing your life away. You didn't sign those damned papers yet, did you?"

"I fail to see how buying a small upscale hotel is *throwing my life away.*" She hadn't had strong feelings about the purchase one way or the other, thinking it was something to do with her life, a task she'd grow into, but the more her father had harangued about it, the more she'd wanted to do it. If Beau had come all the way to New York just to harangue, as well, then it had definitely been a wasted trip.

"Now, don't go gettin' your dander up," he said, seeing how her backbone had grown all rigid. "If you want to own a hotel, that's fine with me. But you're going to do it back in Jackson, where I can keep an eye on you. That's what your daddy wants." He swallowed, looking as though his next words were stuck in his throat and he had to force them out with a crowbar. "That's what I want, too."

The coffee machine gurgled to its conclusion, giving her an excuse to rise and do something besides look him in the eye. She poured two cups, set them on the table, and took her seat once again before saying wearily, "We've been through this, Beau. I don't belong in Jackson. You don't want me there."

"I do, too."

"Okay, then," she said calmly, perfectly willing to put him in the hot seat, "tell me where I'd fit in your life."

"Smack dab in the center."

"The center of what?"

"Of everything."

"I don't have any idea what that means," she said, sipping her hot coffee too fast, wanting it to burn on the way down, "and I don't think you know, either."

"It means that maybe"—he shifted uncomfortably—
" . . . maybe I missed you."

"I missed you, too, but so what?"

"And maybe I want you to come back with me."

"To do what?"

"How about running your bakery—like we talked about before you left?" He dug into the pocket of his jeans and pulled out a key, which he laid next to her coffee mug.

Allison stared at it, afraid to touch it. "What's that?"

"The key to the front door of the place. I bought it for you, had it remodeled like we talked about. It turned out real cute, too. It's got all these little round tables, checkered tablecloths, and red umbrellas.

Prints of different spots in France." He blushed slightly. "I did it just in case you changed your mind and came back. I wanted it to be a surprise."

Allison didn't think it was possible for the Beau she knew to flush with embarrassment, but he was. He'd laid out megabucks for a commercial property, paid to fix it up, all hoping for . . . what? "Why would you do such a thing?"

He cleared his throat. "I guess when you left, I hoped maybe you didn't mean to go. That maybe you'd get back here to New York and realize that you'd made a mistake."

"Why didn't you call or write?"

"You told me not to!"

"Since when did you ever listen to what I said about anything?" she asked, shaking her head in disbelief. He only did exactly what he wanted to do—no matter what. If he'd truly wanted her back in Jackson, he would have asked it in a heartbeat. She couldn't fathom what was driving him now. "If you wanted me to come back, why couldn't you just say so?"

"I'm sayin' it now. I want you to come home with me."

Tears welled in her eyes. Struggling for control, she stood and moved toward the counter, fiddling with the cord on the toaster and taking deep breaths until she had her swirling emotions under control enough to speak. Softly, she begged, "Don't do this, Beau. Don't ask me to make this decision."

"Why shouldn't I?"

"You know why."

"No, I don't," he said. "You tell me."

"Because I'd like to come home with you more than anything, but I need to have all of you, and you're just not willing to give me all. I can't share you with the rest of the women in the world."

"Who says you'd have to share?"

Something about the way he asked the question had her whirling back around, her eyes widened in surprise. On the table was a small black case with a diamond engagement ring centered for display. He took it out, stuck it on the end of his pinkie finger and wiggled it at her as he pushed his chair back from the table and patted his thigh.

"Come on over here, darlin'."

"No," she said, shaking her head. "No way. You're not doing this to me." But even as she said it she was taking a few slow steps across the kitchen, the ring reeling her in as though it had magical powers.

"I'm only doing what I should have done three months ago."

"It's all or nothing with me, Harley Beaudine. You know that."

"I surely do."

"It's going to take more than a diamond ring. You're going to have to marry me."

"I realize that."

"But you don't want to ever get married! You don't want to do this!"

"Don't I?" he asked, one corner of his beautiful mouth lifting in a slow smile. "Wild horses couldn't drag me into an airport, but I rode on *five* airplanes just to be able to get here on time. Now, you tell me, does that sound like I *want* to be doing this, or not?"

"Five?" she asked, shocked and surprised, her heart thudding with joyful trepidation. "You rode on *five* airplanes just for me?"

"Yes," he said, grouchy because he'd had to do something so nerve-shattering just to get to her. "And when we go home, we're taking the train!"

Shifting in the chair again, he tried to find a comfortable spot, but was unable to. Looking like a man on his way to the gallows, he said, "Now, why don't you come over here so I can ask you proper? We have to do it sitting down. My knees are knockin' too hard to stand."

He was offering her the only thing she truly wanted in the world. Still, she hesitated. Quietly, she offered, "This is your last chance to back out, Beau. If you ask me, I'm saying yes."

"Good, because I won't accept any other answer."

"No going back. No changing your mind. No ten year engagement that's never going to end."

"I'll marry you this afternoon, if we can find a preacher."

"And when we say our vows, it will be forever."

"It'd better be."

"And no other women. Ever! If I so much as see your lips on somebody else, I'm gone."

"I realize that. I don't want anybody else. I don't need anybody else. Just you." Gradually, with each word, he was luring her closer, until she was finally near enough for him to reach out and take her hand. He pulled it to his lips and kissed the backs of her fingers, then turned it and kissed the palm. His eyes were a darker blue than she'd ever seen them, shining and intense, and the look he was giving her took her breath.

He said, "You told me once that you loved me. Did you mean it?"

"Yes," she answered, no doubt about it, no need to waver.

"Do you still?"

"Each and every day of my life," she said, sinking onto his lap and resting a loving hand against his stubbled cheek. "And longer than that."

"Well, I love you, too. I promise that I will each and every day of *my* life. And longer than that," he echoed. He kissed her on the forehead, on each cheek, and then pulled away, his tender gaze searching hers.

After an eternal pause, when she began to suspect he was too terrified to ever speak the words she was dying to hear, when she could hear only her pulse pounding in her ears, he finally said it. "Allison, will you marry me?" A quick affirmative response almost escaped her lips, but he shushed her by laying his fingertips against her mouth and adding, "Think before you answer. I'm only doin' this once in my life, so you'd better mean it."

Her heart felt too big for her chest. "I'll want a big wedding."

"You got it."

"A fancy one. With tuxedos and attendants and a dinner and a band. The whole ball of wax."

"No problem."

"With all my cousins and uncles and everybody in attendance. I want Patty to stand up with me, and my father to give me away." At his nod of agreement, she continued. "I want to have a family."

"You'd better."

"Three kids."

"Four," he insisted.

"It's for life, Harley."

"Forever."

"Then, yes, I'll marry you." With her acceptance, sweat pooled on his brow, he started to shake, and he hung his head, resting his forehead against her chest. She ran a comforting hand through his hair. "Are you all right?"

The low chuckle told her he was, but he still didn't look at her as he responded, "I've never been through anything so scary in my life. I'd rather live through another plane crash."

She laughed, full and long and loud, and—when he had finally recovered enough to raise his head—she promised, "Everything will be okay."

"I know it will," he said, smiling in return. He stood her on her feet and rose, as well, asking, "Where's your phone?"

"Over there." She waved toward the counter.

"Take it off the hook."

"Why?" she asked, transfixed by the predatory gleam that had suddenly come into his eye.

"'Cuz you're busy. And you don't want to be interrupted." He swung her off her feet, and she squealed with the delight of it, loving the feeling of once again being sheltered in the circle of his arms.

"What are you doing?" she asked, knowing full well what he intended.

"I'm completely drained, honey," he said, taking a deep breath and letting it out slowly. "After all that, I think I need to lie down for a spell. Where's your bedroom?"

She pointed down the hall.

HER FIRST TASTE IN DESIRE . . .
Once, Penelope Westmoreland seemed certain to
land a first-class husband. Now her only marriage
prospect is a lecherous, aging earl—the complete
opposite of the bold American who comes to her
rescue one night. Tall, muscular, and thoroughly
male, Lucas Pendleton unleashes a wanton
hunger in Penelope. She impulsively agrees to
elope with him, giving herself completely to a
man whose sexual expertise leaves her breathless.

ONLY LEAVES HER BEGGING FOR MORE . . .
Lucas Pendleton intended to force the philandering Duke of Roswell to make amends for wronging
Lucas's sister. Seducing the duke's daughter into a
ruinous charade of a marriage was never his plan,
though each sizzling tryst makes him wish their
union were real. Beautiful Penelope embraces
every carnal lesson he imparts, teaching him
plenty in the process. But when she discovers his
deception, will he be able to convince her that a
liaison begun in lies has become a true, lasting love?

**Please turn the page for an exciting sneak peek of
Cheryl Holt's
MY TRUE LOVE,
coming in January 2008!**

Chapter 1

Lucas Pendleton hurried quietly down the long corridor, counting the doors he passed, looking for movement and checking for hiding places in case a servant came wandering by. Luckily he'd not seen another living soul since sneaking inside.

Laughter came from somewhere far off in the grand house. A handful of silver clanged on china, and he paused, listening for footsteps, but none came in his direction. He took a deep breath, let it out, then started off again.

So far, the hastily drawn map he'd coaxed from the tavern maid, Peggy, had proved to be surprisingly accurate. The alley, the mews, the unlocked back gate, the concealing hedges, the open entrance off the terrace, all had been located in exactly the spots she'd indicated. According to her calculations, the library would be just ahead on the right. Very soon he'd be inside, where, according to Peggy, he would not have long to wait for the duke to make an appearance, as he purportedly did after each evening's meal.

He hoped the girl was as well-informed about the exalted man's personal habits as she was about his house. If she was mistaken and the duke didn't show his face, Lucas was prepared to wait hours, or even days, if that's how long it took to force a confrontation.

As he thought of Peggy, the plump, friendly young woman he'd cajoled and seduced in order to obtain the necessary information about Harold Westmoreland, the Duke of Roswell, he felt double stabs of guilt and regret. A bag of coins was being delivered to her just about then, along with his carefully penned good-bye note, and the combination would ease some of her upset. Although Peg was hardly an innocent, he still hated using her as he had, but he hadn't been able to find anyone else who possessed the knowledge he needed to get him safely in and out of the manor.

His dispute with the Duke of Roswell was a family matter, and where Lucas's family was concerned, he would take any risk, shoulder any task, carry any burden in his efforts to protect them. His parents had died when he was a young boy, causing him and his brother and sister to endure the hardest of childhoods. Lucas had grown up knowing that he would eventually assume the care of his two younger siblings, and that's exactly what he'd done. For years their lives and happiness had been all he cared about, and if he had to deceive a kind person such as Peggy in order to discharge his responsibilities to one of them, so be it. There was no other choice.

In all the weeks he'd been in London, trying and failing to arrange a valid appointment with Harold

Westmoreland, it had quickly become apparent that he was going to have to use alternate methods to obtain his meeting. Westmoreland was too wealthy, too powerful for a man such as himself to gain an audience if the duke wasn't willing to grant it.

Lucas had knocked on the duke's door numerous times without being admitted. He'd written a dozen unanswered letters and finally taken to watching the duke and tracking his movements, attempting to find a means by which their paths would cross, but Westmoreland never went anywhere alone. He was always surrounded by armed servants, fit and serious-looking, who appeared to know their jobs and understand their duties, the main one apparently to prevent the rabble from approaching their distinguished employer.

If they had been on more equal terms, if Lucas had brought along a cadre of his own men instead of just his brother, Matthew, he might have been successful in arranging a showdown. As it was, he was an American, an outsider, highly visible because of his clothing and accent. He couldn't infiltrate the duke's world by himself.

Before coming to England, he and Matthew had agreed that they would try to keep the affair as quiet as possible. The duke was married, had two grown children, and Lucas and his brother had no desire to embarrass them or to cause any sort of public uproar. They had simply intended to resolve the problem with a minimum of fuss and bother.

What they hadn't counted on was that the duke could not have cared less that a pair of upstart Americans wanted to speak with him. In the times they'd rapped on Westmoreland's door, politely re-

questing a meeting and having it denied, it wasn't
as though Lucas could blurt out to a doorman the
important reason for his solicitation, not unless he
wanted all of London to know their business. They
had eventually decided to resort to more effective
measures, but it would certainly have been prudent
to have brought along a few more hands to set to
the job.

While Matthew was highly competent in carrying
out any kind of dubious enterprise, and exactly the
type of man you wanted protecting your backside,
there were only the two of them. They hardly had
the forces to overwhelm the duke's guards, so Lucas
hadn't been able to do more than catch an occasional glimpse of Westmoreland as he went to and
from his carriage.

"But that's about to change," he murmured to
himself.

Stopping short, he looked up and down the hall,
then slipped into the library. A hasty scan indicated
that no one was there. A fire burned in the grate, a
brandy had been poured and awaited the duke's
pleasure, sitting as it was in the center of the large
desk. Lucas thought about downing the amber
liquid himself and leaving the empty glass for the
duke to discover, but he didn't. Much as he relished
the idea of committing that one small, rude act, he
dared not. He wanted no trace of alcohol dulling his
senses.

He walked to the end of the room in order to
hide behind the heavy velvet drapes, but as he
passed, he couldn't help but observe the opulence
of the surroundings. With each step he'd taken
through the vast structure, his eyes had lingered

on costly objects. The place was quiet and cold as a tomb and seemed much like a museum, packed as it was with treasures and valuables—artifacts, knick-knacks, paintings, rugs. The wallpaper shimmered with gold embossing, the brass fittings glimmered in the dim lights. Everything was dusted, polished, expensive, and displayed with the obvious intent of letting others perceive just how large a fortune the man enjoyed, how supreme and omnipotent he was because of it.

The luxurious ambiance only strengthened Lucas's resolve. The man could pay. The man *would* pay. If it was the last thing Lucas ever did in his life, he would see to it that the Duke of Roswell lived up to the obligations he had incurred to Lucas's family.

His wait was not long. In minutes the library door opened, and footsteps crossed the floor, coming around the desk. Wanting to be certain it was Westmoreland and not a servant, Lucas glanced out from his clandestine location just in time to observe the back of the duke's head as he settled himself in the large chair. Sighing wearily as if he were carrying a huge weight on his shoulders, he leaned against the soft leather, closed his eyes, and relaxed for a moment before reaching for the glass of liquor.

Lucas watched furtively as the infusion of drink visibly caused the tension to leave the duke's body. Lucas waited while Westmoreland sampled the beverage a few more times, then set the heavy crystal on the desk. Only after he'd steepled his fingers over his stomach did Lucas make his move.

With a silent tread he was away from the curtain and behind the other man, the barrel of his pistol dug hard into the duke's neck. "Don't move," he

warned, "or I'll blow your head off." Westmoreland
shifted slightly, and Lucas pressed the barrel
deeper into his throat. "I mean it. I'll kill you without a thought."

"I believe you," Westmoreland responded, instantly growing still as a statue. "What do you want?"

"Put your hands where I can see them." Westmoreland didn't budge, so Lucas ordered, "On the desk!
Now!" The man leaned forward as much as he could
with the gun hovering so intimately against his skin,
and obeyed by resting his palms against the dark ma-
hogany.

"If it's coin you're seeking," Westmoreland said
carefully, "I don't keep any in here. . . ."

"Be silent!" Lucas advised. "I want you to look
upon my face"—the duke's brows rose at this—"so
I'm coming around the desk. Keep your hands in
plain sight and keep your mouth closed unless I ask
you to speak." Westmoreland's gaze flew to the
door, and he wondered at his chances if he called
for help. "Don't even think about it," Lucas threatened. "I'll kill you before anyone can make it
through. It matters not what happens to me after
that, and it won't matter to you much either. You'll
be long dead before they arrive."

"All right," Westmoreland said with a hint of a
nod. "Please explain yourself."

Slowly Lucas removed the pistol, then tucked it
into the waist of his trousers. In his thirty years he'd
used a weapon numerous times and knew he could
retrieve it in an instant if need be, but he truly
hoped he wouldn't be required to shoot the despi-
cable swine. Much as he would like to see West-

moreland cold and in the ground, Lucas would much rather have him alive and repenting his sins.

Keeping a wary eye on the duke, he took one step, then another, until they were face-to-face for the very first time. To his great surprise, Westmoreland wasn't anything like he'd expected. Certainly he appeared wealthy and refined, dressed as he was for supper in a dark blue velvet jacket. Set against it, the white of his shirt was dazzling, the knot at his neck intricate and perfectly tied. But he was a much younger man than Lucas had imagined him to be.

Although he had heard the man was only forty-five, for some reason he'd gotten it into his head that Westmoreland was decrepit and elderly. While Lucas had wanted him to be old and disgusting, the duke seemed active and actually quite handsome. Lucas had fed his anger and outrage off visions of an ancient, experienced lecher who pleasured his sick physical appetite at the expense of innocent young women, but this man seemed capable of nothing of the sort. He was the absolute representation of an English gentleman.

Slender and roguish, he was one of those lucky fellows who grew better-looking with age. Obviously of aristocratic blood, with high cheekbones and a patrician nose, he was the type of comely devil over whom women swooned. His full head of white-blond hair just going to silver was tied back in a short tail. His eyes were a deep sapphire, the shade enhanced by the blue of his jacket. They showed evidence of a keen, shrewd intelligence, taking in all the details and nuances of the situation and missing nothing.

There was an aura of command and strength about him, indicating he was comfortable with his position in life. Most likely he'd have been enormously successful at any endeavor, even if he'd been born without all the trappings afforded by his fortune and pedigree. A powerful individual, he was clearly used to giving orders and getting his own way. He would be a tough adversary, but then, Lucas had suspected he would be, and he was not daunted by the idea.

In his struggles as a boy, unwillingly conscripted to the hard life of a sailor, and later as a young man starting and running his own shipping business, he'd repeatedly gone up against the worst class of villains, brutes who were a thousand times more ruthless and vicious than this highborn man could ever be. Nothing scared Lucas anymore, especially not the rich, pampered nobleman sitting before him.

"I apologize for all this drama," Lucas asserted, "but I have been trying to arrange an appointment with you for weeks."

Westmoreland shrugged. "I am a busy man."

"My name is Lucas Pendleton," he said tersely. If his identity meant anything at all to Westmoreland, he didn't indicate it by so much as a blink. Deep down Lucas had been hoping that the duke was afraid to meet because he knew who Lucas was, why he'd crossed an ocean to seek an audience, what kinds of demands he would make, but Westmoreland showed no reaction.

"How do you do?" the duke said, nodding his head in polite recognition of the introduction.

"My sister was Caroline Pendleton," Lucas declared, but still the bastard didn't move a muscle, and Lucas's anger came to a quick boil. "Before you have time to think of some inane response, let me tell you that if you pretend you don't know who she was, I shall come around this immaculate desk, wrap my two hands about your throat, and squeeze until there is not a single breath left in your body."

Harold Westmoreland glared into the eyes of the enraged man before him, and all he could wonder was why the fates had conspired to bring about such a dreadful encounter at just that moment. Hadn't the family supper he'd just survived, attended by his daughter Penelope's new and extremely horrid fiancé, been quite enough torture for the evening? Would his torment never cease? How much emotional upheaval could one man be expected to endure in a single night?

He hated the fact that he was sitting while his foe was standing, because their positions put him at too much of a disadvantage, yet he didn't think rising to face Pendleton would be a good idea. Harold liked to flaunt his rank in order to keep others cowed, but Pendleton clearly placed no importance on titles or position. If he had, he would never have dared commit so outrageous an act as breaking into Harold's home. No, Harold's usual haughty attitude would hardly work, but his height wouldn't intimidate either.

Pendleton was over six feet tall. Harold three inches or more shorter, so he couldn't overawe the knave with excessive size. Even if they were of the same build, he had none of the younger man's impressive, lithe, predatory grace. Pendleton moved like a stalking cat, tanned, lanky, and fit, with the type of solid torso that comes only from a lifetime of strenuous employment. Given those broad shoulders, long, muscled arms, and strong fingers, Harold felt quite certain that Pendleton could easily carry out the threat he had just made about strangulation.

The scoundrel's nerve and physique were just two of the reasons Harold stayed seated. There was a third: Pendleton was filled with righteous indignation. The man was like a lethal keg of gunpowder ready to blow, and Harold couldn't expect to avoid an explosion except by remaining cool and calm.

"I know Caroline," he admitted cautiously. "A lovely young woman. An American, I believe. I met her several years ago when she was here visiting her English cousins."

"Yes," Lucas said, filled with relief that Westmoreland had admitted the acquaintance. There'd be no cause to beat it out of him.

"I haven't seen her in a very long time," Harold said, stalling, trying to recall everything he could about her. There had been so many women in his life that sometimes it was difficult to distinguish one from the next, but not in this case. Upon seeing the brother with all his long, dark hair and those intense brown eyes, the sister was easily remembered. Beautiful and graceful, in her early twenties, she was thin and tall, having no similarities to the pale blond English beauties with whom he typically consorted. She'd had a quiet, interesting manner about her, a good sense of humor, was easy to talk with and easy to like. All in all, she was exactly the kind of female he often wished he'd been allowed to marry.

Unbidden, a smile flickered and, as rapidly as it came, he suppressed it. Once Caroline Pendleton had learned the ways of intimate affairs, she'd become a passionate, involved mistress—although he hardly intended to mention such a tidbit to her outraged male family member.

Ah, Caroline, what a sweetheart she had been! How joyously their pretty summer had passed. And how quickly! Pulling himself back from his hasty, delicious reverie, he queried, "How is she?"

"She's dead."

"You have my sympathies," Harold said, trying to show little sentiment himself. "My condolences to your family."

"We don't want your condolences," Lucas said hotly. "Wouldn't you like to know how she died?"

"If you would like to tell me," Harold responded, hesitant now, beginning to fear where this might be leading.

"She died in childbirth," Lucas said, finally getting the reaction for which he'd been waiting. The duke went completely still, not breathing, not flinching, simply processing. Lucas could almost hear the wheels spinning inside Westmoreland's head as he added, "Approximately six months after leaving England."

"Isn't that interesting?" Harold said weakly, not meaning it, and suddenly feeling as though he might become ill. Swallowing, he asked, "How long ago was that?"

"Almost five years."

"Then, I must beg your pardon," he blustered, "but I'm extremely confused about what brings you here. I assume it has something to do with Caroline's death, but I fail to see what any of it has to do with me. . . ."

"Shut your lying mouth," Lucas barked, wishing he had the fortitude to kill Westmoreland then and there for what had happened to Caroline. Sarcastic, and intentionally wanting to goad, he used Westmoreland's given name. "It's a *boy*, Harold. Congratulations." Before the duke could comment, Lucas retrieved his pistol once again and aimed it directly at the man's chest. "He's four years old now, almost five, and if you say that he is not yours, I will put a ball through your heart before you can draw your next breath."

Harold ran his tongue over his bottom lip, his mind briskly calculating whether it was possible. Could he have left her with a bastard child?

Their affair had been exactly the kind he liked best: short and sweet with no chance for lingering affection and no opportunity for hanging on after he was ready for the woman to be gone. Rarely had he been alone with Caroline, their handful of assignations so risky, their time together curtailed by her return to America. There had been so much more he could have taught her, so much more he had wanted her to experience.

But a child? No, it simply couldn't be. He refused to accept it.

If such a disastrous event had occurred, why would she not have written once she became aware of her condition? Just as abruptly, he realized that perhaps she had, but with the vagaries of ocean travel he had never received her message. Which was just as well. What could he have done anyway?

Staring down the barrel of a loaded pistol cast a definite pall over his usual assuredness. Prudently he began, "I'm not saying I'm not the lad's father—"

"Harry," Lucas interjected. "His name is Harry.
She asked us to name him after you," although that
wasn't entirely true. Caroline had never admitted
who the father had been. Lucas had used a variety
of threats in attempting to learn the answer, but
she'd refused to tell, correctly assuming that Lucas
would want to exact revenge against the man who
had compromised her while she had been so far
from home and away from the protection of her
two older brothers.

On her deathbed, with practically her last breath,
she had requested that her male babe be named
Harold and referred to as Harry, but she had not
explained why. It was only years later, when Lucas
had come across the letter she'd written but never
sent, that he had discovered his nephew's paternity.

"Well . . ." Harold murmured, for once at a loss
for words. They glared at each other angrily, neither willing to be the first to look away, and Harold
had to suppress a surge of admiration for the reckless American. Few men of his acquaintance were
brave enough to challenge him in such a fashion.

Pendleton was either immensely courageous or
completely mad. Perhaps it was a combination of
both.

Finally Harold asked, "What is it you want
from me?"

One utterance described all that Lucas required.
"Recognition."

Harold snorted in disbelief. "You can't mean it!"

"I am serious." Lucas's finger flexed on the trig-
ger. "Deadly serious."

"I have no intention of claiming the child," Harold
insisted, suddenly feeling more bold. A chap like

Pendleton, who was seeking a father's declaration for his illegitimate nephew, couldn't get it from a dead man. No matter how much Pendleton swaggered or prognosticated, he wouldn't kill the only person who could confirm or deny the allegation, and Harold wasn't about to confirm anything.

As far as he was aware, he had sired one other bastard child, a grown daughter named Maggie. Despite their rocky past, they managed to lump along rather well, but he still hadn't publicly declared himself to be her father, even though she was now an accepted member of society and married to the Marquis of Belmont. She'd been born years earlier to a mistress before Harold had wed, and if he hadn't gifted *her* with paternal identification, he was hardly about to take such a drastic step on behalf of this foreign upstart over a boy he'd never met and who hadn't existed for him until the past few minutes.

"And I think I've heard enough," he said, confidently coming to his feet. "It's time for you to go. I will *never* acknowledge the boy. Despite what you say or how fervently you press, you will never convince me that I am the bastard's father."

Lucas let pass the slight over Harry's birth. There were other, bigger issues to address, and the facts clearly indicated that Harry *was* a bastard. But Westmoreland was going to ease the lad's way. Lucas would see to it if it took every last breath, his very last penny. He reached into the pocket of his vest and pulled out a miniature that had been painted a few months earlier, just before they'd set sail from Virginia, headed for London.

"Look at that boy's face," Lucas said. He tossed the likeness onto the desk, where it landed with a damning thunk. "Look into those blue eyes and then have the gall to tell me he is not your son."

Tentatively Harold picked up the gold frame and perused the rendering. It might have been a portrait of himself at the same age. Still, he felt compelled to assert, "No one will ever believe you."

"We'll see, won't we?" Lucas said, trusting that the unpleasantness would never become public gossip, that it could be resolved peacefully and privately. "I realize you would not wish to embarrass your wife and family with the details of Harry's birth. I understand your concerns. Therefore, I have no need for you to make any general announcements. I'm happy to handle it confidentially, just between us."

"You are mad!" Harold sneered, thinking now that the American was insane after all. He'd listened to enough nonsense and wanted only that the blowhard be dispatched without delay.

"Jensen!" he shouted at the top of his lungs, calling for his butler, but the man was probably far away, in another part of the house, and unlikely to have heard his summons. Harold yelled again, hoping in vain that someone, *anyone*, might come to his aid, but chances were remote. As per his standing order, he wasn't to be disturbed for any reason during this regular respite of quiet in the evening. No servant would be lurking outside the door.

To summon assistance he needed to reach the bellpull on the other side of the room, but Pendleton would never allow that. Harold knew he was already pushing his luck by bellowing for Jensen, but he hadn't been shot outright for his bald action, so he was greatly encouraged. Pendleton wasn't quite as ruthless as he was trying to appear, but he was foolhardy. He couldn't know how isolated they were, that rescue was improbable; at any moment footmen might burst into the room, yet he stood there, calm as you please.

"All I require," Lucas said, completely ignoring Westmoreland's outburst, "is your signature on papers I've prepared." His eyes narrowed in disgust. How he ached to kill the man that very second! But he had sense enough to know he couldn't, not when he had yet to obtain what he had come for. Later he could call out Westmoreland, exacting his final retribution, but only after the entire impasse was successfully concluded.

He continued. "You will admit that you are the boy's father. You will put funds into a trust account for him that will remain sealed until his twenty-first birthday. You will also pay the start-up costs of whatever business he chooses to undertake as an adult. Other than that, you will never hear from us."

"Why don't I believe you?" Harold scoffed. "You're nothing but a bloodsucking blackmailer."

Westmoreland's volume was rising with each word. Lucas listened carefully, and off in the distance he could hear people rushing down the cavernous hall. Only seconds remained. "If you refuse to comply with my terms, I shall exact my revenge publicly." He leaned closer, pressing his thighs into the edge of the desk and adding quietly, "On your family."

"You wouldn't dare!"

"Wouldn't I?" Lucas asked. "I have not killed you today, but I don't think you should question my resolve." He turned toward the fireplace. It took up a good share of one wall. Above it hung a portrait of the woman Lucas knew to be the duke's wife. Lucas aimed and fired, hitting the posed duchess right in the heart. Westmoreland was so shocked that he gasped and fell back into his chair. From out in the hall came clamoring and noises, but Lucas didn't mind, for he was ready to depart. Reaching behind his back, he pulled out a second pistol and pointed it at the duke.

"I'll give you three days to consider your answer," he said, then walked to the door and opened it as though he hadn't a care in the world. Casually glancing out, he saw two maids huddled on the stairs, a third hurrying down. "I'll kill anyone who follows me," he pronounced loudly, tipping his head toward the cowering women and causing all three to jump. Over his shoulder he glared at Westmoreland a final time. "I'll send word on how you can reach me with your decision."

With that he was off and running, disappearing from the enormous house as quickly and easily as he'd come.

Frozen in his chair, Harold watched the blackguard go, but he didn't give chase as he supposed he should have. The room was filled with smoke, and his ears were ringing from the sound of the blast. He didn't know why the exhibition had left him so shaken. Pendleton had only shot at a harmless painting—one of which Harold had never been fond—but there was something extremely disturbing and violent about the act. Yet, Pendleton hadn't batted an eye while committing it, hadn't so much as flinched when the pistol banged and jerked so loudly.

Harold's knees had turned to jelly, and he couldn't seem to raise the alarm so that others would attempt to catch the lunatic, which was probably just as well. Pendleton was deranged, and heaven forbid that any of the servants come face-to-face with the madman. There was no telling what he might do.

All Harold could accomplish was to sit speechlessly, steadying his breathing. Many minutes later Jensen appeared, his supper interrupted by recent events, a napkin still dangling from his collar. Several curious footmen and maids fluttered behind him in the doorway, trying to see what had occurred.

On seeing that the duke was alive and in one piece, the short, squat, unflappable butler calmed himself, instantly halting while straightening his jacket by tugging at its hem.

"Your Grace," he said with a slight bow, his usual reserve firmly in place, "may I inquire, are you all right?"

"Yes, Jensen."

"May I get you anything?"

"A brandy, please."

"Very good, Your Grace." He flashed a menacing glance to those peeking around him, and they scattered like leaves in the wind, then he went to the sideboard and poured, filling the glass nearly to the rim.

Harold took a long gulp, draining the drink in a single swallow, letting the burn sizzle though his stomach and instantly go to work on his shattered nerves. Severely frazzled, he rested his head in his hands.

Another bastard child! he raged, bemoaning his luck. *Would they now start coming out of the woodwork?*

What had been the Good Lord's reasoning to create mortal man with such overpowering physical needs and drives, only to leave unwanted children as the result? Harold was only human after all. How could he be expected to resist the luscious temptation offered by the Caroline Pendletons of the world?

He looked up, found the butler waiting patiently for orders. "We've had an unwelcome visitor, Jensen."

"I surmised as much," the butler affirmed, his eyes straying to the ruined portrait and back again without betraying a flicker of curiosity.

"Send word around to my man, Purdy. I absolutely must consult with him this evening. I need him to find information on an American. He goes by the name of Lucas Pendleton."

"I'll have the message delivered immediately."

Harold stared at the man's napkin, still immaculately folded under his chin. "That will be all," he said. "You may return to your meal."

"Thank you, milord." Jensen took a step toward the hallway before looking back at Harold with no hint of any emotion showing on his worn face. "And the painting, milord, of Her Grace. Should I have it removed?"

"Later."

"Very good, sir. I bid you good evening."

He walked out and the door clicked shut, leaving Harold alone with his calamitous, guilty introspection.

Chapter 2

Penelope Westmoreland strolled along the rear wall of her father's dark garden. The air was moist and cool, and she suppressed a shiver—one that was not entirely from the cold—and pulled her black sable cloak more tightly about her shoulders. It was an exotic piece of fur given to her as a gift by a Russian countess, and she ran her hand across the soft nap, thinking how perfectly it contrasted with her virginal white gown and long, blond hair, making her flawless skin appear pale and translucent.

The meal she'd just eaten in her parents' lavish dining room had been a tedious affair, as she'd known it would be, so she wasn't certain why she'd gone to so much trouble with her appearance. Habit, she supposed, and she had to admit that she'd looked beautiful with her hair swept up on her head, the two ringlets dangling on her bare shoulders exactly as they were supposed to. She'd worn a new dress that had been expertly tailored by the finest French modiste in London, and it was styled to show off the newer, trimmer figure she'd acquired; her personal debacles of the past three years had caused her to lose weight.

Even her jewelry had been dazzling, all those strings and bangles and combs of pearls. The very finest, most exquisite pieces had been taken from the family vault just for that evening's special engagement supper.

No doubt about it, she had looked exceptional. Custom of a lifetime had required that she not appear at her father's table unless she was magnificently turned out. She had always been the wealthiest, the prettiest, the most sought after girl in the world, but not any longer, so adorning herself meticulously hardly seemed worth the effort.

At age twenty, and quickly marching toward twenty-one, she was well past her prime, far beyond those first heady days of her debut three years earlier, where the only thing that had mattered was what gown she would wear to what event. Those times of innocent flirtation and romance were gone, but how she wished she could recapture some of the excitement they had engendered!

As the only daughter of the Duke of Roswell, she had been fawned over wherever she went. Hostesses had begged her to attend their soirees, other girls jealously regarded her across crowded ballrooms, wondering which of the men they wanted for themselves might be considering Penny instead. And there had been so many.

The gentlemen had lined up, making marriage offers to her father, while she in return had passed her leisurely hours doing nothing more strenuous than having her skin creamed and her body perfumed, reviewing invitations with her mother, orchestrating her fate, and setting the standard in appearance and affluence that others could only blindly follow.

But that thrilling era was behind her.

She rarely went out anymore, because when she did, people laughed at her behind her back, pointing and sniggering over her plight. The women she'd grown up around, whom she'd always considered friends and admirers, weren't that at all. They were married, most having already produced the heirs expected of them, and they were ready to gloat, happy to rejoice over how far Penny had fallen from her lofty beginnings. A vicious lot, their malice was frightening to see, their words painful to hear, their dislike palpable.

Where once on a Saturday evening she would have passed from ball to supper to ball and danced till dawn, now she was merely tired, distressed, and wished only to be left alone while she figured out what course of action she could take to keep the future from rushing toward her. With the ferocity of an approaching storm, her destiny was bearing down, and very like a force of nature, she could deduce no method for steering it in another direction.

Even though it was March, her mother had had lamps lit along the walkways so that guests could enjoy an evening stroll, but Penny had been the only one to slip outside. Many of the tapers had burned down, and they gave off just enough light to mark the path but were dim enough to provide her with privacy. An added benefit, the multiple shrubs and hedges shielded her from view from the back of the house. Still, she cautiously glanced toward it. If Edward, her current fiancé, saw her and came out into the garden, she wasn't certain she could be responsible for her actions.

"Oh, Father," she murmured, shaking her head as she recalled how unperturbed the duke had appeared throughout the wretched meal they'd just endured. "How could you do this to me?"

If he had his way, she would be wed in June, at

last. After all the cancellations, the machinations, the plotting and planning, it would finally happen. Once upon a time she had truly believed that marriage to a gentleman of their social class was the one and only occurrence that could make her happy. Now she shuddered at the thought.

It would be her third attempt at making a trip to the altar. On the first occasion, she had been betrothed to Adam St. Clair, the Marquis of Belmont, the man she had dreamed of having as her husband from the time she was a child. Adam was more than a decade older, sophisticated, and worldly in every manner she was not. The proposed union had been a typical arrangement, but she'd believed herself to be madly in love, and she'd naively assumed Adam would grow to love her in return.

During those marvelous months of their engagement she'd been deliriously ecstatic, certain she had made the grandest match in history, reveling in the envy of others, flaunting her good luck wherever she went.

But to her mortification, Adam cried off at the last moment, deciding instead to commit the unspeakable act of marrying his mistress. Just a week before what would have been the most splendid wedding ever held in London, she'd been jilted.

Although her father had spread the appropriate stories, saying Penny had decided they didn't suit, everyone knew the truth: Adam preferred someone else, and Penny's life had never been the same since. For months she hid in her rooms, refusing to venture out, unwilling to suffer the stares, finger-pointing, and crude remarks made just on the edge of her hearing, remarks that never failed to cut like the sharpest sword.

Then her father had come up with an excellent solution. Another man was willing to have her despite

the embarrassment of what had happened with Adam.
The candidate was a viscount who would become an
earl someday, and he was close to her own age. Penny
had been exhilarated, convinced that a good marriage
would end her ongoing humiliation. Her husband-to-
be lived and worked on his family's properties in Jamaica, and Penny decided that if nothing else, she
could return to Jamaica with him and remove herself
from the taunting, hateful eyes of Polite Society.

However, her second union was not to be either.
Her swain was supposedly killed in an accident
before he could make it to England for the nup-
tials. Her parents insisted that his carriage had
overturned on a slick road, but after the furor had
died down, she began to hear shocking stories
about him. That he had been a gambler, a drunkard, a womanizer and wastrel, sent abroad by his
London relatives because they couldn't abide his
behavior. He had not been killed in an accident at
all but had met his death while dueling over a
woman—another man's wife.

While she'd never confessed as much to a single
soul, she was relieved to have narrowly escaped
being joined to the ne'er-do-well. She refused to
accept her mother's type of existence, one of
painfully whiling away the years in silent torment
and pretending not to notice or care that her husband dallied with every lightskirted woman who
caught his eye. Penny would rather be dead than
suffer such a circumstance.

Finally, for the third attempt, her father had chosen
Edward Simpson. He had just turned sixty-three
the previous month. A widower three times over, he
was bald and obese but also a wealthy and powerful earl,
his fortune said to be equal to that of her father. At a
more innocent time in her life, and despite his ad-

vanced age, she might have been excited and impressed by the prospect of becoming his countess. No longer.

Now she simply wanted to run away in order to avoid the coming calamity. After her second engagement had fallen through, she had begged the duke to secure another with someone who could quell the whispers and gossip, but she never imagined Edward would be the kind of man her father would select. On one melancholic occasion she had dared ask why, and he had answered honestly and brutally, as was his usual style.

No one else would have her.

The duke insisted that she wed a man of sufficient rank and prosperity, but in any given year there were not many marriageable men who met his exacting standards. Of those who were available, who were younger and would make her an appropriate husband, none was interested. For an unattached noble son seeking matrimony, there was a large assemblage of acceptable, unencumbered females from which to choose a bride, and Penny was no longer part of that group.

For the past three years she couldn't help but hear what people were saying about her: that she was jinxed, that she was bad luck, that she was a pompous, demanding shrew who was only getting what she deserved. Some even whispered that she'd been compromised, and that's why the duke couldn't find her a husband. The very idea made her laugh aloud, as she sometimes wondered if she wasn't perhaps the oldest living virgin in England. Gads, she was almost twenty-one, and she'd never even been properly kissed.

The wind rustled the trees, sending a blast of frigid air swirling through the garden, and she looked up at the sky, fearing the rain that had threatened all day would finally fall. How she hoped not! Foul weather would force her inside—to where Edward would be waiting. If she ran into him, she'd have to plead a headache and make an attempt for her room, but her mother would never allow her to escape the small party. The gathering was for the two of them, a signal to family and friends that the prenuptial festivities were about to officially begin.

Just then a shadow came down the path, and she hesitated, a bit unnerved. Who else might be out in the yard? When the form took shape, to her great dismay, she saw Edward approaching.

From the time she was still in the nursery, she had been acquainted with him as a colleague of her father's, though she'd not really known much about him. But with the engagement, he had been spending time in their home, and she was disheartened to discover that he was a drunkard, a glutton, a man of strong opinions and short temper who seemed to be always undressing her with his eyes and muttering sexual comments under his breath. On the few occasions he'd managed to get her alone, he'd taken physical advantage, attempting to kiss and paw at her. Just the thought of his touch started her shivering anew.

Had her father understood the kind of man Edward was when he arranged the marriage? Had he known of the drinking, the lewd language, the bouts of temperament? Had he known and, having no regard for Penny, gone ahead anyway? She wanted to hope that the duke was just learning, as she was, what her fiancé was truly like. After passing three hours at the supper table with Edward, she wanted the duke to be as miserable as she, but she was only fooling herself. Her father was perfectly content to have the entire affair proceed as planned.

The previous month, when she'd first been informed of her father's decision, no amount of pleading or arguing could change his mind. She'd stoically accepted Edward's proposal, sitting silent and graceful through the whole nightmare, letting Edward kiss her briefly on the mouth after she'd said yes, trying to smile while drinking sherry with the family to celebrate the news.

Edward had stood next to her through the ordeal, holding her hand or touching her shoulder, back, or waist, as though their arrangement had immediately given him special authority over her person. The afternoon had dragged on for an eternity, and once he'd departed, she'd run to her room, vomited again and again into the chamber pot, cried for hours, then remained in bed for two days, until the duke appeared and threatened to beat her if she didn't rise and carry on.

After all the scheming her father had instigated, after all the orders he'd forced her to obey, after all the paths he'd led her down while she'd blindly followed, here came her final reward: This man with the foul breath, body stench, lack of hair, and rotund figure, this elderly, obnoxious gentleman, was her father's idea of a suitable husband. And as Penny watched him approach, a drink in hand, the odor of alcohol lingering strongly, she couldn't help wondering if perhaps her father hated her. If perhaps he always had. If perhaps he'd never cared for her one whit.

"There you are, my little ducky," Edward said, slurring his words, stumbling and staggering. "I asked about you, but no one seemed to know where you'd gone."

"I needed some fresh air," she said, meaning it.

"You should have asked me to join you. I would have been more than happy to accompany you out of doors."

"Thank you," she murmured. "Next time I'll remember to invite you."

She wasn't certain how to deal with him. Although she'd never heard any whispers about him being abusive with his previous wives, she suspected that his temper could be formidable. He scared her, and she always felt the need to be on guard.

In his presence she never knew what to say or how to act. He constantly turned the conversation to physical topics, about her looks or size or some such. The manner in which he regarded her made her queasy, as though he were evaluating her for their wedding night, wishing he could find the opportunity to hurry things along.

"You misunderstand," he said, suddenly seeming more menacing. "I'll not have you walking about in the dark by yourself. Even on your father's property."

"All right," she said, thinking it best to agree. "I'll not do it again."

"That's my girl," he chided, his hulking figure blocking out the lights from the house. Her sense of unease grew in direct proportion to his nearness. "I like a child who knows how to do as she's told. Do you know how to do as you're told, my darling little Penny?"

"Of course," she said, smiling hesitantly.

She took a step back, and he moved with her. They were at the far end of the garden. Behind her there was a large expanse of high brick wall. The mansion was too distant for anyone to hear if she called out, and the only avenue for evasion was to slip by Edward and run in the direction from which he'd come.

"You'll be a fast learner, won't you, Penelope?" he asked.

His question sounded mean and frightening, and she couldn't help remembering how much he'd drunk during supper, how long the men had been at their port after the women had left the dining room. He had to be deep in his cups.

Feigning a chill, she pulled her cloak tighter. "It's getting rather cool, isn't it? Would you escort me back to the party?"

He laughed low in his throat, then reached out and twirled one of her ringlets around his finger, winding it tighter to the point where it started to hurt. Using it as leverage, he drew her close, until the flare of her skirt tangled around his thighs. "I don't want us to go just yet."

"I do," she insisted, feeling outright afraid.

"I think I'll steal a little kiss while we're here. You don't mind, do you, dearie? I've had so few opportunities to get you by yourself, and I've been eager to sample a little taste of what I'm buying."

The crudeness of his comment set her temper flaring, and she shook off her trepidation and tried to shove past, but he grabbed her arm. "Good night, Edward," she said in her fiercest tone, the one that always set others to trembling, but it had no effect on him.

"I'm not ready for you to leave," he said, his eyes glittering with a sickening carnal desire.

"You're drunk," was her reply.

"Not as drunk as I intend to be," he snickered.

"And you're being rude. Good night," she repeated more forcefully, trying to jerk away, but he only strengthened his grip, his fingers digging in hard. "Let go of me!" she demanded. "You're hurting my arm."

"Then do as I say," he ordered, "and I won't have to hold you so tightly." Instantly she relaxed, and his grasp lessened too. "See? You're learning already."

She bolted, but for an intoxicated man he reacted swiftly. There was a bench next to them, and he wrestled her onto it, forcing her down, then stretching out on top of her. Their bodies were on the smooth stone, their legs off on the grass. Before she realized what he intended, his mouth descended on hers, and she was invaded by his tongue working back and forth in a vulgar rhythm. He tasted like rancid tobacco, stale liquor, and unclean teeth, and by the time he pulled his lips away and began painfully biting and sucking against her neck, she was gagging and choking with disgust.

"Help me," she cried. "Please . . . someone . . ." But his large, fleshy hand covered her mouth, and she was silenced. Between her legs he was rocking his hips, and she could feel the hard ridge in his trousers that her French maid, Colette, was always yammering on about.

"What a wildcat you are." He breathed heavily, the putrid smell of his breath wafting over her face with each exhale. "We shall have many lovely hours of bed play between us. I can hardly wait."

The man was revolting! To think he dared treat her this way! He imagined he could steal a bit of her virtue on a garden bench as if she were some lowborn serving girl!

Completely outraged, she struggled in earnest but made little headway. He was too heavy to dislodge. She kicked with her legs and turned her head back and forth, finally managing to bite his hand. He angrily yanked it away, and she was able to call out. "Help! Someone!"

Suddenly Edward vanished. One moment he was there, the next he wasn't. Shakily she rose onto her elbow, only to behold another man picking him up by the lapels of his jacket. The force of it popped the fine stitching along the seams.

"What the bloody hell . . ." Edward muttered just as a fist connected with his stomach. The blow doubled him over, and the unknown attacker struck again, a severe right to the chin that sent Edward flying into the shrubbery.

The stranger was dressed all in black, from shirt to trousers to knee-high boots. His long hair looked black as well and was tied back with a black ribbon. His eyes were two dark pools gleaming with outrage and threat. With his high forehead, strong cheekbones, and aristocratic nose, he was very likely the most handsome man she'd ever seen.

Tall and broad-shouldered, his muscles thoroughly defined, he towered over Edward, protecting her and shielding her from further harm. Although he didn't know her or anything about her, and had absolutely no reason to intervene on her behalf, there he stood—her protector and savior. He was a magnificent specimen of potent male fury, shaking slightly, poised on the balls of his feet, and ready to pounce again at any second.

"Are you all right, miss?" he asked in an accented voice, probably American. It was a deep, rich baritone that floated on the night air and skidded across her frazzled nerve endings in a soothing way.

"Yes . . . no . . ." She shook her head, unable to assemble a coherent thought. "I mean, he didn't have time to hurt me. I was just frightened . . . very frightened. . . ." Holding her terror at bay, she shuddered violently. "If you hadn't come along, I don't know what might have happened."

He turned his attention back to Edward, who was still cowering in the bushes. Crisp with affront, he kicked out with the toe of his boot, landing a hard thump against Edward's side, causing the other man to wince and recoil further.

"Wait! Stop!" Edward complained, holding up

both hands in surrender. "It was just a bit of love play . . . I didn't mean any harm by it. . . ."

The foreigner reached down, grabbed him by the center of his shirt, and with one hand lifted him up until they were eye to eye.

"Apologize to the lady," he commanded in a manner that brooked no refusal.

Edward swallowed firmly, glanced her way, then mumbled, "I apologize."

The stranger lowered him until his feet touched the ground. "Bloody, drunken sot," he growled. "Get back to the house."

Edward tried to bluster, tugging at the bottom of his vest, patting at his thin, mussed hair. "How dare you lay a hand on me! Don't you know who I am?"

"No," the American said between clenched teeth, "and I don't give a rat's ass." He tipped his head slightly in Penny's direction. "Begging your pardon, miss."

"I say," Edward whined, "you can't just come up to me and do whatever you please!"

"I just did," the foreigner said dangerously, "and I'll not be responsible for my future actions if you don't immediately depart. I'm sickened by the sight of you."

Edward hesitated, glaring at her as if his comeuppance were all her fault. The malice in his stare caused her to shift back as though he'd slapped her. He made a move toward her, but the stranger stepped in front of him, blocking his view and his advance.

"This is your last warning," the interloper asserted. "If I see your face again this night, you're a dead man!"

Apparently Edward believed the warning, for he started backing down the path, keeping a wary eye on his tormentor. The American hurried him along by giving him a shove that sent him floundering, but he regained his balance and lumbered away, finally realizing he would be greatly out of his league in trying to do battle with a sober, much younger man.

Lucas watched him go, every muscle primed and ready for a fight, every sense prepared and alert for the possibility that the coward might return, but apparently the windbag was tough only when roughing up young women. He scurried toward the grand domicile, slinking away like a whipped dog.

Once Lucas ascertained that the other man posed no further threat, he turned his attention to the victim. She remained sitting, shivering, a hand to her mouth, her eyes wide and fearful.

"Are you all right?" he asked again more softly. He took a step closer, not wanting to frighten her any more than she already had been, and when she didn't shy away, he seated himself next to her.

"Yes, just terribly shaken," she admitted, unable to meet his gaze, as though she had somehow been to blame for what had happened.

Although he knew he should make good his escape from Harold Westmoreland, he couldn't abandon her until he was absolutely convinced that she was unharmed. He'd always been a pushover for damsels in distress, having made a fool of himself on numerous occasions for various women who found themselves in dire straits. This instance seemed no different. Cursing himself for the idiot he appeared to be, he stayed despite every instinct telling him to flee.

For the time being he felt secure enough. As far as he could surmise, after Lucas' dramatic exit Westmoreland had not raised the alarm, so he had a few moments to spare. Refuge was a mere leap away, his route to safety carefully planned and ready to be executed. At the first sign of threat, he'd be over the wall and swallowed up by the night.

He wondered about the fetching girl he'd chanced

upon. From her clothing, jewelry, and demeanor, she was obviously from a wealthy family. Her fur cloak alone was probably worth more than he'd earn in his entire life. Very likely she was a supper guest of the Westmorelands. But who was she?

She was young, too young to be by herself with such an older man. Had the cad lured her outside? Had she come willingly, innocently unaware of his dubious intentions? Had she run into him by accident and the knave taken drunken advantage? He couldn't help speculating as to who her parents might be, and what kind of people they were that they had allowed such a dastardly misadventure to occur practically under their noses.

"Would you like me to walk you to the house?" The offer was perilous, but he could hardly leave her huddled up and anxious in the dark.

"No," she said, refusing with a shake of her head. "I'll be fine. I just need a moment to gather myself together."

"But someone should know what happened," he said. "Is your father about?"

"He wouldn't care, I shouldn't think."

"You must be joking."

"No, I'm not. Unfortunately." Her eyes glistened with unshed tears. "That man you chased off is my fiancé. My father selected him for me."

"Now I know you're joking," he insisted.

"I'm not. They're longtime acquaintances. My father knows exactly the sort of man Edward is, yet he arranged a marriage anyway."

Just then the clouds decided to part, and a sliver of moon broke through. Its brilliant glow shone down on her, and he felt his breath catch. In the shadows her beauty had been hinted at, but in the fuller light she was spectacular. Her face was perfectly formed, heart-shaped, and lovely, with creamy skin, high cheekbones, a small nose upturned at the end, and generous pouting lips, the kind meant for kissing and no other task.

Her hair had come loose during the skirmish, and it hung long and free, so blond that it looked silver, and she seemed to shimmer with an unearthly luminescence. Though the moon was bright, he could not distinguish the color of her eyes, but he suspected they would be blue, a deep, dark sapphire that would only add to her allure. She stared at him, courageously fighting the tears that clung to her lashes.

"Oh, dear Lord," she exhaled softly, "what am I going to do?" Leaning forward, she rested her arms on her thighs, her shoulders sagging, her head down. "The wedding is in three months. I don't see how I shall he able to carry on until then. And after . . . oh, I can't bear to think about after. . . ."

"Is there anyone you can talk to?" he asked. "Anyone you can turn to for help?"

"No. There's no one," she said, and the admission was the last straw. The tears she'd so carefully held at bay began to fall, looking like tiny diamonds as they splashed down her cheeks. There was only a pair at first, then another and another, until it was a raging torrent of despair.

She even cries prettily, he thought, completely touched. He knew he should leave her to her own devices. A woman's tears always made him feel helpless and out of his element, but he couldn't forsake her during this private moment of sorrow.

"Here now, love," he said quietly, "it's not as bad as all that."

"It's worse," she said. "It's so much worse."

It appeared that her heart was breaking, that she'd been carrying the weight of the world on her shoulders and had finally collapsed from the strain of it. "Have a good cry, then," he advised. "You'll feel better."

He dug around in his clothing, surprised to discover that he actually had a kerchief. Tugging it out, he gave it a shake, then tucked it into her hand. She pressed it to her face and wept for a time, making no sound, as though sobbing were an indignity far beneath her position. Without thinking, he rested his palm on her back, stroking up and down, comforting her as one might a small child who's had a terrible upset. After a lengthy time the emotional upheaval began to wane, and he could sense her relaxation.

"I'm sorry," she said, giving him a somber half-smile. "I didn't mean to make such a scene." She dabbed at her eyes, willing her tears to return to the reservoir from which they'd sprung.

"What's your name, lass?" he queried, deciding that she was without a doubt the most enchanting woman he'd ever met, and that he'd have to see her again.

"Penelope," she said. "Penelope Westmoreland."

The name hit him in the center of his chest like a physical blow. His heart skipped several beats, and he had to force the air out of his lungs. Striving to remain calm, he asked, "Harold is your father?"

"Yes," she said, obviously not finding it odd that he would know her father's name. Most people did. The duke was famous and infamous.

She straightened, fiddling with her skirts, and finally turned to look at him. As she shifted, he couldn't help but notice what should have been apparent from the beginning of the encounter. Of course she was a Westmoreland! His young nephew, Harry, was her double. In her face, hair, and eyes he could see how the boy would look when he was grown, but that was hardly surprising. Miss West-moreland was, after all, Harry's half sister.

Just then, a commotion erupted from the house, and he stared over his shoulder. Several figures were milling about on the terrace. One of them was the duke, and he was flanked by several men who looked armed and determined. Immediately he jumped to his feet. "I have to go," he announced.

"What?" she asked as she stood, confused by the sudden change of circumstance. They'd been conversing so pleasantly, and she couldn't remember the last time she'd felt so uninhibited in the company of another. In a few short minutes she'd admitted secrets to the stranger that she'd never disclosed to anyone.

"I have to go," he repeated, peeking warily through the hedges.

From a distance she heard the duke's voice calling, "Penny? Are you out there?"

"That's my father," she explained, gazing up in consternation at her handsome protector. "He can't be looking for you! Edward wouldn't have had the audacity to say anything about what happened."

"I doubt if it was anything your Edward might have said or done," Lucas responded, flashing her the jaunty smile that had never failed to melt a female heart, "but your father and his men *are* looking for me." He gauged the brick wall and the leap he'd be required to make, then smiled at her again. "I need a head start in order to be safely away. Please don't tell anyone you saw me."

"I won't," she vowed, not knowing what he was doing in their garden, where he'd come from, or where he was going, but in a world where no one cared about her, he'd become a fast friend. She'd protect him no matter the cost, despite the risk to herself.